Midnight Sleeper

Visions of the Jazz Age

Vol. 1

Raeder Lomax

Copyright © 2016 Raeder Lomax
All rights reserved.
Book Design: Mary Smith
Photography: Wikipedia Commons Reuse
ISBN: **1533259909**
ISBN 13: **9781533259905**
Library of Congress Control Number: **XXXXX (If applicable)**
LCCN Imprint Name: **City and State (If applicable)**

Backstory

Midnight Sleeper is a journey into a moment of time when steam locomotives, ocean liners, drop-waist dresses, bobbed hair, bootleg whiskey, wood, and leather were as common as plastic and the Internet are today. The United States was a rawer place, heavier in the natural scents, more infected, rougher to the touch, manual, ethnically tribal, newly suburban, and tolerant of bigotry and social exclusion, yet an intensely inventive era that introduced electrical household appliances, the automobile, and radio on a mass scale. Television was invented (1925). Passenger aviation was first getting off the ground. Sound recording merged with film. Franchised restaurants were becoming a nationwide phenomenon. There were few, if any, safety laws. Construction workers often fell to their deaths, and death was misunderstood in its causes and was quite often a result of the pleasures that were its sources. It was a funky age, a sharp pivot from Victorian repression and feminine domesticity. Flappers—those young women who were stenographers, shop girls, beauticians, athletes, artists, coeds, budding scientists, doctors, and lawyers—took the first steps to free themselves of the traditionally limited roles that had defined women since the dawn of civilization. They left home not with a husband but with the notion of earning money and taking control of their lives. No longer could society force them into mummifying bustles, room-size hoops, or lengthy trains that dragged across the floor with penalties if any flesh was revealed below the waist. Flappers of the Jazz Age dressed themselves for themselves, showed leg, and wore the new drop-waist dresses that moved the eye from the traditional focus—above the waistline—down to the groin, and if the old guard was offended, too bad. The floodgates had been opened. The Nineteenth Amendment to the Constitution was enacted, in 1920, which gave women the right to vote; yet, insidiously, that same year, the Eighteenth Amendment, Prohibition, also became law—a notion of fantasy more to do with nativism and turning the clock back than sobering up a nation already sober. Add to this the Pullman porter (mainly Afro-Americans) who worked on the railroad, and we have a nation of all races on the move, where intimacy and service become functions of each other and of this story. America, through technology and self-reinvention, took the first steps to free itself of the rigid past so that the fault-lines that rocked the Jazz Age became the stuff that is now legendary, and now is the soul of this book.

Midnight Sleeper (prequel to *Stand Your Ground*) is based on an incident that occurred in Clarksdale, Mississippi in December of 1925. Several historical names, in this book, have been kept for authenticity: Al Nachman, Vince Brocato, Grover and Tom Nicholas, Mrs. Brewer, Sheriff Glass, E. C. Yellowley (all Mississippians), Texas Guinan, Dorothy (Dottie) Parker, Robert Benchley, Barney Gallant, Max Steuer, and the bold Billy C. Hopson.

99¢ Price Deals at **www.RaederLomax.com.** Get on the list **NOW!** And get notified of the exact day.

Railroad and Jazz Age Slang (or some of it)

Bakehead: Fireman on a coal steam locomotive.

Beehive: Railroad yard office.

Big E's: Engineer (from the big letter E on their Brotherhood of Locomotive Engineer union button).

Boomers: Itinerant/seasonal railroad workers also known as drifters, who travel where work is needed.

Bug Slinger: Switchman or brakeman.

Busthead: Contraband liquor generally not of good quality.

Buzzard's Roost: Yardmaster's office.

Cinder Dick: Railroad cop or detective.

Cinder Snapper: Passenger who rides on the open platforms of an observation car and falls off when drunk.

Coffin Varnish: Bad quality liquor.

Consist: The train or equipment of a train.

Deadheading: Railroad worker or Pullman porter who is traveling on the railroad, free of charge, to a work assignment.

Dinger: Train conductor or Pullman conductor (see below).

Dope Monkey: Car inspector.

Drop Table Shop: Where train cars are hoisted onto big tables for workers to make repairs.

Gandy Dancer: Track repairmen.

Grave Digger: Medical Doctor.

Lynching: Hanging by rope or any other means of murder by an angry mob.

Mud Hop: Yard clerk.

Paddy Roller (Patrollers): White men of the pre–Civil War South who patrolled the roads to make sure slaves had passes and were not runaways.

Panther Piss: Bad quality liquor.

Pullman conductor: Passenger trains had two conductors. The Pullman conductor took the fares and was responsible for passenger service. The train conductor was responsible for the operation of the train and worked for the train line that leased the passenger cars and crew from the Pullman Palace Car Company.

Rap the stack: Wide-open throttle for extra speed.

Speed Gauger: Locomotive engineer.

Straw Boss: Foreman of a small yard gang, who moved or coupled trains or did other related work.

Sweat: Bad quality liquor, but also a term for any kind of alcohol.

STOP: Morse code, early on, did not have a symbol for "." to indicate the end of a sentence. All telegrams used capital letters.

Suit-in-law: Lawsuit.

T-straps: Women's heeled shoes. The top strap was to keep the shoe on while doing the Charleston. The shoe was all the rage from 1925 and on.

Nothing in his life became him like the leaving it.

1.4 *Macbeth*

Clarksdale, Mississippi
December 28, 1925

1

Morning light poured into the bare Mississippi cotton fields as Clementine LaHood walked through the back door of her three-plow dogtrot farmhouse. Freshly picked collard greens and orange pippins from the orchard were bunched in her apron. She set them aside on the kitchen table as the first of her children came running down the stairway that her husband, Beau, had promised to fix. The bannister squeaked with each touch of his hand. The children followed him and tumbled down the stairs. They stopped at the kitchen door. An out-of-breath Western Union boy stood between them and their mother, the telegram already out of his brown leather bag.

"I'll take that," Beau said. He signed the receipt book and walked around his children, who were eyeing the white boy's Western Union Messenger Special bicycle by the doorway. Beau handed him a nickel, but the boy's eyes were on the stovetop skillet. Clementine reached for a biscuit and shooed him out the door. Then she turned her anger to Beau. "You can tell the Pullman Company to go to hell."

"I haven't even opened the telegram."

"Then don't strain your eyes. I'm mighty tired of you out on the road all the time. Us got five chil'un, 'nother on the way. Pullman said you got the whole week of Christmas off includin' New Year's. Now, you out the door again."

This wasn't the first time Beau had run afoul of his wife since he had taken the offer to work on the railroad, in the summer of 1915, when he was a bellhop at the Alcázar Hotel in downtown Clarksdale. A Pullman train executive, having just arrived from Chicago, pointed his ten-cent cigar at Beau and said, "A Pullman porter is the very best job a colored boy can get, and no white man has got a chance at it. Each section-train you have up to thirty-two folks, and on compartment and drawing room cars, you've got the finest of people who think nothing of handing you two bits to warm the baby's milk." The Pullman executive stepped back and took in Beau—all six-feet-four of him. Beau's deep, soft voice and still eyes, the kind a barn owl has when it's hungry, impressed him. He tossed a coin at Beau as if he were about to call heads or tails on his future. "I'm offering you a job, boy, not time to dawdle. Let me know, and I'll send you over to the depot. Have the superintendent sign you up for training, tomorrow morning. You'll be rich in no time." Later that day, Beau showed Clementine the Pullman application along with her new engagement ring and the notice for the training school he would have to immediately attend. He told his bride-to-be that they would have to put off their honeymoon for the moment—ten years, now.

Clementine said, "Why they always have to call on you when somebody don't show up? Ain't they got nobody else can do the job?"

Beau said, "I'm first porter on the Twentieth Century. Only the best men work on that line, and there's always too few to go

10

round durin' the holidays when men, for some reason, suddenly get too sick to work."

"Why don't *you* suddenly get sick for some reason?"

"I just told you. Anyway, it's holiday time. Folks tip plenty well."

"How do you celebrate the holidays with your family middle of January?"

"By thinkin' of the money I made durin' the holidays," Beau replied, glancing at his twenty-three-jewel Illinois railroad pocket watch. The 1:13 Yellow Dog connection to New York wouldn't be rolling into town for some time yet.

"What about Lindsay's trial today?" Clementine said. "Or is the train more important than your oldest friend?"

"I'm on my way to see him now."

"The trial starts when you're leavin' town."

"I'm gonna see him at the jailhouse, now. I can't talk to him at the trial."

Clementine put several biscuits on a plate and a cup of coffee on the kitchen table. She said, "I don't know why they botherin' with a trial. Everybody know them cotton scales at the Prevette plantation ain't accurate." She pulled a cornbread skillet off the coal stovetop. "Grover Nicholas, the boss overseer, is the one to fault. That white boy didn't give a damn. And now poor Lindsay's gonna pay for it with his life."

"You tested the scales?"

"*No* and I don't have to. Grover Nicholas owed Lindsay

pickin' wages, plain and simple. That's why Lindsay raised hell, and he's good at raisin' hell but never at raisin' Cain. Them white folk know who killed Grover, and they ain't sayin' nothin', but why am I wastin' my time tellin' you?" She headed to the larder.

"You found out who killed Grover Nicholas?"

"Al Nachman's partner, Vince Brocato, was just here askin' questions iffen I seen a white man named Marston Cobb. He the one killed Grover Nicholas." She came out with a bag of sugar. "And he's gettin' hunted right this moment." Coon dogs were barking in the distance.

"Why didn't you tell me Brocato was here?"

"Because your *Highness* was in the bathtub." She opened a kitchen cabinet. "You hear them dogs?" She took out plates.

"I heard them before, but I didn't know they was huntin' a person."

"Well, they is, and Brocato said for you to come by his office before you run off on the train. Somethin' Al Nachman needs you to do concernin' this whole trouble." Clementine set the table. "We owe Nachman big for doin' the legal work to get this land, so you better be there."

"I'll see him soon as I get done seein' Lindsay at the jailhouse." He looked down at the floor where something should have been.

Clementine walked on over to the alcove, then tossed his grip into the middle of the kitchen as if it had a disease. "Go on. *Leave.* I got things to do."

"Everythin' is in here?"

Clementine opened up the grip. She called out each item as if she were hawking them. "Razor blades, iodine, bandages, Kotex, aspirins, antacids, combs, nail files, hand cream, Brilliantine, chewing gum, cherry-scented red lip paint, blush, Minx mascara, cigarettes, pints of whisky. There anythin' missin', you let me know." She dropped the grip again for good measure.

"You'll break them bottles."

"*I'll* break first."

Beau lifted his grip and felt for any broken glass, and then he said, "You got the medicine in there?"

"You ain't supposed to give no medicine to no passengers."

"Tell that to all the posh grannies and soused ballplayers I saved."

"You should charge 'em, Beau, instead of givin' it all away."

"I do. They calls it tips."

Clementine pointed to a leather box inside the grip. "There's enough slippery elm, poke salad root, and mayapple to save all of New York and Chicago." She picked up the grip, set it by the back door, and then let out a wail as if she were singing the blues. "I wish you had a job that brought you home every night. I wish I wasn't home all alone with five children. I wish I had somebody here to give me five minutes of my own time." The words were brittle from having been sung so often.

"Clementine, you do the wishin'. I'll do the work." Beau stepped out the backdoor as the children gathered around him to say good-bye.

2

Jess Earl turned the Alcázar Hotel's 1922 Ford Huckster Depot Hack off of Dog Bog Road and onto a dirt path rutted by hooves, automobile tires, and wagon wheels. The bare fields cleared a path all the way down to the valley. Gone were the rows of pickers and sharp bolls that scratched fingers from plucking out the cotton, as too the boys on mules who hauled gunnysacks over powdery dirt roads that floured their britches. Winter had settled in, and, as always, it seemed to last forever. Jess Earl stopped the Huckster and honked the horn. A milking cow joined in with its low lonely wail as a strong gust of wind blew and stretched the trees one way and then the other. Jess Earl said to the tall man who was testing the planks on the veranda that were warped and overdue for repair, "You ridin' the 1:13 Yellow Dog?"

Beau buttoned up his winter coat, grabbed his grip, and headed toward the Huckster. "Yeah, didn't you get the note I gave to the Western Union boy?"

"That's why I'm here." There was something else Jess Earl wanted to say as he stared at the Pullman porter hat in Beau's hand, but it would have to wait. "You can forget about gettin' into the trial, Beau. Judge don't want no fuss, so he ain't lettin' in no one but family."

"Judge say that?"

"This mornin' at the Alcázar where he's keepin'."

Beau got into the front seat of the Huckster. "Grover Nicholas got a big family."

Jess Earl put the Huckster in gear and said, "So does Lindsay. That's why the judge ain't lettin' his in for fear both'll kill the other. Sheriff Glass gonna have a deputy at every door."

"You just take me to the jailhouse, Jess. I'll deal with the sheriff."

"Beau, you lookin' for trouble with that attitude."

"Don't argue with me. Just take me there."

Jess Earl put the Huckster in gear, and they rode off—with worry now the third passenger. He turned onto Dog Bog Road, and then slowed to a stop. White folk were walking by, and he didn't dare to get them dusted. "You do know the trial's been moved up from eleven o'clock?"

"No, I don't."

"Judge moved it up to nine."

"He can do that?"

"Can do what he wants," Jess Earl said.

Beau thought it odd the way the civilian world could change something on a moment's notice. The Pullman Company had conditioned him for exactness. Whether it was how many inches to fold the bedsheets when making up a berth or how to serve a bottle of soda: *The label must always face the passenger with no more than three ice cubes in a glass*, but one thing was for sure: anyone working or living outside the railroad would say one thing or the other and without the slightest care. Ten o'clock could be eleven o'clock. On time could be any time. Not if you worked on the railroad. Not if you wanted to arrive on time and alive.

Jess Earl felt it was time to tell Beau. "Guess what?"

"What?"

"I applied for the job."

"What job?"

"Went on down to the Pullman District Superintendent. Told him you was my best friend."

"I don't think you got what it takes to be a Pullman porter, Jess."

"Beau, why can't you say nothing nice about me?"

"Just get me to the jailhouse before the trial starts. I'll see what I can do about sayin' somethin' nice."

Beau leaned back into the stiff front seat and set his eyes on the empty cotton fields and the Mississippi River beyond. He had seen more of the continental United States than most people had in a lifetime and certainly more than anyone in his family, including his granny, Ella, who, in the winter of '61, was stunned to hear that a war had been started, never once thinking there was any place else beyond the Delta. Sixty-four years later, her grandson, Beau, had seen nearly all a person could see, and it was beginning to look the same. Granny Ella told him more than once, "Then you ain't lookin' in the right places, son."

Jess Earl pulled up in front of the jailhouse. It gave him a chill. He had heard all sorts of tales, true or not, of what they did to a man once inside who wouldn't cooperate or had yet come to terms with his crime, especially if he wasn't white. "I guess I better wait for you."

Beau said, "No, you go on back to the hotel."

"Gonna be a lot of time after you see Lindsay. Stop by. I got somethin' else I need to say."

"I gotta see someone after. Then I'll stop by," Beau replied, hopping out of the Huckster.

"Beau…?"

"What?"

"I'm serious about becomin' a Pullman porter."

"So's a lot of folk."

"Granny Ella said she saw it in a vision—you and me workin' together, Beau."

"When did she tell you that?"

"When I took her to Doc Ketter."

"What was wrong with her?"

"Nothin'."

"So then why'd you take her to him?"

"Doc wanted some more of her poke salad root."

Beau laughed all the way to the jailhouse.

3

Sheriff Glass, round and soft from sitting long hours waiting for something to happen in a town that hid like a cat on a mouse, leaned back into his big wooden swivel chair and looked up at the tall black man standing in front of his desk, grip in hand, wearing a New York tailored suit. He had heard about the local Pullman porter who acted as if he owned the railroad and had money to boot. The deputies who were boiling their morning coffee by the coal stove kept an eye on Beau as if he were about to do something crazy. Sheriff Glass said, "Boy, you just don't come walking on in here telling me what to do."

"Sheriff, sir, I just want to see my old friend. I don't mean to disturb nobody. Please, sir. Just a few minutes. That's all I'm askin'." Beau took out a small package; something he hadn't planned to do. The sheriff stared at the offering. Beau lied, "Just some hot biscuits my wife made for you." Clementine had specially prepared them for Lindsay Coleman.

Sheriff Glass allowed Beau to set the biscuits on his desk. They were warm and smelled awfully good to the deputies with their empty coffee cups and half-eaten breakfasts of cold cornbread spread with bucket lard. The sheriff picked up a biscuit and set it in his mouth. It fell apart on his tongue, and for a moment he was lost in the buttery softness of something so good that a childlike smile appeared on his face. Then he said to Beau, "How the hell does a Pullman porter buy a plot of land and live like a white man?"

"I sure don't feel white."

"I don't give a damn how you feel. The law catches up with

niggers who think they're too smart. I don't even have to go looking for 'em." He stood up and gave Beau's suit the once over, including the stylish brogues Beau had bought in a closeout sale in a Manhattan store that sold to whites, blacks, or Chinese as long as they had greenbacks. Sheriff Glass said, "Just where did you get the money for such fancy attire?"

"Working hard on the railroad, sir."

"They don't pay y'all that much. Forty, fifty dollars a month, I know that."

"Yessir, but you got to look your best for Pullman or they fire you. See, I represent the company."

Sheriff Glass said, "Well, you don't represent shit here. A lot of white boys work hard, and they don't live like you."

"Folks tip me well, sir."

"Well, I'll give you a tip, and it ain't one you can spend on fancy nigger clothes. I find out you're up to something no good, I'll have your ass locked up like Lindsay Coleman. Is that understood, boy?" he said, pointing to the jail door over to his left.

"Yessir."

"Now, turn around and put your arms up as high as they can go."

The deputies walked over and pulled Beau's pockets inside out, which caused his money roll and coins to scatter underneath the desks and tables. They found an expensive fountain pen that an ink salesman had given Beau as a tip. A Pullman timetable for the eastern seaboard and a letter of transit they gave a quick read, before crunching them into a ball and stuffing them into his coat pocket. The deputies scuffed his brand-new brogues for good measure, but Beau was too smart to fall into their trap. He knew, all too well, they were trying to goad him into a fight so they could lock him up. When the deputies were finished, they told him to fetch his things. Beau got down on his hands and knees and stretched his arms under the desks and tables for the loose coins and scattered bills that were hard to reach. The deputies laughed at him in that nasty pitch folks have when fun is being made at someone else's expense. One of them said to Sheriff Glass, who was eating his second biscuit, "Ain't nothin' on the nigger, Sheriff," laughing at the cheap pun.

Sheriff Glass then said, "Get up, boy."

Beau didn't bother with the coins he couldn't reach, but he couldn't forget that each one had been earned for a pair of shoes shined, a dress pressed in a hurry, a deep stain removed from a tie, or a quick run into a station to pick up something for a crying baby.

"I'll give you five minutes, boy. That's all," the sheriff said. "Otherwise we'll find a cell for you and something else to wear."

"Sir—"

"Did you *hear* me?"

"Yessir, but I also heard they moved the trial up to nine this mornin'."

"That ain't no concern of yours. You leave your grip right where it is."

"Yessir." Beau set it down, worried they'd force it open while he was gone and have more fun at his expense.

A deputy took Beau to Lindsay's jail cell and unlocked the door. Lindsay was all alone on a mangy iron cot in the corner. He quickly got up. "Man, is it good to see you!" he said, putting his arms around his old friend.

The deputy closed the cell door and locked it. Beau was shocked to see how much thinner and tired Lindsay looked. Even his big bright smile couldn't hide the worry and fear that had turned a proud face into a haggard and weak sore. His once bright, happy eyes were now dim with injury. His fingernails were long and dirty. His clothes were shabby. The air was tight with foul aggressive odors. A shaft of light from the small window imprinted the outside world onto the dark grimy floor.

Beau said, "I hear they gonna acquit you?"

"My lawyer, Al Nachman, says he got what he needs to do it, too."

"Yeah, but how's he gonna convince a white jury that you didn't do somethin' the whole town believes you done?"

Lindsay said, "Nachman got some outside expert. Gonna show that Grover Nicholas was stabbed by a person at least five-ten. Somethin' to do about the angle of the knife and how it got into Grover."

Beau looked down at his friend, maybe five feet five inches tall, thin as a rail. "What if the jury don't buy it?"

"Then I'm almost dead."

"What do you mean *almost* dead?"

"See, Jubal Laiter was in the fields the day Grover Nicholas was stabbed to death. He had a tare in his picker's bag, so he was late in comin' back. On his way to the bale house, he saw the murder happen in the path between the fields. Jubal said Marston Cobb, a new overseer who come down from Chicago, was bickerin' with Grover Nicholas, his brother-in-law, and it weren't the first time, neither."

"Bickerin' over what?"

Lindsay replied, "Over Grover Nicholas's sister, Euphia Cobb."

"What about her?"

"She's married to this Marston Cobb," Lindsay said. "Word is he been chasin' that rich Prevette girl who's cousin to 'em all. So Grover Nicholas warns his brother-in-law, this Marston Cobb, more'an once in the fields, until it got out of hand one day when Cobb pulled out a hunting knife and killed Grover. Jubal saw it all go down, but he didn't want to say nothin' for fear of gettin' lynched. But in time, with his conscience gettin' to him, he went to my folks, and they brought him to Al Nachman, where he got Jubal to sign a legal document swearin' he seen the whole murder happen and describes it down to the last detail. So I'm feelin' pretty good I'm gonna be a free man after the trial this mornin'."

Beau said, "When did you find this out?"

"Nachman was here tellin' me this all, and everybody know he was the best district attorney we ever had."

Beau said, "I hear the judge won't allow no one at the trial other than them selected by him."

"That's because he don't want my people sittin' in the same courthouse as Grover Nicholas's. Afraid there gonna be a ruckus inside should the verdict don't go their way. See, everyone knows Tom Nicholas is real angry 'bout his brother gettin' killed. Word's out he gonna do somethin', too. That's why Sheriff Glass gonna have the court doors guarded all around with deputies, should somebody get the wrong idea."

Beau said, "I heard the trial's been moved up to this mornin'."

"It's fixin' to start exactly at nine."

Beau checked his railroad watch that was deep in his vest pocket: 8:25 a.m.

"Beau?"

"What?"

Lindsay peered out the small tight window where freedom awaited. "We gonna have us a big party once I get outta here, this afternoon."

Beau touched his old friend's shoulder and admired the hope in his voice. "You're goddamn right we gonna have a big party," trying to sound as convincing as he could, then seeing flashes of the past when they were kids catching flatheads by hand in the Yazoo River or just sitting back and talking about the crazy things boys do when the world, for a moment, feels like it's theirs.

Lindsay put a hand on his old friend. "I just can't believe this happened to me, Beau. I ain't never hurt nobody in my life."

"I know that, Lindsay, but white folks, well, I heard they was all upset about you makin' a fuss over back wages, and it got to 'em."

24

"*Upset?*"

"That's what they say."

"Beau, I got *three* kids."

"I know you do."

"I got every right to be upset."

Beau said, "It ain't never about bein' right. You know that."

"The hell's it about then?"

"It's about you *thinkin'* you got the right."

"Well, I *do*."

"And look where it got you."

"Beau, you ain't sayin' I shouldn't of asked what was owed me?"

"No, but you ask a white man more'an once and he takes it as in insult."

"Too bad."

Beau said, "Too bad for you."

"Whose side are you on, Beau?"

"Side that stays alive."

The deputy opened the jail cell. "Let's go, nigger. Time is up."

Lindsay shouted, "Y'all give white prisoners all day for a visit! My friend only been here a few minutes! That ain't fair!"

Beau quickly got in-between Lindsay and the deputy. "He didn't mean nothin' by that, sir." The deputy pushed Beau to the side and struck Lindsay hard. He fell onto the cot and hit his head against the rusted iron bed frame. The gash gave blood, but that didn't concern the deputy, whose sneer, narrow with impudence and resentment, was full of the notion that niggers never learned. He lifted Lindsay off the cot and, with a tight fist, hit him hard in the gut. Lindsay folded over and dropped his head into his lap. Once again he was quiet and in his place. The deputy opened the cell door. Beau put his hand on Lindsay's shoulder and almost wept. "See ya at the big party, brother."

4

Nachman & Brocato, esquires, were located in a two-story brick building that had once been a slave auction house. It was right off the Cotton Exchange. Beau turned the corner of Delta Avenue and hurried up the worn wooden steps to the second floor, where slaves had once been quartered until sold. A queasy feeling overcame him as he knocked on the frosted glass door with its newly stenciled names. He knew dead people weren't supposed to appear out of nowhere, nor could the energy of the past remain and infect the present. The smart folks all said, "If you can't see it, then it can't exist." Nevertheless, Beau could see the slaves through the closed door and hear the traders and plantation owners dicker before the block: "I'll buy those boys over there, but not if I have to take the parents. The mother's got a bad ankle. See how she puts her weight on her stronger foot? And the father's eyes are no good. He might be able to see far away, but how's he gonna pick cotton if he can't see his own hand? Sell him to a one-acre farmer." Just then the door to Al Nachman's office opened. A young woman with alert eyes said, "There something you want, boy?"

"My name is Beau LaHood, miss."

The legal secretary shut the door for a moment to speak with Al Nachman, and then she reopened it. "You may come in."

Beau stepped into the office. There were coffee cups, half-eaten sandwiches, overflowing ashtrays, and empty bottles of root beer scattered over tabletops and chairs. It looked more like the quarters of an army on the march than a law office. Al Nachman's desk was just off to the right. A candlestick telephone was clutched in his left hand. He wore a three-piece charcoal gray suit with an Arrow Collar that pinched the knot of his tie so that it didn't lie flat and dull, but it was his unruly jet black hair that made him look like a man in a hurry as he swept his hands through the trial papers on his desk. Vince Brocato, Al's partner, was on his way out. Al lowered the telephone and said to him, "I'll be at the courthouse shortly," Then he turned back to Mrs. Brewer, the previous governor's wife, who was on the other end of the line, and said, "You're talking as if I'm still the district attorney, Mrs. Brewer…Well, you'll have to go to the new governor and get me the authority to do that…I know, but if y'all can get it done by tonight, then I can go after Cobb out of state…Well, Sheriff Glass couldn't find him…No, but Vince Brocato was over there early this morning, and Euphia Nicholas, I mean Euphia Cobb, told him she hopes her husband never returns." Al motioned for Beau to sit down. "Mrs. Brewer, get me the authority, first…Fine, see you at the trial." Al hung up and noticed the grip beside Beau. "You coming or going?"

"Goin', sir."

"10:13 to Meridian?"

"1:13."

"That was Mrs. Brewer, the previous governor's wife, on the line. She's now head of the Mississippi League of Women Voters and has got a lot of power in this state and is mighty annoyed about the situation with Lindsay Coleman. She wants to make sure that he gets acquitted of murder—now, don't look so sad. Things are going to be all right."

"You mean the way her husband, the old governor, got them colored boys acquitted a few years back?"

"Exactly."

"Can you get me a seat at the trial this mornin'?"

"I'm sorry, Beau, but the judge has set a limit, and I'm not about to approach him at this particular moment, especially when I know there will be an acquittal. I'm sure you can understand the risk I would be putting Lindsay in if I brought someone into the trial not permitted."

"You really think Lindsay's chances are that good?"

"There's not a jury can rule otherwise, and if they do, the judge will overturn the verdict."

Beau said, "Well, I was just in the jailhouse to visit Lindsay, and when I walked out, I felt Lindsay was dreamin' about gettin' freed. I don't know if you been there, but it's filthy. They also roughed him up bad."

"Mrs. Brewer knows all about the conditions over there and what goes on."

"She been there herself?"

"Yes, and she assured me there's going to be a lot of changes after the trial."

There was a big hopeful smile on Beau's face. "When do you figure the trial will be over?"

"The jury should be in with its verdict by noon, latest. And don't worry that its makeup is all white. I've got this case won as it stands, but I *do* need your help with something else," Al replied, opening his briefcase. "Vince Brocato was down at your farm this morning, looking for this man. We thought maybe you'd have seen him, since you live on the road to the Nicholas people," taking out a photograph. "Clementine told Brocato that she hadn't seen him. Have you?"

Beau studied the image of the overseer standing in a cotton field with pickers. His shirtsleeves were rolled up. His vest was unbuttoned. His hatband was stained with sweat, and his eyes squinted from the strong midday sun. The man seemed wary as if he had compromised something by allowing his photograph to be taken. Al showed Beau another photograph taken at the man's wedding to Euphia Nicholas. His dark curly hair made Beau think of John Wilkes Booth, the man who shot Lincoln.

"Funny."

"What?"

"I seen this man at the depot, often enough."

"Here in town?"

"Yessir."

"The man's an overseer at the Prevette plantation," Al said. "What would he be doing down at the depot?"

"I don't know, but I seen him many a time at the depot talkin' to porters."

"Ever talk to you, Beau?"

"Nossir, but for some reason he always talkin' to the porters on the Illinois Central goin' to Chicago or out west."

30

"You have any idea why he'd be speaking to them?"

"Absolutely none."

"But you found it curious?

"Oh yessir, I did. The man always had a strange look, too. I once seen him take a coin out of his pocket and put it in a porter's hand like there was some big promise to be kept."

"What promise would that be?"

"I wouldn't know, Mr. Nachman. Go down to the depot and ask an Illinois Central porter headin' to Chicago and maybe you'll find out."

"The man in the photograph is from Chicago," Al said. "His name is Marston Cobb, and he's the one who murdered Grover Nicholas."

"Lindsay said as much."

"I don't have time to go into all the details now, Beau, but Marston Cobb just might be on the train. We tried finding him earlier this morning. Maybe he'll be on the 10:13. I don't know; I've got someone down there keeping an eye out for him. Now, if should you see him on the 1:13, or any other transfer, I want you to immediately wire me. But if you feel doing so will jeopardize your job with Pullman, then you just go on your way as if you'd never spoken to me."

Beau was deadheading to New York, which meant he wouldn't be working and would have a lot of time on his hands to keep an eye out for Marston Cobb. Beau knew all the porters as well as the conductors. Sooner or later, they all needed something, so friendships were made to take care of those needs, needs that served the railroad, too, and it was in this manner the porters survived and endured as a group when mistakes were made or common sense deferred to more corrosive impulses. Beau said, "I'll see what I can do, but you got to remember, all I can do is to wire you his whereabouts. Can't do nothin' stronger than that."

"That's more than enough, Beau."

"You absolutely sure you can't get me into the trial this mornin'?"

"I can't, Beau," Al replied, putting on his hat and coat and heading to the door. "But if you wait here, I'll call you soon as the verdict arrives, and then you can come on down and celebrate. How's that?"

"Fair enough, but please don't forget to call me, Mr. Nachman. I'll be here waitin'."

"I won't forget, Beau." Al then told his legal secretary, "Make sure my friend here feels at home, and put up some coffee for him." Then turning back to Beau. "Don't you worry. In a few hours Lindsay's going to be a free man."

The legal secretary shut the door behind Al and said to Beau, "You may sit on the chair near the couch and read a magazine, but it *must* stay in the office."

Beau stared at the hard-back wooden chair, small for a man his size. He would've much preferred the soft comfort of the big leather couch to stretch out his long legs and put up his arms. The legal secretary returned to her desk and got back to work. The Franklin Argand stove and the coffeepot were just a yard or so away, but it might as well have been several thousand. Beau waited a spell and then gave up on the coffee. He walked over to the nearest window and gazed out into yonder sky. The road to heaven looked easier than the one that led to town where decency seemed to be a coin seldom spent. Huge clouds herded and blocked the sun. The only sound came from the pounding of the legal secretary's Underwood typewriter and the shifting of its shiny metal return bar. Beau took off his overcoat and folded it neatly on the wooden chair and sat down. The next several hours he went through every magazine on the coffee table: *The Saturday Evening Post, Life, Judge, Radio News, Colliers, Farm & Fireside, Country Home, Country Life, and Popular Science,* before drifting off into a hazy sleep. He awoke several times and not to a passenger calling for an aspirin or a tonic to get back to sleep but to a dim heavy dream weaving in and out of his dozing mind. He kept seeing himself in a jail cell. A deputy was peering into the small gap in the door. He laughed and then walked away as he jingled his keys like spare coins. Then something raw and unsettling forced Beau to sit straight up. It came in rapid succession and plugged the air with a fierceness and intensity that made him rise to his feet and open his eyes as if mortal danger were inches away. The legal secretary's chair had been pushed away from her desk. Her coat was no longer on the tree. Her cigarette was burning in the ashtray. The time on the American Oak Regulator wall clock was 12:45 p.m.; way past the time Al Nachman said he would be calling in with the verdict. Beau seized his grip and quickly went down the stairs. He followed the people who were running toward the courthouse. They turned the corner of Desoto and found a large group of white people pushing up against one another to get a better look at what had happened. A man in the crowd turned around and shouted, "Here comes the nigger's friend!"

Beau hollered to Al, whom he could see standing tall above the others. "*What* was the verdict?"

One of the white men laughed. "You're looking at it, boy."

Another said, "He got his acquittal, all right," as the crowd let Beau in so he could have a first-hand look at Lindsay in the gutter, whose body was twisted from over two dozen cartridges fired in rapid succession. His clothing and skin were scattered on the street in chunks of raw bloody pieces. A voice loaded with swagger brayed, "*You're* next, nigger."

Beau stepped away from the smartly dressed folks who were at the trial and put on his best porter's smile as he tried to contain his anger. "Gentlemen," he said as if addressing the members of the local Rotary Club and not a bunch of fools, "there's a phrase I hear spoken now and again, but I ain't too sure which way it goes. Is it 'Dress up a dog and his tail will stick out?' or is it 'Dress up a cracker and his dick will stick out?'" The crowd went after Beau, whose smile was now a venomous sneer.

Al Nachman and Vince Brocato quickly tried to make a protective ring around Beau, but they got kicked, pummeled, and pushed. The fight turned into a free-for-all, where to turn one way was to get kicked, to turn the other way punched, until one of the deputies, deep into the fray and barely able to balance himself, felt a hand reach for his sidearm. Overwhelmed and unable to separate himself from the entangled mob, the deputy grabbed his weapon and fired successively. Two men fell dead to the ground as another stumbled on—death taking a little longer. The solidarity that had galvanized the crowd before was now gone as the mob dispersed and scattered. It was every man for himself as it always is when self-interest overrides the illusion of unity. Sheriff Glass turned to the deputy, who looked bewildered and confused, his revolver loose in his hand and his eyes full of what he had done. *You stupid ass.*

Al Nachman and Vince Brocato pushed Beau into Al's Ford. They drove hard down 2nd Street onto Delta Avenue to the Clarksdale Yazoo and Mississippi Valley/Illinois Central Passenger Depot. Beau was desperate to know who killed Lindsay. Al said, "Tom Nicholas, Grover's younger brother. He was at the trial and the first to leave when the verdict came in."

Beau said, "Didn't they check for firearms?"

Vince Brocato added, "Everyone had been checked before the trial started."

"Obviously the sheriff didn't check *him*."

Al said, "Tom Nicholas got the gun after he had left the courthouse. Bishop Blakely and Lance Parker were waiting outside for him in an automobile, ready to seize Lindsay, and with the help of the crowd, they drove up several streets, stopped the car, pulled Lindsay out, and fired over two dozen rounds into him at point-blank range."

Beau said, "Where was the damn sheriff? He was supposed to

be protecting Lindsay."

Al said, "He was told something like this could happen, but he said that he was the law and was going to do things his own way."

"Which was to do nothin'."

"Beau, there's four dead now, not just one," Al said. "So there'll be hell to pay on his part…" The sound of an incoming locomotive drowned out his voice.

Beau turned toward the 1:13 Yellow Dog K Class steam locomotive chugging toward the depot. It was a harsh reminder that whatever may happen, the railroad always came first. A long trail of woolly black smoke, about as wide as a small tornado, drifted from the engine stack all the way to the last car of the consist. It suspended into gray clouds and floated away as the swinging bell, atop the locomotive, clanged as the train chugged into the depot and eased to a stop. The doors of the six section and compartment cars swung open. Pullman porters exited in starched white jackets and placed step-boxes on the ground to help passengers on or off. The train conductor, already on the platform, checked his pocket watch and spoke to the soot-faced engineer leaning out of his locomotive cab as the fireman, using a long-spouted can, oiled the brake shoes and wedges of the man-sized locomotive wheels. Beau grabbed his grip and said to Al. "The kin of them boys killed gonna come after me and Jubal Laiter. I want y'all to send Clementine and the chil'un over to my mother and Granny Ella's cabin and then put a watch on Jubal Laiter."

Vince Brocato said, "The deputy shot them, not you, Beau."

"Yeah, but I'm the one who called 'em cracker, and Jubal's the one who told the truth."

Al said, "We'll make sure it's done. You keep an eye out for Marston Cobb."

"I'll do all that I can," Beau replied. He then left the motor car, crossed the tracks, and hoisted himself aboard the train as the whistle blew a third time. A happy voice hollered, "*Beau,* I thought you was home for Christmas!"

Beau looked into the big friendly face of the Pullman porter standing in the vestibule. "You say that every year, Jimmy." Then he noticed a young lady boarding the train, the one his cousin, Julius Stephens, had said was as wise as a tree full of owls.

5

Pullman porter Jimmy Quitman helped Shelby Prevette, the South's wealthiest girl, board the 1:13 Yellow Dog as her mother, Mims, stood by in a streak of stubborn tears, worried that she would never see her nineteen-year-old daughter again. She ordered Julius, the houseman, to run back inside the depot to buy more magazines and candy for Shelby, who already had more than she could carry. Mims's husband, Addison Prevette, was more concerned with his daughter's needs than with his wife's fears. He squeezed a thick roll of bills into Shelby's hand and warned, "If you need any more of this, go into City Bank when you arrive in New York and tell them who you are, but remember, a fool and his money are soon parted."

Shelby leaned out the vestibule. "The only thing parting is this train, Daddy," she responded. "I'll wire y'all as soon as I can," she said, holding onto the long brass vertical handrail and looking out at Clarksdale as if it were for the last time. "And, Daddy, don't forget to change the feed for my horses. I put them all in your barn until I get back. And make sure the gates are up in the south pasture. I don't want to come home and find my stream ruined. And tell Julius I haven't forgotten the key to the trunk. He thinks I left it at my barn."

Mims caught up with the train as it started to leave the station. "What's she talking about, Addie?"

Addison Prevette, just ahead, replied, "Nothing at all." Then turning to Shelby, he said, "I'll make sure, baby doll," blowing a kiss from his gloved hand, sending it express with his deepest breath, thinking of the day she was born. The first time he put her on a mount and the morning hour he gave her his thirty-ought-six center-fire and taught her how to shoot and hunt better than any man in the county. Addison hollered, "Wire me as soon as you get to New York, Shelby!"

"I will. And make sure Mama doesn't open my mail!" she replied, her voice now trailing.

The Yellow Dog K Class locomotive chugged ahead as Julius lagged behind, with the magazines and candy tumbling in his arms. Mims, youthful and as pretty as her nineteen-year-old daughter, haplessly ran after the train as it narrowed into a thin wire.

Addison Prevette said to his wife, "At least Marston can't bother her, now."

Mims wasn't so sure. The last time her nephew Marston Prevette Cobb had come looking for Shelby, he stood imperiously at their front door with all his afflictions, resentments, and high sense of honor in full array as if he had come to evict the family. He told his aunt, by marriage to his uncle, Addie, "You forget that you married up when you married into our family. You, Nicholas people, are just one step above field niggers and as common as pig tracks."

Mims said, "You married down when you married my niece Euphia. Now you're an overseer. Tell that to your high-class mother in Chicago, who has to beg her brother for money, because no one will marry her."

"*You* leave my mother out of this."

"You've been warned more than once to stay out of here."

"You just tell me where Cousin Shelby is," Marston said as he turned his hand into a fist and threatened to step inside the house.

Julius slammed the front door in his face. Marston scurried around the big white house that stood on a thousand acres of pristine pastures and cotton fields. He shattered a window with his fist and reached inside. Julius was already there to push him away. Mims was on the phone with the sheriff, telling him to come quickly, but when Sheriff Glass arrived, Cobb had already departed—not after having shitted on the lawn, his sense of honor and humor at its most twisted.

Mims said to her husband, "But what if Marston found out Shelby's on the train?"

"Did you tell anyone?"

"I...I certainly didn't tell him."

"We made a grave mistake concerning that boy. He should be in jail, and I don't mean just for what he did to our little girl," Addison said, taking his briefcase from the car and walking to his office, thinking of the note his nephew had left him about how he was going to pay for having ruined Marston's and his mother's life—a notion he had cultivated beyond any normal grievance, but then, an injury to a man's honor has no bounds.

Julius said, "What about the missus, Marse Addie?"

"What about her?" he replied, as he crossed the road and left her there.

***

Shelby Prevette leaned over her upholstered section-seat that had cushioned armrests, white linen head covers, and a gold inlay mahogany backboard. She searched for her parents on the platform, but the sharp midday glare blinded her. When it cleared, Clarksdale had all but vanished. Only the stripped cotton fields and gray shuck of winter were left as the parched dryness of despair took hold of the land and the excitement of leaving home turned on itself.

"Everything all right, miss?" Shelby turned away from the window, surprised to find a colored man standing in the aisle. He was no less surprised. Her jet-black bobbed hair was boy-short at the neck, and her full bangs were sharply trimmed above bright blue eyes jumpy as a yearling's. "I thought I saw a tear, miss, that's all."

Shelby was offended at the sight of Beau. His overcoat was a mess from the fight back in Clarksdale. She pushed her peekaboo red cloche down over her eyes.

"I'm a Pullman porter, miss, just not on duty. I'm on my way to the men's lounge where I'll be stayin'. I can have your porter get you somethin' to make you feel more at home."

Shelby had heard all about the men who preyed on women riding alone on a train—something she'd been warned about before leaving home. She peered down the aisle to make sure she was in the right car. Everyone was white, and though it was the ladies' car, husbands and family were allowed passage. "You're in the wrong car, boy," she said, pointing for Beau to leave.

"Yes, miss, but, see, I'm deadheadin' to New York."

"Deadheading...? What's that?"

"It's what we call travelin' when in transit. See, I'm on my way to the last car. But I can send a porter over iffen you be of need of somethin', but you got to give him a minute or so. The train just left the depot, and they got to finish with the baggage."

"I don't care about the baggage, boy. You're not supposed to be in this car," she said, pointing to the two-foot-long slot posted at the end of the car: *White Passengers Only*: a guarantee of protection from all that was considered low, vile, and coarse.

"Well, miss, there ain't no other way of gettin' to the last car other than flyin' in through the window, and I ain't no good at flyin'," showing her his Pullman train credentials.

"You could walk on top of the train."

"I get dizzy, miss. May I ask where ya headin'?"

"None of your business, boy."

"Certainly ain't, but I can get you your porter. Make sure everythin's right on the call chart."

"What's a call chart?"

"When and where you be gettin' off, miss. Everybody on that. This your first time on a train?"

"No, and I didn't run away from home, if that's what you're thinking."

"I don't think that at all, miss." He read the train ticket in her hand: *Miss Shelby La Haut Prevette.*

"How long will it take us to get to New York, boy?"

"Oh, 'bout same as your last trips."

Not appreciating his sarcasm, "How about getting me a drink?"

"I'll have the porter get you some warm milk once everybody's settled in."

"Who said milk?"

"It's good for the nerves on a long trip, miss."

"My nerves are just fine. Rye whiskey is what I want and not coffin varnish."

Beau didn't expect to hear that from a girl who didn't look any more than fifteen years old. "Well, I can't help you with that, miss."

"Baloney. Porters always have something to sell a passenger."

"Iffen I stumble upon somethin', I'll let you know."

"Oh, I'm sure you'll stumble upon something, boy. What's your name, in case I need something?"

"Beau, miss. Beau LaHood. But I'm off duty, so you'll have to get another porter."

"You say *LaHood*?"

"Yes, miss."

She now sat up straight. "Say it again."

"LaHood, miss."

"Where are you from, boy?"

"Clarksdale."

"You not related to a Roy LaHood, are you?"

"Iffen you mean Roy LaHood, my great uncle on the Prevette Plantation, yes."

She stared at Beau as if she should have known him. "How come I've never seen you before?"

"Well, miss, the train got me most of the time, and I rarely get a stretch long enough to visit kin, but I'll be seein' Uncle Roy when

I get back after the holidays. I'm gonna surprise him with some holiday gifts from New York."

"That's kind of you, but it would be kinder if you said your name correctly."

"How should it be said, miss?"

"It's La Haut, not LaHood," saying it the French way, "without the *t*, and my family name is said without stressing the second syllable, contrary to some misguided Francophiles—but then, you knew who I was all along, didn't you?"

"Yes, I did, miss."

"Why is there blood on your coat?"

"There was a lynchin' just outside the courthouse this mornin'."

"A lynching…?"

"Yes, miss. Right in town."

"They tried to lynch you?"

"Not at first."

"What do you mean not at first?"

"See, the man accused of killin' your cousin, Grover, was acquitted. Then he was lynched."

"What does it have to do with you?"

"Well, it's a long story, miss; one that hurts. I won't waste your time lookin' for sympathy."

"You knew the man who was lynched?"

"Oh yes, I did."

"When did this happen?"

"Right after the trial, this mornin'."

"Did you see it happen?"

"I heard the shots."

"I still don't understand what you had to do with it."

"I had nothin' to do with it," Beau said.

"Your coat wasn't torn for nothing."

"No, it wasn't. You see, Tom Nicholas and two others killed Lindsay Coleman after he was acquitted of murderin' your cousin Grover."

"*Tom Nicholas?*"

"Your other cousin, miss."

Tom's boyish face was large in her mind as was the melancholy that made him edgy, impatient, and at times petulant. He took his nightmares awake and his failures broadly, not understanding that life was as much its errors and mishaps as its achievements, but he was no brawler, no brute force of a man. He had love in his heart, and he would have given it freely had he known what free-giving was.

"I better get goin', miss. People gettin' uncomfortable with me in the car."

"How far north are you going, Beau?"

"As I said before, New York."

"Why so far?"

"I'm first porter on the Twentieth Century Limited."

"Oh, I've heard about that train."

"Everybody has, miss."

"I'm going to New York, too."

"I know," pointing to the ticket in her hand and tipping his hat as he went on his way.

The Yellow Dog 10:13 to Meridian

6

Working porters were on call twenty-two hours a day with a guarantee of three hours of sleep, which meant either dozing on a night stool by the car's vestibule at the end of the aisle or staying in the men's lounge should a passenger put in a call. Beau took the leather bench-couch in the lounge and gazed out at the passing landscape, where big stretches of clipped fields were bookmarked by whistle stops, horse-drawn wagons, and hard-top automobiles that kicked the dust tree high, but it was a slow world outside. Time seemed to drip minutes, hours, and then days, so unlike on the railroad where the pressure was relentless and unforgiving.

Jimmy Quitman entered the men's lounge looking worried. Reaching into the pocket of his starched white service jacket for a cigarette, which, he knew, wasn't allowed to be smoked on duty, he said to Beau, "Some crazy woman complainin' she lost a piece of luggage. Shoutin' and callin' me a thief. Sayin' I should be locked up ball'n chain." He hung the call chart on the wall.

Beau said, "Lemme guess. She left it back in Clarksdale?"

"Her mind is what she left. Woman's in section one," as he flipped a page on the call chart. "She now with the dinger in the baggage car, raisin' hell that I'm the devil hisself."

Pullman conductor Earl Eddis entered the men's lounge. Jimmy slipped his unlit cigarette back into his pocket. The conductor, a stout sturdy man with graying hair and a bulldog neck, pulled out his

1911 Elgin Lever Set Railroad Pocket Watch from his vest and checked the time. He said to Beau, "You look like you fell off the train."

"I feel like it."

Conductor Eddis walked over to Beau and set the palm of his hand flat up against the lounge wall where Beau was sitting. "That pretty girl over in section eight, named Miss Prevette…"

"What about her?"

"Took her ticket. Said she wanted something to drink. Said if I didn't have it, I should ask the porters."

"Well, don't ask me."

"Don't be funny, Beau. If you're selling contraband, I'll have you up at the superintendent's office when we pull into Meridian. There's a law called Prohibition, and the Pullman Company obeys it."

Beau said, "Too bad its passengers don't."

"You're not a passenger, Beau. You got any contraband, get rid of it."

"Yessir."

"That don't sound too convincing, Beau."

"*Yessir*."

"Good," He then left the men's lounge.

Beau turned to Jimmy Quitman. "What's with Eddis all of a sudden?"

"You didn't hear?"

"Hear what?"

"There's a suit-in-law against the railroad to do with somebody dyin' from wood alcohol."

Beau said, "Thanks to that stupid law, this whole country's dyin' from bad alcohol."

Jimmy moved aside to let Beau read the call chart. "I thought you wasn't workin', Beau."

"I ain't, but I need to know who's on board."

"You lookin' for somebody?"

"Yeah, his name is Marston Cobb."

Jimmy asked, "Why you lookin' for him?"

"My oldest and closest friend was lynched this mornin'."

"*Lynched?*"

"Shot to pieces for somethin' he didn't do right after an all white jury acquitted him."

"And who's this Marston Cobb?"

"The one who's behind it all. Might be on this train. So I need you to keep an eye out for him."

"What's he look like?"

"Like John Wilkes Booth, without the mustache."

"Beau, we got a lot of miserable passengers without a mustache."

"Good. Let me know which sections or compartments they in."

"You got a picture of him?" Jimmy asked.

"All I got is the one in my mind, and it's beginning to burn a hole through it." Beau returned to the couch-bench and waited. It was all he could do.

***

When Jimmy Quitman returned from the buffet car, Beau had on a clean change of clothing. "Beau, the man you lookin' for, iffen he is on the train, ain't goin' by the name of Cobb."

Beau said, "Where's Eddis?"

"With the big dinger in the first car. Why?"

"I'm gonna have a look myself."

"That Cobb fella ain't on this train, Beau. I was up and down. Spoke to all the porters, and they ain't seen nor heard no one by that name. Eddis see you runnin' about, he'll report you, maybe throw you off the train, and you know that ain't a threat."

"I don't give a damn. None of y'all looked hard enough."

Beau put on his Pullman porter hat so that if a passenger wondered why a colored man was in their car, all he'd have to do is point to the stamped letters above the visor, and if someone couldn't read, Beau would do the favor. He went through every car of the consist, checked every section-seat, and spoke to all the porters who had compartments, and they all swore no one had met the description of Marston Cobb, though they did remind Beau that without a photo they didn't have much to go by. On his way back to Jimmy Quitman's car, Beau ran into Conductor Eddis. "Beau, I thought I told you to stay in Jimmy's car."

"Yessir, you did."

"Then what're you doing here?"

"Stretchin' my legs, sir. Gotta move 'em about or they ache."

"I don't give a damn about your legs. I want you back in Jimmy's car."

"Yessir."

"And what's this I heard about you looking for a murderer? You got some other job besides working for Pullman?"

"Nossir. Just helpin' out Mississippi law enforcement on a request they made because of my workin' on the railroad."

"You got a picture of the man they want?"

"Nossir."

"Well, unless you do, I'm not bothering passengers, especially those in compartment cars, and neither is Jimmy. Because if we're mistaken and pull out the wrong man, Pullman will have our heads. So you just mind your own business and let the law see to this matter. They'll get him sooner or later."

"But Mississippi law specifically asked me to help 'em out on the train so they could get him sooner than later."

"Beau, the train comes first before anything else, and you know that. Now, unless I hear from central, I won't have you moseying about."

"Even iffen a killer's on board?"

"Even if Jesus Christ himself is on board." Eddis left the lounge.

Beau spent the rest of the ride staring out the window.

Meridian, Mississippi
December 28

7

An annoying wind tied a chilly knot around the passengers changing over from the Yellow Dog 10:13. Some remained bundled up on the platform. Others headed into the slim warmth of the station to wait for the Pelican Midnight Sleeper. Porter Jimmy Quitman said to Beau as he stepped off the Yellow Dog, grip in hand, "Well, maybe the man you lookin' for ain't on this train."

The faceless evening sky seemed to agree.

"I'll see you next trip," Beau said as he headed toward the big station doors. He waited until they cleared. Then he went straight for the stationmaster's office. The stationmaster, a rangy man in a long gray overcoat with an even longer face, was warming his hands over a Kalamazoo potbelly stove. The collar of his white shirt was smudged with coal dust, as was his necktie. The stubble on his face had grown prickly and sharp, but his eyes, so used to the night, barely opened. He stoked the stubborn potbelly fire and then reached for the shovel in the coalscuttle bucket right beside the Kal. He turned to Beau as if he'd been rudely pushed. "Whaddya want, boy?"

"Sir, I believe there might be a telegram here for me from Clarksdale."

The stationmaster cupped his long bony fingers over the uneven fire as if to snag the heat. "Telegraph office is closed, boy."

"Yessir, I know, sir, but I believe my boss might have left instructions to leave it with the stationmaster."

"I *am* the stationmaster."

"Yessir, I know, sir."

The stationmaster wiped his hands on a damp towel that hung on a chair made of blackened metal struts. "What's yer name, boy?"

"Name's Beau LaHood, sir."

The stationmaster walked over to his desk that was up against a wide window that faced the platform. A tall wooden crank telephone was mounted on the wall. Below it was a Woodstock typewriter with keys that had been punched too often.

"What's the name of the person you work for, boy?" he asked, sorting through a wooden tray.

"Al Nachman, sir."

"What kinda name is that?"

"I don't know, sir."

The stationmaster said, "There ain't nothing here for you, boy."

"Could be chunked in with 'em others, sir."

"Could be, but it ain't."

"It would be from Clarksdale, sir."

"There's only thing in from Clarksdale, and it's for a lady."

"Would that be Miss Shelby Prevette?"

The stationmaster went back to the stove, picked up the coal shovel, opened the belly hatch, then fed the fire and stoked the embers. "Why do you ask?"

"Well, sir, she ain't but right outside."

The stationmaster looked up from the fire. Beau pointed to the viewing window where a man on the platform was trying to light Shelby's cigarette. She quickly got the conductor to send the man on his way with a threat to have him arrested for harassing a lady. The stationmaster said, "Is that Miss Prevette?"

"Yessir."

The stationmaster was out the door. He gave Shelby a pencil to sign for the telegram. Then she opened it.

Western Union Telegram

CLARKSDALE = MERIDIAN DEC 28 1925
EUPHIA TOLD MARSTON THAT YOU ARE ON YOUR WAY TO NEW YORK STOP OUR ONLY FEAR IS THAT YOU WON'T GET THIS IN TIME STOP WIRE US IMMEDIATELY AS TO YOUR SAFETY AND COME HOME NOW STOP DADDY

Shelby quickly wrote down her reply and gave it to the stationmaster: *"No one will prevent me from going to New York STOP Not Marston not you not anyone STOP We made a bet daddy and I'm going to win it STOP Love Shelby."* Her anger and resolve seemed deeper than the threat Cobb posed. She gave the stationmaster money and sent him off.

A man slapped his hand hard on Beau's shoulder as he walked through the station doors that led to the platform. He angrily said, "Boy, you're not supposed to use the white entrance." Beau turned around and faced a man half his size. He was holding the hand of a little girl dressed in a red plaid winter traveling suit.

"Niggers use the side entrance," another man said.

Beau lied to them. "Yes, but the coloreds' door is jammed. So I had to use this here entrance." The white men looked down the long platform. Beau said, "I got no interest in disturbin' the peace, gentlemen. Please go down and see for yourselves. Colored door won't open."

The man with the child was satisfied the negro had shown enough respect. "Don't make it a habit, boy."

The other man, less satisfied, said, "Or we'll make something of it."

Beau said, "It won't happen again, gentlemen."

They went on their way.

Beau picked up a cigarette lighter with the initials MPC next to Shelby's baggage and handed it to her.

She at first refused it but then took it, thinking something with that much gold shouldn't belong to someone she hated.

Beau carefully panned the platform. "The man just botherin' you, miss, did he go into town?"

"See for yourself."

"I might iffen you help me."

"Help you with what?"

"Findin' Marston Cobb."

Shelby stared at Beau coldly. "Why would *you* be looking for Marston Cobb?"

"Well, miss, before I left Clarksdale, the law asked me to let them know his whereabouts should I see him on the railroad. He's behind the lynchin' back home and the one who killed your cousin Grover."

"You're not the law."

"Don't mean I can't help the law, miss. Was you suppose to meet this Cobb fella here?"

"Of course not."

"So it's just a coincidence him bein' here a moment ago?"

"For him it wasn't."

"I don't understand."

She was now angry and tired of the questioning. "*What* don't you understand?"

"Why wasn't it a coincidence?"

"Because he's been after me for months."

"Why?"

"You just tell the law that I'll kill him the next time he comes near me."

"Why's he after you, miss?"

"He's crazy." Shelby closed her coat and turned the other way. She had nothing more to say.

Beau took out his fountain pen and wrote a message to be wired to Al Nachman. He gave it to one of the porters, heading west, to be sent first thing in the morning. Then he waited for the train like everyone else.

8

A bobbed redhead leaned over the observation deck of the private car and sang *Collegiate*: a frenzied hit song that sounded as though it had been popped out of a champagne bottle and boiled to a bubble with Marcel Waves and saxophones. The Pelican Midnight Sleeper had rolled into Meridian.

Pullman porters alighted from their section and compartment cars with step stools and measured grins. Beau headed toward the train's Pullman conductor, Kurt Thompson, who was busy monitoring the movement of baggage and the boarding of passengers, answering questions, checking tickets, and giving encouragement when needed to confused travelers. He might have been new to the line but not the railroad. He vigorously shook Beau's hand and took his traveling papers. "So you're a Twentieth Century Limited man."

"Yessir, I am."

Conductor Kurt Thompson knew full well that only the best of porters were allocated to that train. Their chief asset was that they knew how to work under extreme pressure with precision and skill and had at least five years of service or had proved themselves otherwise.

Beau said, "I guess they changed conductors on this line."

"Yes, they did. How long have you been on the Twentieth Century, Beau?"

"Since January of 1920, sir."

"Five years means you've got seniority."

"I'm first porter, sir."

"Had a feeling you were. Gets mighty cold up north this time of year."

"Yessir. Sometimes your coat needs a coat."

"I hear there'll be a lot of snow on the rails straight through Albany and Buffalo this season. Traveling could be slow on your line. Dangerous if it should slide. I remember that bust up a few years back when that engine boiler exploded and melted snow for miles."

Beau said, "Long as there ain't a blizzard, everythin' should be fine."

"You know engineer Bob Butterfield?"

"Yessir. He's our top speed gauger. Can rap the stack through an avalanche."

"You know of Conductor Liston Truesdale?"

"Why, yessir, I'm in his crew."

"I'm not surprised. He and I worked the Texas Special and the Sunshine Limited years back."

"I heard about them lines," Beau said. "Lot a trouble back then. Train robbers and hold-up men on horses."

"We had our hands full, but we rode with Fred Heinz. The best man-hunting detective on the continental railroad. Your line has got him now. Heard he shot some freight thieves out of Chicago a few weeks ago."

"Yessir. He was waitin' for 'em in one of the box cars. Haven't had no trouble since."

"Well, you're in good hands, Beau. Liston Truesdale is a Mississippian like ourselves." Then with a thumb to his chest, he said, "You tell him Kurt Thompson says hello."

"Yessir, I will, sir. And glad to meet you, sir."

"You know Johnny Dixon?" nodding to the porter by the car just ahead of the private car.

"I know all the porters on this line, sir. My cousin, Samson Paisley, should be on this consist, as well."

"He is, Beau, but don't you let any porter try to get you to do their work. You're a guest on my train. You just take it easy and sleep all the way up to Bristol."

"Yessir, I'll do that, sir. Thank you, sir."

"Go ahead and board the train, Beau. Ride with Johnny Dixon. You'll have less disturbance in his car. A pleasure to meet you."

"Same to you, sir."

Pullman conductor Kurt Thompson went on down the platform, his eye on the last porter helping the last passenger. He waited until the stair chains of the forward six cars were pulled, before hopping aboard. Then he swayed his big red lantern back and forth and sang *All Aboard* across the long empty platform. The train lurched forward and left a trail of dark-gray smoke that lingered like field crows in the moonlight glow.

9

Beau slipped his suitcase under the dark-brown leather bench-couch in porter Johnny Dixon's men's lounge. "Johnny, what happened to Ridley?"

"He died."

"He *what?*"

"You heard me."

Beau couldn't understand. There was so much life to the Pelican Pullman conductor who had started out as a batboy for the Brooklyn Bridegrooms before moving on to the Boston Beaneaters as a second string shortstop. One day he got beaned in the head with a fastball for standing too close to home plate. On his way back to Brooklyn, to convalesce, a Pullman conductor advised him that it was far safer to work on the railroad than to rely on the mercy of a National League pitcher. He took the advice *and* his glove with him on every trip to show the teams traveling north and south.

Beau said, "The hell happened to him?"

Johnny Dixon said, "Bobby Jenks, sign-out man in New Orleans, told me Ridley's wife walks into their bedroom with a hot drink, thinkin' it was the cold that got to his bones and finds him dead on the floor, cigarette burnin' a hole deep in the carpet."

"He looked fine last time I saw him," Beau said.

"So did last Monday till it rained," Johnny replied as he put up new towels. "Look, Beau, I really need ya to help me out this trip.

Porter assigned to the private car missed his connection. And they got all sorts of demands, inside, like makin' cocktails I never heard of with things I know nothin' of."

"I'll take care of 'em iffen you help me out."

"With that?"

"There was a lynchin' yesterday."

"Where?"

"Clarksdale."

"What happened?"

"My oldest friend was acquitted of a crime and by a white jury at that. Then on his way out the courthouse, he was shot at close range more'n two dozen times. Flesh on him looked like it was tore up by an ice pick. He was my oldest friend, Johnny. We growed up together. Cracker started it all might be on this train. So I needs you to help me find the son of a bitch."

"That why you was checkin' the call sheet before?"

"Yeah, and he goes by the name of Marston Cobb. I'll be checkin' all the other call sheets too."

Conductor Thompson came through the vestibule door that led from the private car. "Johnny, I need you in Russell's car. Says he ain't getting the service he paid for, and I don't like his temper. He's ready to fight again."

"Yessir, I'm on my way."

Conductor Thompson looked from Beau to Johnny Dixon. "Something going on here?"

Johnny replied, "Oh no, sir. I was just about to make up the berths for the Meridian pickup, but I'll go to the private car now."

Conductor Thompson said, "I'll tell your passengers to change, first. That'll give you time so you can take care of Russell and then make up their berths." Then turning to Beau he said, "Keep your eyes open. There was a pretty white woman in Shreveport, working undercover, getting real nice with the porters."

"Entrapment?"

"Yeah, and she nailed a porter who hadn't been on the job for long. Thought he could have a little whoopee on the side. There's something else."

"What, sir?"

"Some rich boy up north is near dead from wood alcohol poisoning. Said he got the contraband on the train from a porter. Pullman's out to get anybody this holiday season who's breaking the slightest rule. So be sharp, Beau."

"I will, sir."

"And if you do find a free berth, and somebody complains there's a negro sleeping next to him, you tell him you work for the railroad and that it's your job to sleep, and if that don't shut him up, then you just send him over to me, and I'll put the fear of God in him."

"Yessir, I will, sir."

"You wanna smoke? Chew gum? Go ahead. You're not on duty. Someone complains? Let me know. I'll set him straight. And if you need to wash up, go ahead and do it here. No need to go all the way up to the mail car."

"White folks won't like it iffen they see me at their sink."

"I'm white and I do." Conductor Kurt Thompson headed up the train.

A moment later Shelby appeared in the entrance of the men's lounge, glowing red, as if something hotter than blood ran through her veins. She said angrily, "The salesman sitting across from me is a pervert, and I want y'all to get rid of him."

Johnny Dixon stuck his head into the men's lounge. "You got a moment, Beau?" Shelby almost hollered, "There's a salesman harassing me in my section, and he must to be thrown off the train!"

"Well," Johnny said, "that'll be hard now that the train's rollin', miss."

"I don't care," Shelby said. "The Pullman Company says that no woman shall get harassed aboard its trains, and this salesman dared to touch me."

Johnny replied, "I'd put you in a compartment, miss, but they's all taken."

Shelby turned to Beau. "How about you helping me?"

Johnny said to Beau, "I'll be in the private car. They need some you-know-what quick," and left the men's lounge.

Beau said to Shelby, "It ain't Marston Cobb botherin' you, miss?"

"No. Some other idiot."

"This is what I'll do, miss. I'll get your berth made up. This way you won't have that passenger in your face. Meantime, you go on up to the club car till it gets done."

"But that means he'll be sleeping right above me."

"Then I'll speak to Conductor Thompson, see maybe we can swap section-seats with a lady passenger for the man who's botherin' you. In fact, I'll make sure that it's done and that it's a lady of quality."

"What if her berth is already made up and she's asleep?"

"I'm sure she'll have the decency to accept the swap, miss."

"I hope so, because I will not ride in that section-seat."

"You mind I ask why you didn't reserve a compartment car beforehand?"

"I had to leave on short notice," Shelby said. "This was all I could get."

"Well, miss, I'll have you swapped out in no time. I done it many a time before."

He led Shelby away from the lounge entrance, but something was still on his mind. "Miss Prevette…?"

"What?"

"I know very little about this Cobb fella other than what he looks like and what he done. I'd sure appreciate you tellin' me somethin' particular about him in case I should run into him."

Shelby said, "All you need to know is that he's the craziest person God ever blew breath into."

"Yes, but does he have any habits…you know…peculiarities? Things that only you could tell me."

"He has a long list of peculiarities."

"Such as what, miss?"

"Such as he perceives insults that don't exist and suffers rejection as if it's life threatening."

"What do you mean?"

"Are you going to get rid of that salesman?"

"I'm doin' that now, miss. I just need to know a few things about this Cobb fella, now that you're here. What about these insults?"

Shelby said, "He'll look for a fight where there isn't one, and he has no loyalty to anyone or anything. Just great hates and a false notion of himself."

"Why is that?"

"I don't know why, Beau, but he can get excited by the smallest snub, and he pretends to have many interests and to understand the complexities of the world, *except* his own."

"Anything else, miss?"

"That's not enough?"

"The more you can tell me, the better," Beau said.

"What about getting rid of that salesman?"

"I will in a second, miss. There anything else you can tell me about Cobb?"

"Are you familiar with braggarts?"

"I've met my share."

"Well, Marston has this infallible sense of purpose, but the longer he talks, the easier it is to see through him, though by then you feel like an idiot for having given him the time of day. So be careful; like many fools, he thinks he knows the world, but only in pieces."

"Has he always been like this?"

"Since a child."

"Has he hurt you?"

"That is why I'm on this train."

"Is he in love with you?"

"If you mean the idea of love and its quick pleasures, then yes." Shelby stepped toward the private car where a Victrola was fiercely playing the Charleston. "What's going on in that private car?"

"Oh, they all havin' a holiday party started last year."

Shelby caught sight of two Broadway showgirls through the fancy cut-glass portal in the vestibule door. They were dancing wildly and splashing their drinks without a care. Shelby stepped aside to let several male passengers into the men's lounge. She beckoned Beau to come closer. "Did you or any of the other porters sell them that champagne?"

"They brought it on their own, miss."

Shelby moved into the vestibule and reached for the interconnecting door handle that led to the private car.

Beau said, "I'm sorry, miss, but you ain't allowed in there." He grabbed the door handle from her as Johnny Dixon exited the private car, all sweaty and out of breath.

"Beau, you don't help me out in there, I'm gonna jump right off this train."

Shelby slipped through the open door.

Beau yelled, "You *can't* go in there, miss!" but Shelby was

66

gone like a duck after a June bug.

Johnny said, "Now there's three crazy girls in that private car."

***

The party came to a crashing halt. A redheaded showgirl from the Follies and Virginia Swain, the renowned Broadway actress, sneered at the stunning upstart boldly making her way into the private car's living room. She was sure that the girl had found out that Russell, the owner of the private car, was a big Broadway producer who had hinted more than once since they departed New Orleans that *What keeps show business going is a girl with a new face,* and for the past several years, Virginia had been that new face when Broadway, overnight, had changed from dowagers in bloomers to flappers in teddies. She was the queen of the long kissing scenes that caused riots with parents of teenagers in from the long-skirted towns of Indiana or Kansas, and she had no desire to lose her top-dog position and get carted off to the lowest vaudeville circuit to do heel-and-toe routines while swinging a cane to the tune of *Who Threw The Overalls in Mrs. Murphy's Chowder?*

Shelby couldn't have cared less. The evening light sharpened her lively inquisitive eyes as her lazy Delta drawl broke the silence. "Pardon me, sir, but I was told the observation deck is yonder way," she said, vaguely pointing to the end of the elegant private car. The two talents, not interested in the crasher, instinctively stood closer together to protect their turf as Russell approached Shelby on little toes. His red Santa cap with its furry white tip bobbed off his nose. A Champagne glass gravely tilted to one side as he said in a parishioner's voice, "I'd be more than glad to show you the way, miss." Russell's eyes were fixated on Shelby's magnificent face as it left a dreamy streak in its path.

"I first must tell you, sir," Shelby warned, "that I had the most frightful incident with a perverted salesman in the next car, but if I am intruding, I shall be on my way to fend off that pervert as well as a delicate lady can all by herself." She patted her brow as if about to faint. Virginia was enraged at the performance, but Russell bought it hook, line, and sinker—he had found his new star. On cue, Shelby wiped away a tear hidden underneath the sorrow of the moment and fluttered her hand as if she were drowning and going under.

Russell—a big Southern man with lips made for having the last word—valiantly came to her rescue. "You're not intruding at all, miss. If the railroad can't offer you safety and comfort, I'll have it done in my private car," he said as he poured her a glass of bubbly. "You're going to spend the rest of your trip here. I'll get the porter to bring your things here immediately—can you do the Charleston?"

Shelby pointed to the Victrola and told Russell's girlfriend, the redhead whose ginned eyes and painted stockings belied her real gifts, "Play it. You'll find out."

10

The morning sun struggled through the dark Tennessee mountains as the Pacific Class 4-6-2 locomotive blew long and short whistle bursts east of Whitman's Junction. Beau turned his sleepy head away from the sharp glare that glazed the men's lounge window. Conductor Kurt Thompson was standing in the doorway and looking very concerned. This bothered Beau, because he had worked with conductors who would, at first, come on friendly and then, all of a sudden, turn short tempered and mean. He remembered one conductor, out of Cheyenne, who had made the extra effort to endear himself with his porters but then reported the slightest misdeed to the local superintendent. There seemed to be an impulse in some people to be seen as good, trusting, and kind but then had a need to punish that impulse. Beau hoped Conductor Thompson wasn't one of them.

"Beau?"

He stood up quickly. "Yessir?"

"Porters been telling me you've been looking at their call charts."

"Just a quick glance, sir."

"Any luck?"

"Nossir."

"Well, I already went through the dining car three times, and if this Cobb fella I been hearing about is eating breakfast, he's having it somewhere else."

Johnny Dixon entered the men's lounge. He was dressed in his starched white rise-collar jacket fixed with four shiny Pullman stamped brass buttons. His face was covered with sweat, and his eyes were weighted with exhaustion.

Conductor Thompson said, "The hell happened to you, Johnny?"

"They still partyin' in there, and I haven't slept in two days."

Conductor Thompson said, "I want you to sit down for half an hour and get some shuteye. I'll cover for you." Then turning to Beau. "What does this Cobb fella look like?"

"Well, he got hot dark eyes and black hair. Wears it a bit long. Sorta curly about the ears and forehead. Got the kind of look someone without mercy has."

Conductor Thompson said, "This is what I can do for you, Beau. I'll knock on every compartment door and say I got a message for this Cobb. Then I'll get the waiters to do the same thing at all the servings. We'll flush him out one way or the other. If he's on this train, we'll get him."

"Thank you, sir. Thank you very much."

"No problem, Beau. This man has to be caught." Conductor Thompson then went on his way.

Johnny sat down next to Beau, ready to collapse.

"You look awful," Beau said.

"They's runnin' crazy as a pig in a peach orchard, and not one of 'em is sober. I told them it's morning already, and they didn't give a damn. Your friend Miss Prevette is tellin' 'em all she's a bootlegger from Chicago."

Beau laughed. "She ain't never been to Chicago, let alone seen no bootlegger."

"Maybe so, but she said she got a tommy gun in her trunk just in case somebody tries and highjacks her shipment. She was so drunk she fanned her arms like she was sprayin' 'em all with lead." Johnny handed Beau a cup. "I could use a drink."

Beau tipped his flask.

"And iffen you got some smokes, all the better, 'cause they're all out," he said as he patted his money pocket. "And if you got another pint handy, they just might want that too," he continued, hearing the private car's buzzer again.

Beau said, "You get 'em breakfast from the dinin' car. I'll sell 'em a carton and some hooch."

Johnny left the men's lounge. "Oh, and that's Virginia Swain in there. She promised to get us free tickets to her new play that's gonna be on Broadway after the previews in Chicago."

Beau said, "Get as many as you can. We'll make money on that, too."

***

Fifteen minutes later, Johnny Dixon returned with a tray crammed with fried eggs, ham, Pullman rolls, a big silver coffeepot, and a weary smile. "Good luck, Beau."

The aisle in Russell's private car was scattered with pillows, blankets, cigarette stubs, and empty glasses. The library walls, inlaid with nymphs and gilded forests of fawns and pre-sin pleasure, were sullied with anything that would stick. The big bathtub of gold fittings and swan faucet was throttled with crushed cigarette butts, empty contraband bottles, and enough ashes to bleach the morning sky gray. Spilled cocktails soiled the carpet runners with spotted stains as if a leopard had been inked and rolled across the floor. Beau opened the door to the observation deck to get some fresh air in the car. Then he headed back to the library where walnut bookcases were flush with leather-bound gold-leaf editions of *Vicomte de Bragelonne*, Harbour's *In the Icy North*, Boileau's *L'Art Poétique*, Wilson's *The Science of Baseball*, and other vanity editions no one bothered to read. Beyond the library, Shelby and Virginia were flat out on the floor. Virginia opened her groggy, sultry eyes. "Where the hell ya think yer going, boy?"

"I got y'all somethin' to eat, Miss Swain," Beau replied as he placed the breakfast tray on a side table.

"I think I'm gonna die from all that coffin varnish you all sold us last night," Virginia said, leading him into her drawing room of polished mahogany with framed field and stream prints that kept the eye busy from one hunt to the next. The bed was fixed, not pulled down. A brown leather side couch and a small secretary desk were off to the side. Beau turned away so Virginia could undress.

"Hey!" she said, searching her room. "Whaddya do with 'em?"

"Do with what, miss?"

"My you-know-whats," she replied, pointing to the dresser.

"This what you're lookin' for, miss?" Beau held up her pink silk pajamas.

"Yeah, unless *you're* gonna wear 'em."

She grabbed the pajama bottom from Beau's hand, slipped off her teddy, fell back on her bed, and wiggled in her legs. She reached over, took the pajama top from Beau, and, after several tries, got her arms into the correct sleeves. "Whaddya do with my script?"

"What script, miss?"

"I put it *right* here," as she crawled to the other end of the bed and stuck her nose over the edge. "I don't learn my lines by the time I get to Chicago, it'll be all your fault."

"I'll help you look for it, miss. What's it look like?"

"Black like you."

"Maybe if you remember what the play's about, you'll remember where it is?"

"It's supposed to be about some soldier with a lot of promise, but the director of it has even less."

"Just back from the war, miss?"

She bumped into Beau. "Hey, watch out!" Her flaxen bob bounced off her sleepy eyes.

"Sorry, miss. He gets into trouble?"

"*Who* gets into trouble?"

"Soldier in your play," Beau replied, now down on the floor with her, searching for the script.

"*Big* trouble."

"You his trouble, miss?"

"Hey, you write this play?"

"No, miss, but when Hollywood sees the sun rise, they always

73

think it's for the first time."

"Yeah, but this is a play, not a movie."

"You'd think…" He pulled up her blanket, and the script tumbled to the floor. "Here it is."

Beau left the drawing room and returned to the men's lounge. Johnny Dixon walked in with Beau's breakfast: a soaked bean sandwich and a cup of black coffee. "I got some good news for you, Beau," he said, but he fell right asleep on the couch.

Clarksdale, Mississippi

11

The last time Clementine LaHood put on a smile, it could barely hang on. This time was no different. Al Nachman said to her, "I wouldn't waste any more time here."

She spread more biscuit dough on the board. "You just think I can get up and go?"

"There's been talk going around."

"What talk?"

"Kin of the boys shot and killed by Sheriff Glass's deputy are fixing to set your house aflame and with y'all in it."

"Iffen the sheriff's deputy shot 'em, why they after *us*?"

"You're being rational, Clementine."

"You want me to be crazy?"

"Of course not," Al said, "but they all see it as Beau's fault for starting the brawl. That's why I need you to get out of here, and I don't mean tomorrow."

"I got five chil'un, Mr. Nachman," Clementine said, wiping her powdery hands on her apron. "You just don't pack 'em up in a second."

"That's why I'm here."

"They ain't horses I can hitch up to a buggy."

"We don't have time to argue, Clementine."

"You barge in on here and expect me all of a sudden to change my life? Well, let me tell you somethin'. Somebody wanna make trouble here, I'll tan his hide so hard it won't hold a shuck."

"Clementine, it's just for a spell in case they show up and try something."

"You mean show up and burn down my house?"

"Or hang y'all in the pippin orchard."

Clementine stared at Al. He had his new federal agent badge in his hand so she would understand the seriousness of the moment. Clementine walked over to the closet, aside the kitchen, and returned with a Remington Model 1889 side-by-side shotgun. "I can hunt, shoot, good as men. I'm kin of Holt Collier 'case you forgot."

"I have no doubt about your abilities, Clementine."

"Holt Collier served the South in time of its need. Was the best horse soldier the South had even though he was black. General Nathan Bedford Forrest said it was an honor to ride beside him. How many white people General Forrest honor like that? *None*."

"The Rebellion's long over, Clementine. What's done is forgotten."

"*I* haven't forgotten. I *damn* well haven't forgotten," she said, putting the shotgun back in the closet and then lifting her apron to wipe her brow. "I'm busy makin' breakfast. You hungry? You can pull up a chair."

"We don't have time for that," Al said. "I just spoke to Beau's mother, Charlotte. Said she'd be more than glad to have y'all over."

"Beau's mama got enough on her plate carin' for Granny Ella. Woman near a hunnert. Runs the whole cabin. I keep tellin' her to write a history instead of talkin' it."

Al said, "You know Granny Ella can't read nor write."

"Well, I surely can't do it for her with five kids, one on the way," cutting the biscuit dough and then greasing the pan with drippings.

"I understand," Al said, "but I can't let you put your family in danger. Now, you hurry up, and let's go."

"You takes care of your family. I sees to my own," she said, lining up eight cuts of dough for the skillet.

"You're being a fool, Clementine."

"You thinks they all don't know where Beau's mammy lives?"

"If you wanna go somewhere else, fine," Al said, "but staying here is out of the question."

"And just what did Beau say to that cracker?"

"What you just said."

"*What* did I say?"

"Cracker."

Clementine walked over to Al. She leaned into him as if she was talking to one of her children. "You know what free speech is?"

"Yes, I do, Clementine."

"Beau got a right to say whatever he wants."

"That's not the point.

"Oh yes, it is."

"Clementine, you just can't go into a theater and yell fire if there's no fire; it's the law of the land."

"But you can kill a nigger 'cause he sassed a white man?"

"You can't do that either."

"They do it *all* the time, Mr. Nachman. Y'all talk freedom, liberty, free speech the way poor folk talk about gettin' rich, but it never happens."

"You're missing the point, Clementine."

"I know what the point is, and it's gettin' duller by the second."

"Then know that Beau told me to move y'all out of here right before he boarded the Yellow Dog. I won't let him down, Clementine. Y'all're going to leave here or I'll have to force y'all out."

Clementine walked over to the window by the kitchen sink and stared out into the gray empty cotton fields. The sky was turning copper from the low burning sun. A flock of purple martins shimmered as they swarmed from tree to tree in soaring dark silhouettes. Clementine turned away from the silent cold fields. She undid her apron and dropped it on the baking table and then put out the fire in the coal stove and left the kitchen. The house was filled with the sound of quick feet and accompanying chatter. Moments later she returned with her five children dressed in coats as the little ones struggled with their sleeves. She held two hastily filled bags in her hands and her Remington under her arm.

Al said, "I'd leave that shotgun locked up in the closet."

Clementine said, "What am I gonna do to protect my family?"

"Get out of here."

She did but took the Remington too and a box of shells.

Pelican Midnight Sleeper

12

Pullman porter Samson Paisley was busy shining shoes that belonged to drummers who rode up and down the lines and stopped off at towns with samples, order sheets, and ready smiles. They knew Episcopalians from Methodists, Unitarians from Congregationalists, Hebrews from atheists, Catholics, Irish or not, and if they didn't know their fellow passenger, they quickly engaged him with a journalist's instinct for information and inside gossip before stepping off the train. Samson picked up his shoe brush and aimed it at his cousin Beau as if he were about to put a shine on him. "You say there was a lynchin' back home? I say business as usual. They killed Lindsay 'cause of honor. That's all a lynchin' is. And for the law of the white man to decide against another white man, well, there ain't no greater insult." He wiped the excess polish off a shoe and put his brush to it. "Beau, you and me is like this here shoe. White man takes it off, he can still walk. But the shoe...it ain't got nowhere to go..."

Beau said, "I ain't no shoe."

"No, but you're like one. There gotta be somethin' in it for you to get goin'." Cousin Samson tossed the dirty towel into the metal grate below the long narrow metal shelf on the lounge wall where six white towels with blue Pullman banners were folded into a flotilla that headed toward the nickel washbasin wedged into the corner panel. "You say the white man you lookin' for is named Cobb?"

"Marston Cobb."

A drummer, hands wide on his hips, entered the men's lounge in his stocking feet. "Boy, you got my shoes?"

Samson handed the man his shone leathers. "You need your suit pressed, sir?"

The drummer flipped him a nickel. "Not now, boy," he replied and left the lounge.

Samson said to Beau, "You speak to Cousin Julius?"

"I'm barely home, and when I am, Clementine rarely lets me out of her sight."

"I bet he know what's goin' on. Colored man know everythin' about the family he work for, but then, you been on the train ten years now. You better go 'n' wire that Nachman fella next stop. Tell him to speak to Cousin Julius. He might lead y'all onto somethin' about the lynchin'. Iffen there's one thing I know—" Samson lowered his voice. Shelby appeared in the doorway. She wore an expensive black Chanel knitwear dress, a shade the old world had only used for mourning, but then, they had reason to mourn. The Kaiser, after the war, may have slipped into Holland to pretend he was a butter-and-beer merchant, while his cousin, the king of England, tiptoed back on the throne with his feather-dusting generals, but no amount of hiding could bring back the forty million dead after four years of slaughter, and no amount of black could offset the grief. The flapper, unencumbered by their bloody past, put her fiery eyes on Beau and scolded him.

"It gives me no pleasure to tell you that everyone has stinging

80

headaches from that coffin varnish you sold us last night."

"I'm sorry, miss, but I never seen no one look better than you after a night out."

"Never mind how I look. I need to speak to you."

"About what, miss?"

"About something on my mind. In the meantime, hurry up with that coffee before we all die."

"I'll have it in no time, miss."

Shelby went on her way.

"Who is she?" Samson asked.

"Miss Shelby Prevette."

"You don't mean Prevette from back home?"

"Yes, I do."

"What she want with you?"

"Don't like the hooch I sold her."

"You didn't answer my question."

"She found out my kin were from her plantation, and well, it brought us closer."

"*How* close?"

"I'm just bein' kindly toward her. Nothin' else."

"For your sake it better be. And be careful you ain't sellin' wood alcohol. Word's out some rich folk got a suit-in-law against the railroad, and they wanna skin us alive."

"I already heard."

Samson finished up the shoe. "What else is goin' on between you and that white girl?"

81

"She's on her way to New York."

"That's not what I asked."

"We just got to talkin'. That's all."

"Well, I'll do you some talkin'. Her daddy's the richest man in the South, and iffen you is so much as suspected of somethin', you'll be lynched, next."

"Samson…sometimes I wish you wasn't my cousin."

"Cousin or not, you do what I say about wirin' Julius. I hear he knows secrets that go back before the Rebellion—things Granny Ella should ever hear would drive her to madness."

"Such as what?"

"Such as how things was back then," Samson said. "I'd look that girl long in the face next time you see her. Seems us is all mixed up together—and I don't mean crazy-in-the-mind mixed-up."

Conductor Kurt Thompson entered the lounge with a telegram. "Mail boss got this last stop, Samson," he said, handing him the wire. Then turning to Beau, "I need to have a word with you."

Samson read the telegram expecting he had been transferred to some commuter line where tipping was nonexistent. "Beau?"

"Bad news, Samson?"

"Maybe," Samson said with a tight smile on his face. "Looks like New York Central's short another hand. I'm gettin' loaned to your ride this New Year's Eve."

Beau said, "You can thank me for that." He followed Conductor Thompson out to the aisle.

Kurt Thomson said, "That fella you been looking for is holed up in the mail car."

"Cobb?"

"Yeah, he got in when they were loading the mail. Seems he knows one or two things about a train. Cap Simon noticed him washing up in the men's lounge of his car. He told Cap he worked in the Chicago freight yards as a dope monkey. Cap asked to shine his shoes and got a nasty reply. Normally, I would have intervened, but I wanted to make sure your man gets to Bristol so you can wire the law back in Clarksdale, but once you're in Bristol, you'll be on your own. The Pullman conductor on the Northeastern Limited may not be as obliging about having a murderer on board."

Beau looked out the window and watched the hills dip and rise. *Iffen it's Raylene Hollis, he won't be.*

Clarksdale, Mississippi

13

A flapper walked into Al Nachman's law office the way good luck turns into bad. Chairs were upturned. Bookshelves were cleared. Papers were strewn like rooftops from a late-fall tornado. She swept her T-straps through the mess and, like two loaded canons, aimed her eyes at Al. He moved off the couch; he was a mess: suit jacket ripped, shoes scuffed, hair tussled, a water bottle flat on his head.

"You *are* Al Nachman?" A cigarette already in her mouth.

"Yes. What can I do for you?" Al patted himself down for a light.

"I was at the trial yesterday. What a goddamn joke." Her eyes searched Al's desk and the shelves behind it. "I could use a drink."

The American Oak Regulator struck nine. "Kind of early for that."

"That's why I need it."

Al took a flask from inside his desk and met it with a glass.

"If it's coffin varnish, you can pour it down the drain," she said, taking in the office. "Who's the decorator?"

"The Klan."

"Paid you a visit?"

"Unannounced. What were you doing at the trial?" He wondered when the woman would introduce herself. Her accent sounded local, but her look was of another world.

She took position by Al's desk. "I like trials," then sat down and crossed her legs. "Especially murder trials. Someone gets murdered, and everyone's innocent."

"Is that why you're here?"

"It's why we're both here," she replied, leaning in for a light. "I was told that I could talk to Al Nachman confidentially," she continued, wondering what the good-looking lawyer would be like in bed. "People say he can be trusted."

"Anyone in particular?"

"People you know."

"There are many people who know me."

"That's why you can be trusted." She blew out a stream of smoke that was blued by a passing cloud. The town was still as a photograph. The skyline two stories high to the edge of town. The winter sky, winter dirty. "I'm Tom Nicholas's sister."

Al sat up.

She fiddled with her gloves. "They say he shot and killed Lindsay Coleman yesterday. Can we play it straight?"

"Sure. That's why you're here."

She said, "You and I both know no one gets hung for killing a niggra. If you want Tom, I can get him for you." She moved up her glass. Al poured her another shot.

"Where is he?"

"Let's negotiate."

"What?"

"My brother."

"Go on."

"I need money."

"There's a bank down the street."

"You're not listening."

"I've listened to every word you've said."

"I need *a lot* of money."

"How much?"

"I get ten thousand."

Al took the flask out of her hand. "That's ten times the average yearly salary around here."

"Then get the average man to find my brother."

"Why should I believe you'd turn in your own brother?"

"He's white. Nothing's going to happen to him."

"I wouldn't be so sure of that," Al said.

She snuffed out her cigarette. Then she got up, feeling stiff, and dropped a card on Al's desk. "I'm staying at the Alcázar."

"I thought you had no money."

"I don't. I'd stay at home, but my mother…she drives me nuts. All day she cries I'm an old maid. I gotta get back to New York where people are sane."

"You need money to live at the Alcázar," Al said.

"You need even more to live in New York. And that's where you come in."

"I think you're getting ahead of yourself."

Pointing to the flask on the desk. "Where can I get more of that?"

"I've got a better idea. What are you doing later?"

"Why?"

"How about supper? My headache should be gone, and maybe your notion of what to do with your brother will be clearer, because from my end all you want is money, and I don't dance that way."

"Then I'll have to warn you, Mr. Nachman."

"Call me Al."

"You'll never get Tom."

Al reached over and gave her his card. "What time do you eat?"

"When I get hungry."

"What time is that?"

"When it happens."

"How will I know?"

"You'll know," she said. "Just mind your potatoes," as she fastened her coat. "There's a hopper at eight. You *do* know how to hop?"

"Black Bottom, Shimmy, Charleston, you name it."

"Good," as she sailed over to the door and moored herself in the foyer. She filled the entrance with smoke and then walked out of it like a genie, "Have you ever been on a roller coaster?"

Al sat back and looked up at the question. "Why?"

"I'm talking about The Cyclone. Coney Island. Ever been there? Coney Island?"

"No."

"It's a mystical experience."

"Coney Island?"

"The roller coaster."

"How so?"

"Riding it is like living your whole life in five minutes."

A Western Union boy entered. "Just came in from Meridian, Mr. Nachman."

Al signed for it. Then he picked up the card left on his desk: *Zola Nicholas Alcázar Hotel Room 24.* The other side was in someone else's handwriting: *Ich werde dich immer lieben.*

The Prevette Estate, Clarksdale

14

Julius spent the day driving through the pouring rain, knocking on doors, searching everywhere for Marston Cobb. It was near dusk when Julius pulled into the Prevette estate. The lights were blurred in the window of Addison Prevette's study. Mrs. Brewer, the elegant, powerful wife of the previous governor, was sitting closest to the window with her gloves still on as she impatiently tapped her fingers on Addison's desk as if she were playing out a tune he needed to hear. Al Nachman was at her side, coat on. Mims, in the far corner, was getting up and leaving the study. She had seen the Pierce-Arrow through the window.

Julius drove on through the carport to the garage. The pouring rain followed him into the mudroom, where he removed his spattered chauffeur boots and britches. Ruby, the house cook and his wife, quickly mopped the water by his feet. "Where the hell have you been?"

"Where you just said and back."

"You is soaked through and through," holding up his coat.

Julius said, "You don't need a wet dog in the house to know it's rainin' outside."

"I know. I got you." Ruby brought Julius his house suit, shoes, tie, and a cup of hot coffee. "You know who been looking all over askin' every five minutes, 'Where's Julius?'"

"Same woman sent me out lookin' for that nuisance, Marston."

Julius walked over to the kitchen entrance and looked down the long hallway. "What's all that noise goin' on in the study?"

"That child, Shelby, causes nothin' but vexation."

Julius laughed deeply and warmly. "Like she never left. I do miss that girl."

Ruby said, "They been goin' on like that an hour in there about that crazy fool Marston and all the trouble this town got into with Grover, and now poor Lindsay dead and them three white boys at the lynchin' killed by that idiot deputy."

Julius said, "Well, that ain't the half of it." He lowered his voice as Mims entered the big kitchen with a face as long as a sermon. She clapped her hands and said to Julius, who looked as wet as a mouse hiding in a hose pipe, "Where have *you* been?"

"Out lookin' for your nephew as you directed, ma'am."

"Where is he?"

"I got no idea and neither does nobody else."

"Well, hurry up and get the Magnolia Belle from the cellar."

"Got to be careful, ma'am," as he made his tie. "Prohibition puttin' a dent on our quality rye. Better to serve up the Coon Hollow or Deuces Wild."

"How about Old Puritan? We must have some of that."

"Marse Addie said not to touch no more pre-1920 rye 'less for special occasions, and I don't think he sees this as one."

"Well, is there any Chicken Cock or Old Tub left?"

"Oh, we got lots 'a that, ma'am."

"Bring it up, then."

Ruby motioned toward the larder. "Everythin's here from the grocer, ma'am. He didn't have no Hall's Dixie Special Coffee. Somethin' to do with the Huckster from Jackson breakin' down in the rain." She handed Mims a carton of Old Gold.

"Then we won't pay him for it." She then turned to Julius, "You delivered the supper invitation for tomorrow night?"

"Left it at the front desk. Said Miss Zola would get it as soon as she awakes."

"*Awakes*? What's my niece doing asleep?"

"Guess she doin' what she shoulda done the night before."

"Did you speak to her?"

"I tried knockin' on the door, ma'am, but she wasn't in or didn't think she had to answer. Bellhop said she never leave her room much. Just a visitor come up now and then."

"*What* visitor?"

Julius said, "Bellhop wasn't sure or he just don't wanna be sure."

"Of what?"

"Bellhop want a nickel every time he open his mouth."

"Well, I'm not surprised. She has a reputation, my niece. I've already gotten several calls concerning her, and she's only two days home."

"I can try later iffen you want, ma'am."

"Don't waste your time, Julius. If my niece wants to remain a spinster all her life, that's my sister's problem, bless her heart. I told her more than once it was a mistake to let Zola go to Europe without being chaperoned."

"Well," Julius said, "I don't as know the Nurse Corp allows chaperones and the like, but Miss Zola should have the invitation for supper by now." He set the liquor glasses on a silver tray and turned toward the noise in the study. "Everywhere I went, ma'am, I was told they ain't see'd Marston, and they was most glad. I guess he left town for good."

Mims said, "Did you go to the plantation store?"

Julius looked up from the towel he was using to wipe down the liquor glasses. "I was over there first thing this mornin' like you directed, ma'am, and then on the way home. That Marston was nowhere to be found. He's gone for good and that's good."

"What about my niece, Euphia? Didn't Marston leave word with her?"

"She wouldn't say nothin' other than she ain't see'd her husband since before the trial, and I don't think she desires to see him no more, anyhow."

"My niece is giving birth soon."

"She most certainly is," Julius said as he helped Mims open the Old Gold carton. "And it's a good thing for Mr. Marston that Miss Shelby was sent away or she'd have killed him herself."

"How do you know that?"

"More'n once every hour she said so."

Mims said, "Well, I don't know what my Shelby ever saw in that monster other than to tease Euphia. She and Shelby are first cousins and ought to get along."

Julius said, "Miss Shelby never saw a thing in that crazy Marston. It was him doin' all the seein'. And there's one thing I knows certain—a boy's looks alone ain't enough for Miss Shelby."

"What do you mean a boy's looks aren't enough for my little girl?"

Julius struck a match. "As bright as this here flame shines, a boy got to shine brighter to get her attention."

"Is that what she said?"

"No, it's what I say," wondering how a mother could know so little about her own child, but then, Shelby took a lot of knowing.

"You go get the whiskey, Julius, and don't you dawdle any."

On his way to the cellar, Julius said, "Ma'am, Sheriff Glass lookin' for your nephew Tom. He fixin' to come by. What should I say?"

"My sister, bless her heart, raised that boy. Tell him to speak to her." Mims then returned to the study.

Julius glanced through the kitchen window into yonder field where the rows of old slave cabins were lined up as before the Rebellion. He counted down seven cabins where Ruby's kin had lived for generations.

Ruby gave Julius a push. "Hurry up with that bourbon."

Julius made his way down the cellar steps. "Cousin Beau's people was in cabin ten. Yours seven. Only ones now left from slavery days is Granny Ella and old Roy, too deaf to hear a canon shot fired."

Ruby said, "Granny Ella was from Stephen's plantation, not

here."

Julius's voice drifted up from the cellar. "Yeah, and that's where all the trouble started."

Alcázar Hotel, Clarksdale

15

Zola had lived in army tents; hospitals; grand hotels; pensiones, where the concierge is the owner and the wife is the cook; Grunewald, Berlin, where the house staff clicks its heels and changes outfits three times a day; and on a yacht in Saint-Jean-Cap-Ferrat, where there is as much wine as there is water. She had been kept, loved, lied to, and promised the world and then watched it all slip away. She went from putting out one fire in her life to the next and, with a drunkard's jog, grabbed onto anything in the way of hope or the next fix. Now, she was in a Mississippi hotel room, watching the evening settle in like ether and wondering why the concessionaire had deliberately disobeyed her request and sent up packets of Marlboros with the legend: *Fit for a king, blended to the queen's taste.* Zola rang the service bell and lit up a smoked Lucky Strike stub from the ashtray. Then she put the candlestick telephone back to her ear and coughed, which sounded like a car that wouldn't start. "You wanna be dumb, Tom? Go ahead," she said to her brother as the annoying strains of mixed melodies drifted in from the band warming up in the ballroom, right below. She wondered if they knew how to play anything else besides *Sweet Georgia Brown* or *If You Knew Susie (Like I know Susie)*. She wondered if Al Nachman would play along with her or would every night be like this for the rest of her life on the phone with some loser, waiting for something real to happen instead of all the dead-end situations that left her broke and alone with has-beens or dead boys. She said to her brother, "How else are we going to get the ten thousand dollars?"

"What if they decide to hang me?"

There was a knock on the door. Zola left her brother on the bed. A bellhop in black pants, red cumberbun, and black bellhop hat cinched to his jaw stood at attention in the doorway. He turned away from Zola's partially opened robe, thinking white women had no problem with black men seeing them half undressed as if they had half a mind when it came to sex. He shifted his gaze to the steamer trunk: clothes tipping over every drawer. The red blossom carpet. The Lake Louise wallpaper and the newly installed telephone so guests could book a compartment or section-seat from their room instead of having to go downstairs to the railroad office.

"I paid for Luckies, *not* this garbage," Zola said, pushing the bag of Marlboros into the bellhop's hands.

The bellhop said, "Man in the concession booth said Marlboros is more ladylike, ma'am."

"Tell the son of a bitch I want Luckies."

"Yessum, I'll tell him."

Zola shut the door on the bellhop and went back to her brother still talking on the phone on the bed. She picked it up. "*Listen* to me, Tom. Sooner or later you have to come home, and the chances of serving time are zero. So let's make the most of this."

Tom said, "You get the ten thousand; we talk."

"Where are you?"

"In someone's house."

"*Where?*"

"They're out at the moment but not for long. Just get the money. Then we can get out of here."

"Say, I'm sick of sitting in my room all day, waiting for you to call. Everybody thinks I got pneumonia."

"Zola, get the jack. Then we can get out of here," Tom said.

"I'll bet Mama knows where you are."

"Leave her out of this."

There was another knock on the door. "Who is it?"

"Al Nachman."

"I'm *not* dressed, Al!" Zola yelled back, worried he had overheard her on the phone.

"You said stop over when hungry."

"*I'm not* hungry. Come back in an hour." She heard the telephone line click on the other end. "Tom? *Tom?*"

Al said, "If you think I'm going to sit around an hour, you're nuts. It's seven o'clock. I'll make us drinks while you dress."

"Got any smokes?"

"Yeah."

"What kind?"

"Luckies."

She opened the door. "*Give 'm* too me."

Al handed her a packet of green-and-red Lucky Strikes and then took the glasses off the water tray. Zola was on her way to the bathroom, a trail of smoke behind her. Al said, "I reserved a table right off the dance floor."

Zola turned on the shower. "I *can't* hear you."

"You want me to put your drink on the bathroom sink?"

"Yes."

"I thought you can't hear me?"

"I hear what I want," and stepped into the shower.

***

Twenty minutes later Zola walked out of the bathroom, glowing like a distant star. She opened the jewelry box in the top drawer of her steamship trunk. "You're the typical American, Al."

"How's so?"

Zola slipped on a gold wrist bracelet with ruby red snake eyes. "You're on time like it's a business appointment," she said, thinking Al's black satin lapels, white wing collar, black bow tie, and black gorge vest made him look more like a silk-stocking district swell than a Southern lawyer. The white handkerchief in his breast pocket peaked like a flame from a blowtorch. "I'm used to European men with their exquisite entries, old-world flourishes, and refined prejudices." She walked over to the divan by the window. Her Parisian beaded evening gown black and silver, V-neck and V-back, scalloped to the heels with a blowout of white feathers that flung off the back of her T-straps like confetti off a float. She seated herself and pointed to the vacancy beside her.

Al obliged. "You've lived in Europe?"

"Yes."

"Where in particular?"

"Where there were no trees."

"Doing what?"

"Surgical nurse, and don't remind me. Every time I think of the Cromwell sisters, I want to jump off a ship, too." Her gaze went out the window. The winter clouds were frozen in the sky. The moon was half asleep and half as bright. "You make a good drink."

"Thanks," Al said. "How long were you over there?"

"Eight years," Zola said, "and when I got back home, all my mother wanted to know was why I hadn't met a nice boy. I said I had, but they were all dead."

"What did you do after the war?"

"Stayed in Paris."

"Why?"

"Because the French, unlike us, are out of adolescence." She finished her drink. Al poured another.

"What do you mean out of adolescence?"

Zola said, "They don't get the jitters when they see nudity. They don't think sex is dirty or of single purpose. They see going to the café, dining, and dress as a ritual to be observed with great passion and love. Walk into any bistro, and it's like entering a chapel. Buy a baguette and a glass of wine and experience communion. But stay away from museums and institutions, anywhere, unless you like getting hustled through endless rooms where you become part of the machine and the instruments of those who control it.

"You don't like art?"

"You're not listening."

"Why did you leave Paris?"

"I never left it."

"You're here."

"Think of Paris as you would home. You leave it for work or to go on a trip, but you return."

Al showed her the card that she had left on his desk and read aloud what was written on the back: "*Ich werde dich immer lieben.*"

Zola turned away as if she'd been hurt.

"Did I say something wrong?"

She quickly rose. "You don't know what you said."

"*I will always love you.*"

"You speak German?"

"Something like it."

Zola took a photograph from the top drawer of her trunk and held it as if it were fragile and about to crumble. "Have you ever had your heart broken?"

"I've been turned down a few times."

"I'm talking about something that sears your heart and leaves a burn that never goes away."

"No."

"Do you know what a rare gift is, Al?"

"What do you mean?"

"It's something that you hold in your hand and, when it leaves, has a life of its own that becomes yours as well."

"I'm not sure what you mean."

"Bartel..."

"Some boy you were in love with?"

"Yes. Some boy I was in love with..." Zola sat down and stared at the photo. She was lost in a world of fragments, selected memories, and a pain that had become acid over time. She sadly remembered, "Bartel was brilliant and savvied the intricacies of international life with five languages at his command. He took me to Grunewald, Berlin to meet his family, where we spent mornings in his garden, afternoons in the cafés on Potsdamer Platz, and evenings in cabarets on Kurfüstendamm Strasse, where Jazz and German are spoken with a fuel of its own making. It was a privilege and an honor to be accepted into his world of influential, well-educated people, whose resources, culturally and intellectually, extended to all the friends and people he knew—so unlike the small-minded, petty, hateful, incurious, self-righteous people I grew up with, who know little of the world and even less of themselves. But Berlin is lucky. It's a city reborn out of chaos and war. It's mad, giddy, academic, artistic, scientifically inclined, and raging with intellectual intrigue and a peculiar talent for invention and discovery that is absolutely maddening. I'm going back, and soon. I may even forget Paris."

"Y'all got married?"

"No."

"Why not?"

"It's a long story."

"I've got time."

Zola reached for her drink. "We went to St. Moritz for our engagement."

"I hear it's a swell place."

"Oh it's more than that. The village is like some Hansel and Gretel dreamland set around a frozen lake. The mountains are sugar coated under pillow-puff cotton skies. I thought I was in heaven or someplace better."

"What happened?"

"We went skiing one afternoon and missed the turnoff and went down this long terrible ice patch. There was no way to turn or stop without tumbling over, and Bartel did exactly that. He skidded head over heels, and I followed suit. Hours later I woke up with the sun at the other end of the sky, the wind on my face, and Bartel dead. The lights in the village below were aglow, and somehow—and I don't know how—I made it down that treacherous, difficult, unforgiving mountain into the village where everyone was dressed to the nines, while I'm running around the nighttime streets like a mad dog from hell." She tenderly put the photo of Bartel back into the trunk drawer. Then she turned around. "You've got the ten thousand?"

"No."

Zola pulled lip paint, cosmetics, combs, brushes, and clothing from the drawers of her trunk until she found a large billfold and held it high as though it was full of demons. "This is all I have, Al. Worthless Deutsche Marks," as she dropped them in a flurry. "You could have bought all of Berlin with this, once. Now, all you can do is watch it burn."

Al rose from his chair. "The Europeans did it to themselves.

They had everything in the world but then, out of boredom, blew their brains out."

"It's pretty rough over here too," meaning herself. Her poverty not yet his concern. She followed him out the door, down the flight of stairs, and entered the ballroom. She put her hand in his and glided onto the dance floor. "Ten thousand dollars could make life so easy for us, Al. Those Deutsche Marks are worthless."

"So is your proposition…"

16

"**Say, what's the big idea** stealing all my smokes?" Virginia Swain said as she threw the green-and-red tin of Lucky Strike Flat Fifties across the couch.

Shelby ducked. "Hey, watch out!"

Virginia hollered, "First ya tell Russell all that hooey about some murderer after ya. Then ya tell everybody ya got a tommy gun in your trunk, all the while stealing my smokes. How'd ya get in here anyway, Miss Nobody?"

"Same way you did," Shelby replied, turning the pages of the magazine *Smart Set*.

"Well, I didn't say stay over."

"Old man Russell did, and this is his private car end to end."

Virginia looked under the bed. "Where the hell's my dress from last night? Ya take that too?"

"Nope, and you look better in pajamas."

"*Get outta* my room."

"I'm staying *right* here."

"The party's over, Miss Nobody, and I mean now!" Standing nose to nose with Shelby.

"Well, if I'm Nobody, and you were drowning right now, there'd be *nobody* to save you," Shelby said, now back on the bed turning the pages of *Smart Set*, eating an apple. Virginia was at the doorway.

"Get out or I'm gonna have your ass thrown off the train," Virginia said, pointing the way.

"You seem to forget old man Russell said I wasn't leaving his private car until we got to New York," Shelby said, staring at Virginia like an eye doctor. "In fact, there are a lot of other things you didn't hear while you were knocked out, but you'll find out soon enough. Says right here,"—she shook a copy of *Photoplay*—"why so many stage girls can't break into moving pictures. You may be okay head-on, but your honker's got a bump on it and ruins the close-ups unless the movie's about bananas."

Virginia jumped on Shelby. Shelby flipped her over.

"*Get off* me, ya goddamn Mississippi hick!"

Shelby pushed the magazine silhouette of a girl with a perfect profile onto Virginia's face. "*See?* I got the face they're looking for...!"

"You got a face like a monkey!"

"What you need is a good spanking!" Shelby hollered.

"Get *off* me!"

"I'm staying right where I am."

Porter Johnny Dixon appeared in the drawing-room entrance. "Where do you want me to put this, Miss Prevette?" Beau was right behind Johnny, holding up her trunk.

Shelby pointed to Virginia's trunk as if it were contaminated. "That's where. And make it quick."

Virginia yelled, "*Hey*, what's the big idea!" Johnny moved out her trunk.

He said, "It's Mr. Russell's big idea, miss. See, the redhead has moved in with him, so you got her room now."

"Well, I'll fix that," Virginia said and headed to the bathroom to put something on.

Johnny said, "Mr. Russell done fixed it all up already."

Virginia stuck her head out the bathroom door. "Who asked *you*?"

"Nobody," Johnny said, "but we gonna be in Bristol soon, and this car gonna be decoupled and switched to the Northeastern Limited for New York. So I'm here to tell y'all can either stay here or board the Northeastern and wait in the club car. They got a nice buffet, comfortable chairs. Might even make some new friends."

Virginia hollered from inside the bathroom, "I can't wait!"

***

The Northeastern Club Car

Virginia made her entrance and pulled out a cigarette lighter that she had pinched from Shelby. On cue, a fistful of sparked lighters and lit matches materialized. "Hey! That belongs to me!" the owner of the empty hand said as he pointed to his initials MPC engraved on the gold lighter, his moist, open hand anxiously waiting for custody. "My little cousin swiped it from me back in Meridian."

Virginia eyed the strange-looking fellow, theatrical and fishy. There was a hollowness to his eye like someone blind who cannot see ahead. "*Which* little cousin?"

Cobb said, "Miss Shelby Prevette. A girl full of mischief and incredible beauty—a mischief in itself. You see, the naughty little thing likes to play hide and seek, and I can't find her. She has this terrible disease that only a specialist in New York can cure, and I've been petitioned to make sure that she arrives in Manhattan alive and not dead. Should you know where she is, then you are morally obliged to inform me as soon as possible."

Virginia snarled, "Where's her mother and father if she's that sick?"

"On the next train. They had some affairs to settle prior to leaving. Now, will you kindly tell me which car my little darling cousin is hiding?"

Virginia, no dumb Dora, remembered what Shelby had told her the night before. "Hey, you the one been following her?"

"*Ohhh*, you mean that awful boyfriend of hers, Wallace Thornby. He's sick over her imminent death and refuses to stay at home. You see, the little sneak stole into the train. When I find him, I'm going to rearrange his goddamn teeth."

"What's the matter with her if she's so sick?"

"I'll tell you on the way to her car."

Virginia said, "You'll tell me right now or you're going nowhere."

"Well, it's a long story," Cobb said, "with a lot of big medical words, but to put it simply, it's a disease of the blood, and long in the family. Her grandmother died of it."

"You mean to tell me her grannie was dead at age nineteen?"

"You can live as long as twenty."

"You a doctor?"

"Yeah, I'm a doctor, and if the little brat smokes or drinks, it worsens her condition, and she risks dying instantly of thrombosis."

"The hell's that?"

"I don't have time to go through third-year medical school."

"Well," Virginia said, "if that's true, she's been dead a long time, because she smoked ten packets of cigarettes last night, drank three bottles of champagne, and a pint of stump hole whiskey to boot. I think maybe she's got some other disease. But she's all yours if ya want her. And tell her folks they should be glad the little brat's dying."

They continued down the train through the dining car past waiters busy setting tables with white linen and sparkling silverware. The aroma of freshly baked Pullman dinner rolls and butter sweetened the air.

Clarksdale, Mississippi

17

The Prevette three-story house was built of dry yellow pine and cypress first-growth lumber painted whisper white, and in the evening light its windows glowed like first-time lovers. It boasted sunrooms sheltered by big red maples and dogwoods that pasted lavish shadows over balconies with tables for breakfast or lunch. The ground floor had two separate living rooms: one for the family, the other for visitors, and unlike the older ante-bellum houses, the Prevette residence was contemporary in design: it focused on family, not historical reinvention. There were many rooms: one for opening presents; another for Addison's book-lined study, a snug reading room with sliding ladders for out-of-reach tomes; and an entertainment room with a Baldwin baby grand, a Grebe Synchrophase radio, and a Victrola with records stacked in rows against the wall. The family room, just off the living room, boasted a well-decorated Christmas tree that made merry of everything else. There were big couches, small couches, cozy couches, soft center room carpets, lightweight drapes that spread open with a touch of the hand, but, most of all, sunshine that casted, what Shelby called, Cubist shadows. Each room was filled with flowers that maids watered to a schedule. There were no dark colors. White was the base of everything, with only the coolest of blues or the most radiant of yellows or greens. Mims, who had loved brown, now hated brown. The furniture had to be understated, unobtrusive. No monumental wood carvings with scrolling, fringed, or braided keep-it-dark-all-day imbrications as Shelby had instructed her mother. She kept her away from the kitsch. The English manor style that was now all the rage. The notion that good living had to be replicated by people who charged by the hour or the swatch, and there weren't too many of them in Mississippi, anyway. Shelby deftly pushed her mother in the other direction, that of the Bauhaus rebellion from Weimar, now of Dessau, that at first shocked Mims, who then welcomed it when she realized that she would be way ahead of everyone else. And now that Mims had excellent taste, she got wise and spent hours reading with her eldest daughter the latest magazines with the latest notions of fashion and design that Shelby translated in rooms with circuit boards so anyone could be reached in any part of the house with just a lift of the phone and a touch of the finger, for this was a house of long extended hallways and high ceilings that wound through a spill of light that poured from an endless sky over sprawling fields where a step garden led to a bathhouse and a grand swimming pool. Further on was the tennis court where the groundskeeper had yet to replace the sagging net still on order. Then the stables, riding rings, expansive meadows with livestock, cotton fields, and an older barn built before the Rebellion, which Shelby had recently refurbished, that sat by a cool steady stream lapping over small rambling stones that gave good water any time of year. The approach to the house was set on a long sloping brick driveway that in inclement weather allowed water to run off the sides.

Jess Earl turned back to the lady sitting tightly in the passenger seat of the Huckster. "Here we are, ma'am. Heaven on earth. Careful now," he said, helping her out and guiding her to the main walkway in the perimeter of the beaming house lights. "What time you want me to pick you up, ma'am?"

"I thought this was your last ride of the night."

"For two dollars I could work somethin' out."

"For two dollars I'll see myself home," Zola said as she headed to the front door and touched the electric bell that went off in the kitchen and valet room. Ruby nudged Julius, who was staring out the window and watching the fading moon highlight the rough edges of the old slave cabins in yonder field.

"Julius, you gonna stand there and daydream all night?" Ruby covered the dishes of black-eyed peas, fried cabbage, and mashed potatoes. She moved the roast leg of lamb from the oven to the table as the drippings in the pan saturated the air with piquant aroma.

"I'm on my way now," Julius said as he walked off in his starched white coat and black tie and went through the long main white hall where wide-plank maple floors shone under brightly lit ceilings. He made his way to the front door and peered through the spy windows on either side. He glimpsed an exotic creature shimmering under the hazy evening lamps. Gone was the long hair with bouncing ringlets, the black stockings, lace boots, and ankle-length dress. The farm-girl face—chubby at the jowls, rosy in the cheeks, and honeyed at the chin—had vanished like the century before. In its place was a starry aura tucked under a coal-gray cloche with a black seal brim pinned with a sparkling faux sapphire. The woman's potent green eyes were sharp in the evening light as she stood in-quartata in black leather T-straps sewn with strips of silver decorative leather. Her black chinchilla coat with bushy white fox-fur wristlets and matching white collar went all the way down her hips and met in point so that, from afar, she seemed to be tucked inside a cupid heart. With extreme caution, Julius opened the door and spoke to the apparition before him. "Good evening, ma'am," he said, not sure the woman wasn't fairy dust having just fallen from the December sky.

"Remember me?" Her local accent gave her away.

"Miss *Zola*?" Julius was wide with wonder.

"Have I changed that much?"

"Been almost nine years now, Miss Zola."

"I see you've been counting."

"Not a day I haven't. When the weather's fair and the air's warm, I looks out and thinks of the days us all spent up at Moon Lake. Y'all swimmin' and frolickin' and jumpin' in your uncle's old Packard, tryin' to steal it away from me. Little Shelby on my lap, tryin' to steer it from my hands. You coverin' my eyes so I can't see. Everybody hollerin' their head off. I sho' miss them days, Miss Zola. But time catches up and swallows you whole."

"You were the best uncle we ever had."

"Monkey's uncle you mean," Julius said, laughing louder than he should have.

Zola stepped inside the house. "My, my! This is some house. Where is everybody?" Her eyes followed the bright white walls up the broad grand stairway that had a polished wood banister that curved off into some intermediate kingdom.

Julius said, "Miss Shelby ain't here, and young John is spendin' Christmas in Natchez with cousins. But Little Martha is upstairs."

"You've got some gray in your hair now, Uncle Julius."

"Comes on its own, Miss Zola."

"Where's Shelby?"

"Oh, she ain't here."

"That's what I heard," Zola said, "but I don't always believe what I hear. How is the little troublemaker?"

"Well, Miss Shelby ain't little no more and neither is trouble."

Zola took in the vaulted ceiling that led straight up to the top floor where the pitched windows framed an illuminated sky. "I feel like I'm in some other world. Some timeless dimension."

"Well, your aunt finally put her foot down. Said she was tired of livin' like a bachelor. Told your Uncle Addie to spend some money or she gonna move Miss Shelby and young John into a nice house all by theirselves. It was done gettin' built just when you left for the war. Once you get used to it, it ain't that big. But it's all modern and everythin's plugged in. Includin' the washer. Little Martha was born upstairs."

"Where exactly is the mischief-maker?"

"Oh, she's with her mama, gettin' ready for bed. She had a long day with her daddy, learnin' how to ride her new twelve-hander she got for Christmas."

"I meant Shelby, bless her heart, not Martha. I hear Martha's very serious, though I don't know if she's as much fun."

"Just as much fun as y'all was, miss," Julius replied, laughing at a memory they both shared.

Zola said, "I was told Shelby's on a train to New York."

"It's true. Her daddy got a hotel all fixed up for her there. See, what happened is," he said, now leaning in, "Miss Shelby *had* to go."

"Why?"

"Well, there been some goin's-on here," Julius said, "that ain't yet to be resolved."

"Can you fill me in on what started all the recent trouble?"

"Oh, I wouldn't know where to begin, Miss Zola. Eight years is some time."

Zola took Julius away from the stairway to have a closer word with him. "Tell me what really happened between that crazy Marston and Shelby."

"Well, I don't know other than there been a heap of trouble over them two," he replied as he helped Zola off with her coat.

"How did it all start?"

"Kinda on its own."

"Why don't you tell me, Julius?"

"Well…"

"Go on. I won't say a word."

"See, us had the usual big Christmas party last year, and me and Ruby and the help was in and out with the eggnog and sweets as it is." Julius took Zola's coat and hung it in the big front closet.

"Go on."

"Well, I did notice how that Marston boy was always gettin' closer to your cousin."

"In front of the family?"

"You know how it is."

"How *what* is, Julius?"

"The way folks is at a party."

"Remind me."

"See, what that crazy Marston done was to first come to Miss Shelby with a word as family does and then with more than a word."

"And?"

"Set hisself right down next to her, and wherever she was, he was."

"In front of everyone?"

"Oh yes," Julius said. "So the little devil your cousin is, she hollers across the room and asks your sister, Euphia, how you was doin' in Europe, and Miss Euphia hollers back, 'Zola writes you all the time. Why ask me?' Now, it don't take much to figure the reason Miss Shelby asked her was not to find out nothin' about you but so your sister, Euphia, would have to turn her way and see that crazy husband of hers sittin' right next to Miss Shelby. Well, it went on like that for some time until your Uncle Addie had to have a word with her just where that Christmas tree is now standin'."

"What did my uncle say?"

"I don't know exactly, but Miss Shelby, always one step ahead, walked away from her daddy, and when she was far enough, she shouted across the livin' room so all could hear, 'I don't walk in

Marston's britches, Daddy. They get over to me on their own.' Folks all laughed. But not your sister. She left the house, never to be seen here again."

"Did Marston come around to visit Shelby?"

"Oh yes."

"More than once?"

"Like a buzzard in a boneyard. One day he come to the front door and demands to see her, but she was done with him after ridin' with him just once. Pointed to her head like he was loco. So I told that crazy Marston she gone visitin', and he said he heard she was drivin' around with some other boy, and I said it shouldn't bother him none since he's a married man and is her first cousin, to boot. Well, he got so ornery, we had to call the sheriff, and more'n once. I knew then that Marston boy was on the verge of doin' somethin' no good, and that's just what he done."

"What?"

"Somethin' awful, but your aunt, Mims…well…she just prefer things to remain quiet and in a way she ain't wrong. So it all got hushed up. Then that Marston boy sends your uncle a note sayin' one day he gonna make everyone pay for keepin' him out of the house just because he loves his first cousin Shelby, even though the year before he was off tellin' everyone how much in love he is with Euphia and then married her. We shook heads at the notion, but crazy folk got their own logic that makes all the sense to them. That's about the time your brother Grover come on over and he and your Uncle Addie sat down for a spell and your brother swore a whole lot sayin' he was fixin' to have a duel with that ornery Marston boy because of the way him and his younger sister and the whole family was gettin' dishonored. Your Uncle Addie said he wouldn't mind a duel, but he preferred Miss Shelby be the one drawin' the pistol. That's when things started gettin' dicey."

"What do you mean 'dicey'?"

"They found your poor brother, Grover, murdered in the cotton fields. First thing they all wanted to do was to lynch a colored boy, named Lindsay Coleman, who been makin' a fuss his wages been shorted 'cause your brother didn't weigh his cotton sack right, and that does happen now and then, but Al Nachman, you don't know him…"

"Yes, I do."

"You *do*?"

A voice came from upstairs. "Julius…?"

Julius approached the edge of the big stairway. "Yes, ma'am?"

"Has my niece arrived?"

"Oh yes," as he looked up toward the second floor where Mims was standing in her dinner dress. Little Martha was at her side, in pajamas and robe, rubbing her sleepy eyes. "Miss Zola's right here. Takin' her coat, just now."

Zola nudged him. "Then what happened?"

"I better see to your aunt. She sounds upset."

117

18

There were a few things Mims Nicholas Prevette didn't allow at the dining room table. Zola thought it should have been her aunt. "What's *wrong* with the way I'm sitting?"

"A lady doesn't sit with her limbs crossed."

"They call them legs now, Aunt Mims."

"Not in this house. And your back." Mims pointed as if a mouse had jumped on the table.

"What about it?"

"It's *touching* your chair."

Julius came in with the main course.

"Julius, what do you think of my back touching my chair?" Zola asked.

"Oh, I think Ruby made the best roast ever, Miss Zola," as he set a plate before her.

Mims said, "A lady *doesn't* touch the back of her chair when sitting."

"Funny, we never worried about that in France."

"You're not in France." Mims rose from her chair and put her forefinger between Zola's back and chair. "I want an inch. No less. Now lean forward." She wiggled her exacting finger in the allotted space.

"*J'en ai marre*," Zola sniped.

"Speak *English*." Mims inspected her niece's legs. "Stockings are not to be rolled down to the knees. I can see your thighs."

"That's the whole point, Aunt Mims."

"Uncross your legs."

"*Du gehst mir auf die Nerven.*"

"*Uncross* your legs."

Zola crossed them the other way. "*Why* won't y'all answer my question?"

"You're *leaning* against your chair, again."

Zola leaned forward and uncrossed her legs. "What happened to Shelby?"

Mims sat down and turned to her husband. "As we said, he did something awful."

"When did Marston do this awful thing?"

Addison said, "When is not the point."

"Was he arrested?"

Mims said to her niece, "Let's just say we couldn't risk having the whole world know."

"Know what?"

"We'd rather not say," Mims said.

"Why not?"

"Because we want Shelby to find a respectable husband one day."

"Y'all don't mean Marston had his way with her?"

"We don't mean any such thing," Mims said.

Addison tried to change the subject. "Tell me you haven't missed Ruby's cooking."

"It's the only thing I've missed. Mama told me had you not fired brother Tom, he would never have gone to Chicago and brought

Marston back with him."

"Tom quit," Addison said. "He wasn't fired."

"That's not what I heard."

"We hear what we want to hear."

"Mama gave me the impression that you ignored him."

"Then your mother, Zola, with all due respect, is a fool," Addison said. "And if you believe her, *you're* a fool, too. I tried everything to teach Tom a trade, but he's lazy. So he ran off to Chicago and didn't fare any better. Then he brought back my irritable nephew, who became my obligation to find work, which I did, and then for some strange reason, your sister, Euphia, found him attractive. I'm not saying Marston can't be charming at times, but charming people quite often have the ability to hide their more viler side."

Mims said, "Then Marston decided Euphia wasn't good enough for him. So he went after his first cousin."

Zola said, "Maybe Shelby allowed him."

"Shelby *didn't* allow Marston anything."

"Mama said she took rides with him."

"My sister, bless her heart, is confused," Mims said. "Shelby took only *one* ride and that was it. Then we couldn't keep Marston away. So your brother, Grover, took the appropriate action."

"And Marston killed him for it," Zola said.

Mims said, "The community believes it was that colored boy, Lindsay Coleman."

"Who cares what the community believes?"

"We do," Mims said. "We *live* in it."

Addison intervened, "The point is, had we taken another course of action, we would have been forced to bring up Shelby's predicament concerning Marston. So your aunt decided it would have been better to not have any filth floating around. I know that may sound unethical to some ears, but since people are not rational and pay no heed to reason, we must consider what people will think not what they should think."

Zola said, "I completely agree that people are irrational, but y'all don't mean to tell me y'all let a colored boy get arrested for something he didn't do."

"You forget. He was acquitted," Mims said.

"You're missing the point—he's *dead*."

Mims said, "Why don't you eat your supper? Ruby made it just for you."

"I'll eat it when I'm ready, thank you. It was more than clear, at the trial, that it was Marston who committed the crime and not Lindsay Coleman. That colored boy, Jubal Laiter, saw the whole thing."

"He's a liar," Mims said. "Niggras can act dumber than a monkey when they want to."

Zola reminded her, "Common notion is that they already are dumber than monkeys."

"That's beside the point."

"Not as far as I'm concerned," Zola said. "Y'all committed a crime by not acting against Marston."

Mims said, "Don't talk so high. Your brother, Tom, is in big trouble. *He* killed that colored boy Lindsay Coleman."

"Lucky for Tom we're not living up north," Zola said. "Yankees hang white people for murder."

"They electrocute them," Mims corrected.

"Well, at least they do something."

"You're talking about your brother, Zola."

"Nothing's going to happen to him. He's white."

Addison said, "Why don't we talk about something else?"

Mims said to Zola, "Let's talk about you."

"What about me?"

"I'm very troubled," Mims said.

"What about?"

"Why aren't you working in a hospital? From what we've all heard, you were a brilliant nurse."

"I was, but the war's over. Start one, and I'll get back to work."

"You don't need a war to get back to work," Mims said.

"*I* do."

"As usual, you're not making any sense."

"Aunt Mims, nothing makes sense once you've seen the senselessness of it all."

"Nonsense. You've frightened everyone in town with your sleeping all day at the hotel and having male visitors. I'm not suggesting anything, but it doesn't take much for anyone to imagine what you and that Jew were doing."

"Just whom are you referring to?"

"You know *exactly* whom," Mims said.

"No, I don't."

"That *kike*."

"Which kike?"

"The one you've been fucking."

Zola rose from the table, the anger in her eyes bare to see. "*Aunt Mims*, you seem to forget there was a time when you didn't wear shoes to the outhouse."

Mims rose from the table, ready to slap her niece. Addison ordered his wife to sit down.

Mims said to her husband, "I've had *enough* of her insolence."

Addison replied, "*I'm* the one who invited her for supper. Now *sit* down." Any further protest would have to wait for when bedroom doors were closed. Addison turned to his niece-in-law and said, "Please…sit down." Zola retook her seat. Addison waited until the room was, once again, calm before he spoke. Then he said, "The reason you're here, Zola, is to commend you for your actions in France—the selfless caring of our wounded and dying boys…the giving of yourself while so many others hadn't. It not only was honorable but also showed that you have character. But the war is over. And we all must come to terms with it sooner or later. I was in Cuba in '98, and even though what had happened there can't be compared to the devastation in Europe, the madness, nonetheless, was evident in both conflicts, and in that the experiences were equivalent…But it's been seven years since the armistice, Zola. And I've always loved you, and I've always believed in you. And I will do all that I can to help you resume a normal life, again. As someone who served, I have an obligation. But eight years of roaming the world can take its toll, and you're almost thirty now, which is an old maid in anyone's book, but with your looks, it shouldn't be hard for me to find you a husband who won't ask any more from you than to have his pipe and slippers and a hot meal ready after a hard day's work."

Zola pushed away her plate. "I'm not interested."

"Nonsense," Addison said, "once you've settled in, I'll get to work finding you someone suitable who will care, protect, and love you. It would be remiss of me to allow you to live in shame for the rest of your life."

Zola reached for her handbag and fumbled for a cigarette.

Mims said, "There's *no* smoking at the supper table."

"Isn't there *anything* you can do in this house?"

Addison took out his cigarettes and pushed them toward her.

"Thank you, Uncle Addie."

Addison said, "In the meantime, I'll do whatever I can to find you a suitable hospital for you to continue your work, and if you should prefer one outside of home, I will do what I can to get you a position there. No one will turn down a girl as valiant as you. I *won't* let them. But you've only been home for a few days. So give yourself some time. Then we'll take the next step." Addison waited for Zola to say something. Instead, her eyes were aimed nowhere. He resumed his meal, as did his wife. The room remained silent except for the clinking of knives and forks and the heavy drift of smoke that hung over the table. Then a quick flash of light bounced off the window, and like a brush it painted its bright light over each pane in search of someone or something inside the room as the shrill sound of barking dogs filled the land as men in long winter coats carried bright lanterns that painted long beams of light onto the hard winter ground.

Zola turned to her uncle. "It's a bit late to go hunting."

Julius entered the dining room, his eyes on the window. "They's all headed out to the cabins, Marse Addie."

Addison rose from the table. "I'll speak to Sheriff Glass."

"Sheriff Glass ain't out there."

"Who is it then?"

"I don't know, but they got shotguns and high-caliber rifles."

***

The coon dogs howled and beat their paws against the old logs of the slave cabin. Special agents posted themselves on either side of the cabin's only door. One stood guard by the boarded window. Al Nachman was holding a shirt to the dogs' noses. He hollered, "*Tom Nicholas*, come out with your hands up!"

An agent said, "He might not be in there, sir."

Another said, "Scent can fool the dogs if a man's been in a place long enough."

"He's in there," Al said.

Addison Prevette trundled down the road, full of his supper. "The hell are you doing on my property, Nachman?"

"Tell the boy it's over," Al said as he handed Addison the warrant for Tom Nicholas's arrest: dead or alive.

Addison read it in the lantern's glow. "You could've at least had the courtesy to call me, first."

"Mr. Prevette, the courtesy now belongs to you. Tell your nephew to get out of that cabin or he's in for a sorry haul."

Addison Prevette approached the cabin. The dogs bayed and nipped at his heels. He had to kick them away. "*Tom!* Listen to me, son! There are armed agents out here, and they mean business. They've got a warrant to take you in dead or alive." He waited for a response. "Guess the boy's not in there, Mr. Nachman."

Gunshot came out the window. The nearest agent fell back. The rest fired their weapons in repeated succession. The old door blew into bits and pieces. The agents rushed in.

"Put the light on the boy," Al said.

Tom Nicholas faced the wall, thinking it was the door. His face was full of blood, and his arm was straight out with the same pistol he had used on Lindsay Coleman. One of the agents tapped Tom on the shoulder as another brought him to the ground.

Vince Brocato said, "He needs attention. I'm afraid he can't see."

Al said, "Call Doc Ketter. Tell him to meet us down at the county jail."

They put Tom Nicholas in the backseat of the Ford. Addison Prevette, believing he was owed an explanation, approached Al. "How did you know the boy was in there?"

"Ask the dogs." Al got into the Ford and drove off into the night.

Julius turned away from the kitchen window. There were dishes to be cleared. Coffee and cake to be served—if anyone so desired.

Bristol, Virginia

19

The cold wind blew off the Blue Ridge Mountains into the Bristol Station Western Union office and scattered telegrams fiercely across the floor. The clerk, reaching for as many as he could, said, "Easy with that, or you'll break it." Beau gently shut the door. It had a broken hinge that popped when opened. The clerk put the telegrams back into their proper bins and then resumed his post behind the counter. "There's gonna be snow all along the northeastern corridor this winter. A whole lot of it, too. Not good for the railroad. Not good for me." He held up the newspaper that he'd been reading before the wind had blown everything away.

"Who told you that, sir?"

"Says right here, boy." The clerk held up the broadsheet. "I can tell ya, for sure, if there's a blizzard, people gonna die. That's what happens, and it just ain't right. They should stop the trains. That's what they should do. Stop the damn trains. There's still horses left in this country."

"People die from a lot of things besides the snow, sir." Beau stepped outside. The clerk warned him again. "Easy with that door, or you'll have to pay for it."

Beau stood by the edge of the platform. Cobb was in a fight with Russell, the owner of the private car that was now coupled to the Northeastern Limited to New York. Shelby was inside the car, with her face turned toward the window. Cobb's eyes were grim. His voice pitched with hate as he limped off, fist to the window. "All you rich bastards will pay for this," he warned.

She turned away from the window and disappeared into the car. Beau returned to the Western Union office, careful not to pull the door off its hinge. He said to the clerk, "There's a telegram I'm expecting, sir."

"I know. Been here three times now, you have." The clerk pointed to the window that picture-framed the Northeastern Limited. "You got something to do with all that fighting?"

"Nossir," Beau flatly said.

The clerk placed a telegram on the counter. Beau eagerly picked it up.

Western Union Telegram

CLARKSDALE = BRISTOL STATION DEC 29
BEAU LAHOOD
TOM NICHOLAS APPREHENDED STOP FLYING TO LONG ISLAND DEC 30 STAYING AT BILTMORE HOTEL NY STOP COUSIN JULIUS SENDS REGARDS STOP NACHMAN

"Send a reply, please," Beau said.

The clerk took the pencil from his ear. "Go ahead, boy."

"*Cobb is after SP STOP Failed to get her off the train STOP Said she was going to pay for some trouble she put him through STOP LaHood.*"

The clerk said, "What's this all about?"

"I'm just a porter, sir. I do what I'm told." Beau hurried out the door. Pullman conductor Raylene Hollis, of the Northeastern Limited, waved off the straw boss and sang *All Aboard* down the line as the porters grabbed the stair chains and pulled up the heavy steel steps. The train lurched forward and headed north out of Bristol Station in a slow crunching crawl.

***

Northeastern Limited men's lounge

"Had a feelin' I'd be seein' you, Beau," Porter Joe Dawson said as he gave the passenger standing by the sink another towel.

Beau set down his grip. "You don't mind if I ride in your car to New York, Joe? It's the last car before the private car, so I won't be in no one's way."

"I'd mind if ya didn't," Joe said and turned to the passenger by the sink, "You bump into something, sir?" Joe picked up the man's suit jacket that had fallen to the floor. "I can get this pressed in a jiffy, sir. Get the blood off. Make it brand new like ya just bought it."

The man let out a deep long groan so painful it embarrassed the two porters.

"I don't believe you're a passenger in my car. Are you, sir?"

"I'm not."

"There a problem with the men's lounge in your car, sir?"

"No."

"Mighty long walk to come down here for a wash."

"How would you know it's a long walk?"

"'Cause that's how long it takes." Joe smiled as friendly as he could.

"I like stretching my legs."

"Well, there ain't nothin' wrong stretchin' your legs after a long trip, sir. Ain't that right, Beau?"

Cobb turned to the tall porter.

Joe said, "You headin' to New York, sir, to board an ocean liner for Europe?"

"You ask a lot of questions, boy," Cobb said.

"Just seein' if I can be of help, sir. Lotta folks goin' to Paris. Hear it all the time how cheap it is 'cause of the war. I was there, myself, back in '18."

"You were in France?"

"Yessir. With the three seventieth. The Poilu gave us the Croix de Guerre after that big fight in the Meuse-Argonne. A lot of us was killed, somethin' like twenty-six thousand. But I managed to come through all right. Paris was grand, though. Folks real friendly. I'd love to go back one day. Say hello to all my old friends. Eat some of that long dry bread that just crackles on your tongue. You ever been there, sir?"

"No."

"Well, you need to know of any particular information like where the colonel of our regiment found his pleasure, you just let me know. There's the good places and the bad."

"I suppose you've been to them all?"

"Yessir."

"The good places?"

"Yessir."

"You and the colonel?"

"Everybody, includin' me."

"They let coloreds in whorehouses?"

"Colonel didn't care."

"I'm talking about the whores."

"What about 'em?"

"They slept with niggers?"

The friendly smile dropped off Joe's face. He went over to the lounge bench and picked up a pair of shoes he'd been shining.

"Get me another towel, boy."

Joe looked up at Cobb as if he had just walked in the lounge. "You say somethin', sir?"

"*Get* me another towel."

Beau walked over to Cobb. "There's a rule on the train; you want somethin', you say 'please.'"

"Nigger, you talk as if you fell on your head and got up white. When I tell you to do something, you *do* it."

Beau leveled his fist into Cobb's groin as if he were swinging an axe into a tree. The tough guy from Chicago, all bluster and small antics, fell on his face. "Joe, you got an empty compartment in this car?"

"Compartment B. The couch won't turn down. But watch out.

Hollis likes to sneak in for a quick nap."

"Then he'll have company. Gimme the passkey."

Beau dragged Cobb down the aisle and tied him, with a belt, to the table arch of the empty compartment, and then he stuffed Cobb's mouth. Beau went through Cobb's pockets, looking for train tickets, weapons, letters, anything that might be useful to law enforcement. He found a small black telephone book with most of the numbers crossed out except for Shelby's, a J. Benito of Chicago, and a partial address: Third Avenue, Manhattan, # 6-S scrawled in pencil. He locked the compartment door and went down the aisle.

Joe looked up from the shoes he was shining. "You put him in the empty compartment?"

Beau replied, "Yeah. Gave him some room to think."

The Private Car

20

"**Old man Russell** wants you out of my room. You've got the redhead's now that she's with him all the time, and it's just as nice as mine."

"I don't care," Virginia said as she sat on her old bed. "I want my room back."

Shelby said, "I told you someone dangerous was following me."

"How was I to know he wasn't a medical student?"

"Did that moron look like a doctor?"

"Doctors can look like anything."

Shelby said, "They *don't* look like him."

"Well, I been in the theater all my life, and your cousin put on one hell of an act."

Porter Joe Dawson knocked on the open door. "I got your sandwich, Miss Prevette."

Virginia turned around. "Hey, don't I too rate something to eat?"

Shelby said, "Give her half."

"I want the *whole* sandwich."

Shelby said, "Give her the whole, and bring me another one."

"Same kind, miss?"

"Yes."

Joe Dawson set down the silver tray and left the drawing room. Shelby pulled out a deck of cards and shuffled it under Virginia's nose. "Wanna play?"

Virginia stared at the cards as if they were going to bite her. "*Not* for money." She took the sandwich and checked to see if it had enough mayonnaise. "I want my room back, and I mean it."

Shelby sat across from her on the bed. "If Russell wants to exchange rooms, fine with me."

"Fine with *you*?"

"Yeah, and pay attention, or you'll lose again," Shelby said and dealt Virginia a hand.

"Say, why's your cousin after you, anyway?"

"He's a murderer."

"Baloney."

"Don't believe me," Shelby said. "You want a card?"

"What kinda family you come from?"

"*Do you* want any cards?"

"Are all your cousins murderers?"

"Only two of them."

"*Only* two…" Virginia grabbed the butter knife off the plate. "Ya better not try anything with me, girl."

"Don't worry."

"I'm *damn* worried. Why does your cousin wanna kill you?"

"Just the opposite."

"Whaddya mean just the opposite?"

"Look," Shelby said, "I don't like talking about it."

"Well, *I* do."

"Marston was arrested and thrown in jail, *okay*?"

"For what?"

"For being an asshole."

"What's he doing out on the street if he's an asshole?"

Shelby said, "Because someone was afraid my reputation would get ruined if word got out what he had done to me."

"What did he do to you?"

"Locked me in a cabin for three days until the coon dogs found me—and that's all I'm going to say."

"Why didn't you just lynch him?"

"You can't lynch your cousin."

"Why didn't ya tell me this before?"

"Tell you what?"

"That you were raped."

Shelby lowered her cards. "It's not the kinda thing you go around telling people."

"I would think so in your case."

"Look, some things in life are a serious matter, and they're difficult to deal with emotionally. If you can't understand that, then you can't understand anything." She put her cards face up on the bed. "Three fours."

"You're a cheat."

Shelby picked up Virginia's cards. "Little cards are you friends, but you don't know that."

"Baloney."

Shelby dealt Virginia another hand. They were silent as they rearranged their cards.

"Look, for what it's worth, Virginia, I've been meaning to tell you something."

"You took something else of mine?"

"*No.* Something wrong was done to you despite the urgency of the moment and the danger at hand."

"Oh, that's real big coming from you, Miss Nobody."

"Look, Russell told me to take your room. I didn't ask him for it. He said it had a stronger door."

"Russell told you that baloney?"

"Whether it's baloney or not is not the point."

"It's *still* baloney."

"I *don't* care. I'm trying to have an intelligent conversation with you."

"About what?"

"About when people get desperate. So do the ethics and morals they live by."

"Who said *you* had any?"

"Look, stupid, the instinct for self-preservation overrides any notion of reason and fairness. If you can't understand that, then you're a moron."

"Whatever you say, professor," Virginia replied and finished Shelby's sandwich.

"How many cards do you want?"

"Three."

Shelby dealt three and took one for herself. "So…" she said, offering Virginia a chocolate candy from a newly opened box, "what about this big Broadway hit you were in?"

"Oh, now you got an interest in theater all of a sudden?"

"Yeah, but it's not dancing on my toes."

"What is it then?"

"You and I could make a ton of money."

"Producing plays?"

"No."

"Doing what, then?"

"Let's just say I got an interest in theater—but *not* what you're thinking."

"Say, what's this brain of yours up to now?"

"I'll tell you all about it later," Shelby said, "but I'm taking the New Year's Eve train to Chicago, and I've booked the only drawing room. It's twice the size of a compartment, and it costs a fortune. Now, if you want to get stuck with that dumbbell director you've been telling me about, go ahead. But you're welcome to share my drawing room *and* at no expense."

"Say, I thought you were going to New York, not Chicago."

"I am."

"You're not making sense."

"Yes, I am."

"Then why're you going to Chicago?"

Shelby showed three deuces. "You lose."

Virginia tossed her hand. "This is the last time I play cards with *you*, ya big cheat."

Shelby spread out Virginia's hand. "You blew it."

"Sure, I blew it, and I know why that Cobb locked you in a cabin for three days."

"Why?"

"You're a card cheat."

"Okay, you win the next hand, this room's yours."

Virginia reached out her hand. "Gimme the cards."

"Why?"

"*I'm* dealing."

***

Pullman conductor Raylene Hollis covered a yawn as he went into the free compartment for a quick nap, but the idea of having it with Cobb wasn't going to happen. Raylene Hollis went to the men's lounge and had a word with Joe Dawson, who had a word with Russell from the private car, who, in turn, had a word with Beau, who was having a word with all of them in the free compartment as the Pullman conductor tried to keep Russell away from Cobb, who was gagged and bound under the compartment table. "I wanna know what the hell's going on here, and don't give me no nonsense, Beau."

Beau said to Conductor Hollis, "Well, it's a long story, sir."

Russell didn't care. He pointed to Cobb. "Hollis, throw the son of a bitch off the train, or I'll bust his brains again."

"Let my porter speak, Mr. Russell."

Russell, big as Beau, leaned onto the short Pullman conductor. "I didn't buy a goddamn private car to make it public. Now, get this little shit off the train."

Conductor Hollis said to Beau, "Did you actually see him harass one of the girls?"

Beau and Russell's eyes were in agreement. "Yessir, I did."

Joe said, "And I saw him take a swing at Mr. Russell when he tried to come to the girl's rescue."

Beau said, "We got another problem."

Conductor Hollis said, "What other problem?"

"Man tied up's a wanted murderer."

"The hell are you talking about *wanted* murderer?"

"Been on him since I left Clarksdale," Beau said.

"*Who's* been on him?"

"I've been on him," Beau said. "See, there was a lynchin' back in Clarksdale and—"

Just then Russell stepped in and said to the conductor, "Hey, I thought we settled the matter!"

"Hold on a second, Mr. Russell. I want to hear what my porter has to say," Conductor Hollis replied.

"Who's running this train? You or these porters?" asked Russell.

Beau intervened. "He is, Mr. Russell, but I'm waitin' on a lawman to take this fella back to Mississippi to put him in jail for a murder he committed."

"The hell's a murderer doing on this train, Hollis?" asked Russell.

"That's what I'm trying to find out, Mr. Russell." He then

turned to Beau, who said, "See, there was a lynchin' back home, and the man behind it all is right here on the floor. Now that this compartment's free, why stop the train and get it off schedule?"

"Beau, you haven't been drinking anything, have you? Because if you think you're Sherlock Holmes—"

"I'm tellin' you the truth, sir," Beau cut in. "We stop the train, we gonna be way off schedule. Better to keep him here until New York and let the police have him so he can be sent back to Mississippi with the proper escort."

Russell said to the conductor, "I don't give a damn. I want that little shit thrown off this train or I'll do it myself." He reached for Cobb. Beau, Joe, and Raylene Hollis held him back.

"Easy, Mr. Russell," said the conductor. "This is train business, not yours. Beau, I want you to stay in Joe's car until we arrive in Pennsylvania Station. Mr. Russell, no woman gets harassed on a Pullman train, and no porter tells me what to do. Now, if you really want him thrown off the train, follow me." They headed up the consist to settle the matter, once and for all, with the Northeastern Limited conductor.

Alcázar Hotel, Clarksdale, Mississippi

21

Zola coughed hard into a magazine that was opened to an illustrated advertisement of a doctor wearing a white medical tunic and pince-nez glasses. The ad swore, "20,679 physicians say Luckies are less irritating. It's toasted." Zola was thinking maybe they hadn't toasted her Luckies long enough, or maybe they hadn't spoken to all the other doctors who said that Luckies could kill you, but then, 20,679 was a made-up number by the advertiser and the reason the physician had to be illustrated.

The evening street below was empty except for the pounding rain and negro shoeshine boy waiting for customers outside. He wore an ill-fitting smile and ankle shoes with laces so old they were thrice tied. Even his suspenders failed to keep up his knickerbockers as he crouched under the safety of a ledge that dripped water over his head and onto his small hands. Zola wanted to tell him that she too had to endure the rain and the mud as she tried to keep scalpels, endotracheal tubes, forceps, bone saws, handheld trephines for removing shrapnel from skulls, and other life-redeeming instruments from flying off the portable operating tables while the surgeons sawed, cut, and removed arms, feet, legs, and parts of faces no longer usable nor recognizable. She picked up the candlestick telephone on her night table, called Western Union, and sent a wire to a friend in New York, saying this time she was coming back for good and that she was ready to take the job he had previously offered—*if* it were still available. Then she called the front desk. "Get me a ticket to Pennsylvania Station, right away."

The clerk said, "Won't be a train till tomorrow morning, ma'am."

"Book the first one heading to New York."

"That'll be the 10:13 Yellow Dog, ma'am."

"*Book* it."

The clerk said, "There's someone on his way up to see you."

"I told you to *call* me before sending people up."

"He said I didn't have to."

"*Who* said you didn't have to?"

"Said he knew ya, ma'am."

"Anyone can say that."

"Want me to get him?"

"The hell do you think?"

"He's already up the stairs."

"You're an *idiot*."

"Can't hear ya, ma'am."

There was a knock on the door. Zola slammed the phone on its hook. "Who is it?"

"Al."

"*Scram*."

"Open up."

"*Go to hell*."

Al opened the door. Zola was sitting by the window in her step-in, her skin yellowed from the glare of the streetlights.

Al said, "You don't lock the door?"

"Get lost."

"You like it dark?"

"Pitch black."

Al took a flask from his coat pocket.

"For a government man, don't you think you're breaking the law?"

He pointed at her cheap pint on the dresser. "I wouldn't drink that sweat."

"I'll drink whatever I damn please."

"You'll get sick."

"You'd double-cross your own mother."

"You think murder is a game?"

"I'm talking about your mother."

"I'm talking about Lindsay Coleman."

"Go to hell." The woozy look on her face was a big sore.

"You're a funny person, Zola."

"You're a goddamn bore," she replied, staring out into the wet street.

Al put the good hooch on the dresser. "We got Lance Parker and Bishop Blakely."

"Good for you."

"Parker was having breakfast."

"Isn't that nice."

"Three nice kids and a wife."

"Did you shoot him up like my brother?"

"No, just told him the man he murdered also had three nice kids and a wife. Something to think about when he hangs."

"Hope ya read the kiddies a bedtime story."

"It was morning."

"Try later."

Watching her light another cigarette. "You smoke too much."

Zola said, "You talk too much."

Al walked over to her. "Someone left a note in my office, today," and dropped it on her lap. "Something about finding someone whose ambitions at no time would cause him to cheat, lie, exaggerate, or commit flagrant delusional outbursts of jealously or possessiveness. Someone good, kind, and not expendable like so many who were butchered at the front."

"Get to the point, Al."

"Was it another attempt at bribery?"

"It *wasn't* bribery."

"How would I know with you?"

Zola said, "When I first met you, I thought you were someone special. But then something happened."

"What?"

"The same thing that happened in the war. I saw too much. Now, *get* out."

Al was by the door. "I'm heading to New York, tonight. You need a lift, let me know."

She stared at Al, eyes heavy. "What do you mean *lift*?"

"I'm flying."

"*Who* told you I was leaving?"

"The front-desk clerk."

"What else did he tell you?"

"You give him an earache."

"When are you going?"

"Now."

She reached for her dress and quickly packed.

Al turned on the light. "I thought you didn't like me."

"I *hate* you."

22

The Northeastern Limited breathed hard as it stood on Old Dominion ground. So did its conductor as he guided Pullman conductor Raylene Hollis down the car steps that led to the grading beside the tracks.

Porter Joe Dawson, also holding onto Cobb, said, "Gonna be hard with him actin' up like this." Cobb was struggling to get back on the train.

The Northeastern Limited conductor, just off the embankment, said, "We're gonna be way off schedule if we stand here dickering all day."

They punted Cobb over the grading and watched him roll down the embankment. His hat followed. Then the conductor of the Northeastern waved to the Big E with the coal-flaked face high up in the engine cab. He lowered his goggles and, with his gloved hand, gripped the brass throttle. The hard-chilled flange tread locomotive wheels slowly chugged on into the blue-gray composition of bare trees and marbled winter sky. Marston Cobb, flat out on his back, reached out for the train as it rolled into the sound of its own whistle. Shelby was standing by the baggage-car window, thinking of all the bizarre love letters stuffed into his coat pocket along with his rants, pleas, a long list of threats, and convoluted innuendos. His mad stories of New York with its rumbling elevated trains and five-cent open-top double-decker busses that went all the way down to the canyon—Wall Street—where people took elevators up skyscrapers that had clocks at each stop to tell them what time of floor it was, so unlike Cobb's life a series of incomplete narratives and rewinds that now had him on his ass and riding nowhere.

Shelby said to Beau, "Too bad they didn't break his neck."

"Well, he's off the train now, miss." Beau pointed to the steamship trunk with the brass fittings at the other end of the car. "That the trunk you want, miss?"

Shelby took out the key Julius thought she had forgotten when she had boarded the Yellow Dog back in Clarksdale. "No, the one next to it with the Zürich Dolder Grand Hotel label on the front."

Beau worked his way through the pile of hard valises and trunks. He dragged Shelby's out into the open. He said, "You goin' to Switzerland, miss?"

"No," she replied as she put her key into the center lock and pushed back the drawbolts. She opened the trunk and lifted the protective cover.

Beau saw a row of neatly sealed bottles. "I guess I went and got the wrong trunk, miss."

"Not if I've got the key to it," she replied, taking out one of the eighteen pints of rye whiskey bottles fitted into the top layer and breaking the seal. She pulled the cork and put the bottle to Beau's nose. A spicy scent of smoky heat and slow-burning hickory tickled his senses. She poured a shot into a tumbler and handed it to Beau. The rye went down the way the stars come out at night. He turned to the five-foot-two bootlegger with blue eyes as potent as the spirits in the bottle and thought of all the bootleggers coming and going across Lake Huron by the Canadian border: men with a jeweler's appreciation for hot merchandise and quick money. "That tommy gun I heard about—is it in there too, miss?"

"Never mind what you heard."

He took another sip of the rye and shut his eyes to see how it tasted.

"What you've got in your hand is hundred percent American rye, not what y'all get across the border with ninety percent corn," Shelby said, taking back the pint of rye whiskey along with the tumbler and putting it back into the trunk. She then closed it and locked the drawbolts. Beau was fascinated at how fluidly she moved as if she had done this a hundred times before with a hundred other porters. "I've read that Canadian producers sell whiskey for thirty-six dollars a case to American bootleggers. A quart goes on the streets anywhere from thirty dollars to as much as one hundred dollars, or more if it's from overseas, depending upon where and to whom it's marketed and sold. But the gain is far better in New York," thinking of the prices listed in *Billboard* and *Variety*, to name a few weeklies.

"Your numbers are good, miss. Very good. But them gangsters'll cut your throat iffen they see you tryin' to cut in on their racket."

"You must really think I'm dumb, Beau."

He didn't. He'd been underestimating her ever since she got on board the Yellow Dog back in Clarksdale.

"How many pints do you go through on an average trip, Beau?"

"There ain't no average trip."

Shelby said, "There *must* be an average. There's always an average."

"Well, sometimes you get folks dry as the law. Others, they as thirsty as a fish on its way out the broiler. I don't know iffen there's an average, but you got to play each ride by ear."

"What do you mean?"

Beau said, "I mean there's always passengers makin' unreasonable demands. Some thinkin' they should be waited on hand and foot. Others comin' across kind and pleasant but never tip. Others who mind their own business and for very good reason. Then there's the undercover inspectors. Women put onboard to see which porters will do somethin' stupid like make an advance or try and sell 'em somethin' that ain't allowed on the train. Male inspectors got their own tricks, and when we find either aboard, we wave a white table napkin out the window at an oncomin' train to let 'em know it's a female inspector, or wave our hats upside down for a male inspector. But sellin' contraband, well, that's a tricky business, and I always try to get to know my passengers first, but iffen there's the slightest doubt, I won't sell 'em nothin'. And I don't never sell to kids. That's trouble guaranteed. So there ain't no average aboard the train—especially when it comes to drink of quality."

Shelby said, "Well, I'm going to change all that. But, first, I need a porter who's smart. One who can keep his wits about him. One who's honest in the partaking of money and has the ability to lead, execute, administer, and be cool under pressure. I think you just might be the man, Beau. You can manage your temper. You have patience. You didn't make a fuss about keeping Marston aboard any more than you had to, because you knew you had more to lose if you had persisted. That takes mettle. But then, again, I could be wrong. You tell me. Are you just another fool who goes for glitter and flash? Or are you man enough to look beyond the petty notions and shallow beliefs that choke the life out of everyone else? Because if you are, I'm going to change your life forever."

A block of cold winter air crept through the panels of the baggage car and gripped the whole of Beau's body. He stared into Shelby's overpowering eyes, so blue they cheated his sense of reason. He said, "I'm your man." Satisfied, Shelby headed back to the private car.

23

Samson Paisley took the bean-soaked sandwich from Beau's hand and wiped away a long, gooey drip. "Accordin' to what I hear, y'all eat pretty well on the Twentieth Century."

Beau said to his cousin, "It's a different kinda train, but we got rules just like here."

"You think maybe I could get a permanent position on your ride?"

Not wanting to promise his cousin anything in front of Joe Dawson, he said, "When I own the railroad, I'll let you know."

"Just wanna make a good impression, that's all."

"Don't worry, Samson. Everybody wears a smile, and it ain't 'cause the frown is in the wash. We're gonna be in New York shortly, so we'll have steak for supper." Samson threw away the bean sandwich.

Virginia Swain stepped into the entrance of the men's lounge, her snarl locked and loaded. "The boss wants to see ya."

Beau said, "Y'all friends again?"

"Let's just say I've got a business head of my own," she replied, holding onto a secret with a very broad smile.

***

The private car may have been cleaned up, but it was Shelby in her gold silk empress cape with colliding bolts of colors, which her father had brought back from Paris and that her mother had said would ruin her, that underscored the moment.

"What can I do for you, miss?"

She closed her cape to ward off the chill and then gave Beau a dollar.

"Why, thank you, miss."

The world outside went pitch black as the train descended into the tunnel that stretched between Weehawken, New Jersey, and Manhattan under the Hudson River. The train got louder as the wheels of the "heavyweight" car battered in the tight space.

"Nothin' to worry about, miss. We just in the tunnel. Be out soon enough."

"I urgently need your help, Beau."

"Well, we're just about in New York, miss, so there ain't much I can do for you now."

"I'm talking about tomorrow. I don't know New York, and you know it well."

"Yes, miss, but tomorrow's my day off."

"This is my suite number at the Biltmore Hotel on Madison Avenue," she said, handing him a piece of paper. "It's right next to Grand Central Terminal."

"New York Subway system ain't all that hard to learn, miss. It took me no time at all."

Shelby's high contrast makeup, now all the rage, might have overvalued the ordinariness of the moment, but it was the intensity of her stare that brought out the long knives. "How about I give you five dollars for the day this once?"

"*Five* dollars?"

"For the day, Beau."

"Well, maybe I do have some free time in the mornin'."

"I said for the day, not morning. There's something else."

"What, miss?"

"I'll be traveling to Chicago with you on the Twentieth Century Limited New Year's Eve run."

"I thought you wanted to see New York City."

"I do," Shelby said, "but I need to do a study of how that train of yours operates, and with you on board it will be all the better."

"Well, miss, most nights ain't like New Year's Eve, and it gonna take a lotta ridin' to figure out the trains, no matter what night it is."

"Are you suggesting that I'm incapable?"

"Not at all, miss. Just my job to take the other side now and then to even things out. Two heads better than one."

"All right, but do you know where the Biltmore Hotel is?"

"I most certainly do."

"Be there at half past six."

"Kinda early, half past six in the mornin'. Sights stays open all day."

Shelby spread out a stack of speakeasy membership cards she had gotten from Virginia. "*These* are the sights I want to see."

"Well, they don't open till evenin'. And most good speaks don't get goin' till the wee hours. You won't be needin' to be up at six thirty, miss. You'll already be up."

"There's a reason why I'm going that early, Beau. That's when the liquor is brought to the clubs in laundry bags, and that's when I'll make an introduction of myself."

Natural light flooded the drawing room. Shelby thought something terrible had happened. She turned to the window, unprepared for what she saw.

"We're in New York, miss."

Pennsylvania Station's steep glass-and-iron canopy ceiling pushed everything up into the sky, including Shelby's eyes. People were scurrying every which way through the grand entrance hall that led to the main waiting room that had been inspired by the Roman Baths at Caracalla. Huge brass and wrought-iron staircases decked the station with triumphant sky-high arches modeled after the massive Arch of Constantine in Rome. New York looked majestically surreal and otherworldly as it put its arms around the hurried crowd and the Mississippi girl whose nose touched the window like a snowflake.

"I've never seen anything like this in my life, Beau. It is truly amazing…" Shelby said, her eyes on the crisscrossing beams that joined the glass ceiling as the Northeastern Limited came to a stop, and their long journey from Clarksdale, Mississippi came to an end.

Pennsylvania Station, New York

24

James Gleason, manager of the Pennsylvania Station Western Union office, sat behind a rolltop desk lit by a bendable wire stem lamp that emitted a gauzy yellow glow that softened the clutter of his backroom office. Piles of undelivered telegrams were stacked next to bottles of Skrip, Onoto, Waterman, and Pelikan ink that jostled with paper pinners and bottles of glue. A wire wastebasket, tipsy with crumpled paper, spilled onto the floor. James Gleason reached into the clutter and pulled out a telegram from one of the many small slots above a cluster of tightly fitted drawers. He turned to Beau and spoke in a heavy New York Fourth Ward accent that made him sound as if he were in the middle of an Irish ballad. "I hate when they sit around. They soon enough disappear. And if I should come looking, it's always for nothing." Beau took the wire:

Western Union Telegram
RECEIVED AT PENN STATION = 8 AM DEC 29 1925
BEAU LAHOOD NEW YORK
BLAKELY AND PARKER APPREHENDED STOP
NACHMAN

James Gleason leaned back into his wooden chair, his big face stuffed with a cigar he chewed on more than he smoked. He rubbed the soft dough of his cheeks that were stained pink by years of using a straightedge that cut close to the skin. He looked up into the sorrow of soft barroom light and pointed to the telegram, the expression on his face a mixture of curiosity and disbelief. "The hell's this about, Beau?"

"Nothin' at all, sir."

James Gleason didn't believe him, but he liked Beau. He too knew what a hard life was. He had come through Castle Garden, by the Hudson River in lower Manhattan, from County Roscommon, Ireland, in 1889 as a boy. He spent his teens in a railroad flat in the Irish Fourth Ward, right by the Brooklyn Bridge, famous for the 1863 Draft Riots and other battles, local or political, with seven siblings all quartered in the same room and with more fight than Grant's army. There were no such things as baths, running water, or electricity, and they only changed clothes when they outgrew them. Like a man's color, poverty had its own mark.

"Then how come this was wired to you, Beau?"

"You know what a lynchin' is, sir?"

"Sure. What about it?"

"My oldest friend was lynched. Man who caused the whole thing was on the train. Got thrown off in Virginia."

Gleason held up the telegram. "Nachman, law enforcement?"

"Man gonna catch the son of bitch and hang him."

"Why wasn't he on the train?"

"Who?"

"Nachman."

"He had these others to get, first," Beau said, "and he wasn't sure the murderer would be on the train."

"What do you have to do with it?"

"Everythin'."

"I know, Beau, but you're not law enforcement."

"My job is to let Nachman know if Marston Cobb, the murderer in question, is travelin' on the railroad."

James Gleason said, "Why didn't Nachman put law enforcement on this?"

"The Yellow Dog departed right after the lynchin'. So there was no time. I need some other help, Mr. Gleason."

"With what?"

"The telegraph office in Grand Central Terminal. I can't have 'em play monkey games with me."

"You want me to ask the boys over there to keep an eye out for this Cobb should he walk in?"

"I'd appreciate it. See—" he said, pulling his grip around and setting it on the floor, "Ed Whalen, manager over there, got a problem with colored folk." Beau took out a pint of Shelby's rye whiskey." Gleason took two glasses from the bottom drawer of his rolltop desk. "I could be in that office, no customer there. Whalen act like it's closin' time."

Gleason said, "I'll talk to him. He's a bully, and no one likes him."

"Then why don't they fire him?"

"He runs the office the way the company wants." James

Gleason shifted his attention to the pint of rye whiskey in Beau's hand. "The hell is that? Hair tonic?"

Beau poured him a shot. "You tell me."

Gleason put the glass under his nose. "Where'd you get this sweat?"

"It ain't sweat. It's the real thing."

Gleason swirled a lick around his tongue and waited for the sting to subside. It left a sweet but lingering aftertaste.

"What do you think?"

"Smoky. Strong. Smooth. A crowd pleaser. The hell is the damn proof?"

"One hundred."

"Haven't tasted real rye in years, Beau. You got a hold of some pre-Prohibition keg?"

"No, this is the real thing. Not Canadian product cut with ninety percent corn. This here's unfiltered hundred percent rye made the same way George Washington did back in the old days." Beau remembered a billboard tagline he'd seen before Prohibition. "It's the most American of all spirits and exhibits it in every sip—now your brother, Bradaigh, is head bartender of that popular speak over on Beekman Place just off the East River. I'd like you to let him know I got somethin' real good, not just any old float-in, and its supply is endless."

"Speak to him yourself, Beau. You know him."

"It's always better comin' from you, Mr. Gleason. Your word is better than mine."

"What about this murderer?" Gleason asked, reading the telegram again. "What do you want me to do should he walk in here besides admire his hat and tie?"

"Leave a wire with Al Nachman at the Biltmore soon as possible."

"When do you expect Nachman up here?"

"Tomorrow. December thirtieth."

"And this Cobb fella?"

"I don't know, but some showgirl on the train told him, by mistake, where the girl he's chasin' is stayin' in New York, so he should be up here soon enough."

"Then put the girl in another hotel."

"Then we lose sight of him," Beau said.

"I thought you said this was about a lynching."

"It's a long story." Beau reached for the pint of Belle of Magnolia, but Gleason had his eye on it, so the pint stayed on the rolltop. "Merry Christmas, Mr. Gleason." Beau grabbed his grip and headed out of the backroom office.

"I'll let you know if Bradaigh wants any."

The Shenandoah Valley

25

The new single-engine Stout 2-AT Pullman high-wing conventional gear monoplane may have had an enclosed cabin, but the engine noise buzzed through like a saw. Down below, flat extended fields merged into rippling ridges and cliffs, where hollows and towns popped in and out of hills as if in and out of sleep. Zola more than once complained, "Maybe we should've taken the train." There was no bathroom, just ear-numbing engine noise and freezing air.

It was dusk when they reached the Virginia way station: a shack built of lumber strips and a lot of banging that was attached to a hanger that stored mail and a fuel truck. Al hopped into a waiting 1924 Hudson Super 6 Coach that took him to Bristol Station, while the Stout loaded up with mail and fuel. At Bristol he headed straight to the Western Union office, his badge and a photograph of Marston Cobb in his hand. The clerk looked up from an incoming wire.

Al said, "I'd like to know whether the man in this photograph has been here and whether or not he sent a wire. His name is Cobb. Marston Cobb."

The clerk picked up the photograph and examined the image. "Well, there was one fella kinda resembles him."

"Can you tell me whether or not it's the same person?"

"Well, I don't rightly know now. He looked kinda shabby. I mean he could have been the same fella. I'm not saying he is," shifting the photo, holding it up to the light, and squinting. "There was a nigger from the railroad, who sent a wire with the name Cobb in it. I do remember that."

"To whom was it sent?"

"Some fella by the name of Nachman."

"I'm Nachman."

"Is that right?"

"What about the man in the photograph?"

"Well, fella was here had bruises on his face, so it's hard to know. He'd been in a fight on the train and I was hoping he wasn't looking for one with me. He spoke in an odd way as if he didn't want a soul to hear him; maybe it's over here—the wire he sent," the clerk said, walking to the next desk. "I kept telling the fella to speak up, but it only made him angrier, and when he shows me what he wants sent over the wire, it made no sense. So he walks out, and I thought that was the end of him, when he comes back several minutes later and starts all over again with a new message. This time I process it the way he wants—without even a name." The clerk leaned into Al, confidentially. "Lemme tell ya. I never seen a man fumble so much when it come to pay. Not that he didn't wanna to pay. He just couldn't get his thumbs to split the bills, and then he slams his whole damn roll on the counter and curses something awful. I realized I was dealing with somebody not all there—*if* ya know what I mean."

"How many telegrams did he send?" Al asked.

"Just the one."

"To whom was it addressed?"

161

"I'm still looking." The clerk was at the teletype table, going through several bins that were all part of the weekly file. "Here it is," handing it to Al.

Western Union Telegram

BRISTOL VIRGINIA=DEC 29 1925
J BENITO CHICAGO=DEC 29 1925
MAGNOLIA BELLE HEADING NORTH STOP FOOD GAS CANS MAPS EQUIPMENT CASH STOP WILL CALL YOU AT TELEPHONE EXCHANGE WHERE TO MEET STOP

The clerk said, "After he paid up, he must've went into town 'cause when he come back, he was over there by the water tower, wiping down a new handgun. Probably got it at Hessler's Guns and Ammo. I got a feeling he'll use it too. He got on the first train to New York—is that your man?"

"Close enough," Al said as he left the Western Union office. Outside, passengers in a train heading south were unaware that every move they made was exaggerated by the darkness outside. Al got into the Hudson and drove off, the look on his face a foot deeper than when he had arrived.

Manhattan, New York

26

The Biltmore Hotel, located at 43rd Street and Madison Avenue, was a terracotta showpiece that took up the whole block, with towers boasting views of Long Island, where Gold Coast mansions and lockjaw understudies were waiting to take the social stage. The views of downtown Manhattan were no less imposing with long expansive bridges and endless rows of docks balanced to the north by Central Park right in the panic of crosstown traffic. None of this interested Shelby, who felt as if the bellhop had locked her in London Tower and not the best suite in town. She turned off the Atwater Kent Radio that had a speaker horn and auxiliary earphones. She grabbed her handbag, took a magazine, and headed down to the Biltmore Bar: no longer a men's institution. Prohibition had done away with saloons to the pleasure of all women who, by culture and hard-worn custom, had been excluded from any bar since before the Revolution.

Shelby waded through the crowded watering hole where nearly every man wore black or white tie and every woman a gold silk lamé, crepe, satin, velvet, or sequin beaded drop-waist or teddy-style dress. A bar waiter, a slim pip with black hair parted just off the middle and saturated with Brilliantine guided Shelby to a cozy two-top by the Madison Avenue window. He pulled out a chair. "What's your pleasure, miss?"

"Tell me what you have to drink, please."

The bar waiter assumed Shelby understood the rules. "That all depends, miss."

"On what?"

"You need ginger ale? Let me know," he said as he rung up a smile.

"What do you mean let you know?"

"Maybe sparkling water?" ringing up another smile.

"How much is that?"

"A dollar."

"For *sparkling* water?"

"It's the same everywhere else, miss."

"You're still overcharging by ninety-five cents."

A peevish twist put a dent in the bar waiter's face. He reminded her, "At Barney Gallant's or Texas Guinan's, you'll be dishing out twenty-five dollars for a bottle of something nice. I'd mention some other clubs, but then we'd be here all night."

"So you *do* sell liquor."

The bar waiter wondered if he had a sharp pin from the Anti-Saloon League or one of those new female Prohibition agents waiting to call a raid. "Should you desire any *specific* water, let me know," as he left to consult with the head bartender, who was Upper East Side Irish with thick red hair and strained eyes. He lifted up the bar latch and ambled over to the girl whom he could have fit in his pocket. "Where in the South are you from, miss?"

Not even looking up at the big potato. "Who said I'm from the South?"

"Miss, your drawl is as thick as biscuit dough."

"Yours is as thick as midtown traffic."

The head bartender put his big hands on his hips in an effort to extend his patience. "I'll ask you again. Where are you from?"

"Mississippi."

"Really?" The Irishman wiped his hands across his apron as if they had slipped into something foul. "That's where E. C. Yellowley is from."

"I've never heard of him."

"He just happened to have taken over the Federal Prohibition Office in New York City."

Shelby laughed. "You mean to tell me you had to send a boy all the way from home to clean up this town? I'll have a glass of rye, please."

"How old are you, miss?"

"Is there a drinking age?

The head bartender, finding little humor in her remark, didn't have time to fight with a customer who seemed to be having more fun than he.

Moments later a bottle of ginger ale, a bucket of ice, and a tea cup arrived at the table. The bar waiter said, "That will be three dollars, miss."

Shelby stared at the spill. "For *this*? They sell busthead on the street for that much."

"Oh no, miss. We don't charge anything for *that*, but we do for *this*." The bar waiter pointed to the soda water and bucket of ice.

Shelby smiled for the first time. She now understood how business was done in New York.

***

A rumpled, worn read with a drowsy bow tie matched by even drowsier eyes ambled over to Shelby's table and said, "I see you read quality magazines, miss." He was referring to the December issue of *The New Yorker* that Shelby had brought down with her. The cover illustration was of a rich old daddy in white tie and high hat holding out a handful of pearls to a blushing young showgirl in a pouf-skirt standing by a glittering Christmas tree backlit by diamonds, limousines, an ocean liner, and other necessities for the New Yorker who had no toys and had yet to turn the page. "Did I hear you say you're from Mississippi?"

Shelby took in the mild-mannered man. "Are you, sir?"

"No, I'm not," as he bared a flask. Shelby was surprised he would do that in public. Back home, a flask was hidden and brought out with much caution. He said, "What I have here is pure single malt from Scotland that came off the RMS Majestic this morning on the West Side docks. Now, I couldn't help overhear your conversation with the bartender. He was a bit gruff, but it's a casualty of living in this overcooked town. I would like to apologize for him and offer you something of better quality and of no charge before I take off for my train to Westchester, where my wife has sentenced me for the decade." He poured Shelby a shot in an empty glass. "What brings you all the way up to New York, if I may ask?"

"Have you ever heard of Texas Guinan?"

"I see you've done your homework, miss."

"Do you know her?"

"I just might. Why?"

Shelby said, "She runs the best speak in town, from what I've read. The bar waiter even mentioned her name as well as Barney Gallant's."

"Well, some people think she owns this city. You see, it may rain, but Texas always shines. Would you like to meet her?"

"Could you arrange it?"

The patron was sure he had guessed right about the beautiful young creature who had every man in the bar seriously reconsidering whom he had brought. Her mere presence kept order in the house. There wasn't a man or woman who, at some moment, didn't have eyes on her. "Yes, I could arrange it."

"Then sit down."

The patron pulled out the other chair. "So you want to be a showgirl."

"I couldn't care less about showgirls," Shelby said.

"Then why on earth would you want to meet Texas?"

"I have my reasons."

"You're not some long-lost child of hers, are you?"

"Don't be silly."

"You're not into blackmail?"

"*No.* Get me a meeting with her, and you'll be the first to know why and the first to thank me."

"For what?"

"For something that everyone wants but doesn't have."

The man almost smiled. "You know, you intrigue me."

"In what way, sir?"

"I stop off at this bar every night on my way home, before I take the train. There are girls coming in from every small town, looking for a new life in the city and to be on their own, but there was this one girl—one from Mississippi—who was sitting at the table right over there. She was a very complicated beautiful sad soul with a drawl like yours. At one moment she was the muse, the other a frightened little bird. She's one of those people with no sense of business. Only love, poetry, personal loss, and the ability to bite. She was staying in a tight little room on the third floor of this hotel, and she still owes me one hundred dollars."

"You just give your money away?"

"Let's just say, she and I are determined to never overcome a certain grief."

Shelby said, "I'm sorry to hear that."

"So am I, but she's a wonderful writer. I read the journal she kept about her experiences in the war. She has this uncanny ability to catch a person's character in just a few sentences—and she looks like you when you smile."

"What's her name?"

"Zola."

"*Zola?*"

"Yes. Zola Nicholas."

"Who *are* you?"

The man placed a finger squarely on the cover of *The New Yorker*. "I'm Robert Benchley. I freelance for this start-up magazine. And who are you, may I ask?"

"Shelby Prevette."

"Nice to meet you, Miss Prevette," he said, taking in the Southern girl's impeccable manners, which had the right amount of country-club chill that only wealth and a proper education could breed, but it was her eyes, heavy with process and deep with soul, that kept anyone with less out of the running. "How do you know Zola?"

"She's my cousin! What was she doing in New York?"

"Well, what all people do with great yearning and little money—suffer. One day she suddenly fled town. This morning I get a wire she's on her way back. Don't tell me she's already here?" he asked, thinking they had come up together.

"I didn't even know she was on her way up," Shelby said.

"Then why are you here?"

"I'm here to see Texas Guinan."

"I still can't understand why you'd want to see her, if you're not an aspiring showgirl?"

"Arrange a meeting with her along with Barney Gallant, and you'll find out."

"They don't see just anyone."

"I'm not just anyone."

"Well," he said, tearing out a page from the magazine, "only under one condition, young lady."

"And what is that?"

"Buy a subscription to *The New Yorker* so we can get more advertisers. We're on the verge of collapse."

"Consider it done," Shelby said as she filled out the form. "Why would Zola all of a sudden leave home when she just got back after having been away for eight years? Are we talking about the same person?"

"Well, whether we are or not, she's a strange bird."

"How so?"

"In that she migrates south when everyone else goes north, but I've got a job lined up for her, and if she doesn't take it this time, I'm going to put her over my knees and bring her to her senses," he said, tasting the rye that Shelby had poured from her flask. "Which ship did *this* fall off?"

"The same one from which Miss Guinan will be getting hers." Shelby fanned a dozen or so speakeasy membership cards across the table, all of them low numbered. "How well acquainted are you with these clubs, Mr. Benchley?"

"Where on earth did you get these, young lady?" He touched the cards that weren't already in his wallet.

"Ever hear of Virginia Swain?"

A light went on in Benchley's eyes like in a house that had been dark for months.

Then a bellboy entered the bar with his hands cupped to his

mouth. His voice reached across the room: "*Call for Miss Prevette.*"

"Oh, that's Virginia." Shelby was now on her feet. "We're going to have a quick supper at the Blue Swan, and then I'm off to bed before a long day." She picked up the speakeasy cards. "Meet me tomorrow morning at seven o'clock at my suite, and show me the city, Mr. Benchley. We'll talk some more about why I want to meet Miss Guinan."

"Why so early?"

"Why so late…?" as she made her way out.

Biltmore Hotel, New York
December 30

27

The morning tabloids, one after the other, featured the same splashy cover photo: Broadway star Virginia Swain getting hauled off into a paddy wagon with her eyes aglow from camera flash that lit up the night. Shelby was inside the wagon.

Beau said, "When did they let you out of jail?"

"Around two this morning. I was told no one's kept for long, because the politicians want to get reelected." Shelby turned a page and found more proof that Prohibition was a complete failure. Cocktail shakers and liquor cabinets were brazenly advertised. It was as if sex had been banned, and there were endless ads for baby diapers.

Beau said, "Did they take your name?"

"I told them I was fifteen, so they let me go—though I did meet someone from Wall Street, on the way down to the precinct in the paddy wagon, who's an expert in shorting the market, and he gave me his card, so all was not lost."

"He probably only wants to see more of you, miss."

"His wife thinks so, too." Shelby moved onto Vanity Fair for the social news, amused at how New Yorkers were obsessed with every little detail of their lives—whether it be their diet, the tall building under construction blocking out sunlight, the new Yantorny shoes Mrs. So-and-So wore to that wedding in Oyster Bay, or the woman who sailed to Europe on the SS *France* and had left her Pekingese on Pier 88.

Beau said, "I hope you slept fine with what time you had."

"Better than Virginia. She went to another speak as soon as she got released. By the way, did you know that everyone here is stupid?"

"How's that, miss?"

"At half after four, the operator woke me up with a call for a Mr. Jones. I am not Mr. Jones. The operators just plug the cords into any hole in the switchboard and hope to get the right party."

"Happens in all the hotels, miss. It's the most common complaint." Shelby poured Beau more coffee. "Thank you, miss."

"Sit down, Beau."

"The only place to sit is over there, and that's too far, miss."

"Sit here."

"At *your* table, miss?"

"Yes. Now, what did you have to tell me?"

Taking the furthest chair, he replied, "Your labels, miss. Magnolia Belle Medicinal Rye Whiskey ain't gonna work on a train."

"Why is that?"

"See, there's a cleanin' gang come after every trip, and should they start seein' your product all over, they might get the idea somethin's up, and one of 'em, to score a point, might go to the yardmaster to let him know. It be much better there be no label and that I handle the sellin' of your product on the trip to Chicago, tomorrow."

Shelby grabbed one of the morning editions. "It says right here that the month of December 1925 has had the highest rate of deaths from wood alcohol poisoning since Prohibition went into effect," pointing to a photograph of a bottle of bootleg imitation *Old Kentucky* tagged with phenol and then to a bottle of *Monogram Bourbon* tagged choral hydrate and a bottle of *Gordon & Co's London Dry Gin* that was nothing but ether.

"People knows what they gettin' into, miss."

"You miss the point, Beau."

"What am I missin'?"

"Just last night on my way to my room, I ran into a bootlegger who has a certain habit of riding up and down the elevators all hours of the night, handing out sheets of liquor prices—and I don't mean for quality product but the poison that fills the morgue." She showed Beau the photo in the newspaper with corpses on steel gurneys with drains. She handed him one of the sheets. "We'll get a new label, but it will be called—" she turned toward the window as if the label was being written out in the sky, "*Trusted Rye Whiskey*. I plan on being a trustlegger, not a bootlegger."

"*Trustlegger?*"

"You don't like that?"

"Okay," Beau said, "but don't say I didn't warn you."

"Warn me about what?"

"Look, miss, you go about it the way you think's best. But it's New Year's Eve tomorrow. You think you can get this up and goin' by then, new label and all?"

"I'll be calling a printer as soon as they open and have this done by lunchtime, even if I have to pay him triple, so we can have everything set up by tonight. You'll stay in his shop so he knows not to slack off."

Beau said, "I thought you wanted me to be your tour guide this morning."

"Oh Mr. Benchley will be doing that. He knows this city better than anyone."

"Who's Mr. Benchley?"

"A writer who's got a lot of important people at the tip of his pen."

"Good, because I got to be at Mott Haven Yard later this afternoon—somebody with a big name got a grievance with the New York Central Railroad. One other thing."

"What?"

"I saw Cobb in the lobby on my way up."

"Are you sure it was Marston?"

"Yes."

"Is he staying here?"

"No. I checked with the concierge. But I'll have to insist on you takin' the service elevator till Mr. Nachman gets here. Be for you own good. And I already spoke to the house dick."

"What did he say?"

"What folks always say and do—nothin'." He turned to the door. Someone was knocking.

Shelby reached for the .32 caliber Lemon Squeezer in her handbag that she had bought in Bristol while the train recoupled. "Answer it, Beau."

Beau cautiously approached the door. "Who is it?"

175

"Mr. Benchley."

Shelby said, "Let him in."

Benchley stepped in and almost backed out. "I had a feeling you were up to no good." But then he saw the open trunk filled with pints of rye.

Shelby said, "Still think I'm up to no good…?"

Mott Haven Yard, the Bronx

28

Pullman Conductor Liston Truesdale and New York Central engineer Bob Butterfield were making their way through New York Central's Mott Haven Yard at 153rd Street, where section, compartment, and commuter cars were coming in after trips north and west to be cleaned and refitted. Stepping over the tracks, Bob Butterfield said, "Well, at least we don't have to worry about the cold-set grease. That new dehydrated journal compound M has been lubricating the overheated bearings way above two hundred twelve degrees. Now, unless them gandy dancers decide it's better to sit inside their sheds with wood alcohol this winter, I ain't worried about any trouble on the tracks."

"Didn't notice a thing last trip."

Bob Butterfield said, "'Course ya didn't. You was so liquored up with that Canadian bootleg I coulda pulled out yer front teeth. By the way, I could use a drink now that I got a day off, 'less ya drunk it all yerself."

Liston Truesdale reached into his coat pocket as they climbed aboard the steps of a Glen Class Elmsford Car that had more walnut and gold leaf than the Columbia Club in Midtown Manhattan. Bob Butterfield took the pint of Canadian Rye and put it to his lips. "Still ain't as good as what was made in this country."

Liston Truesdale said, "At least it won't put any holes in your gut and suck out your brains."

"Where'd ya get this sweat? LaSalle?"

"Nah, those bootleggers sell poison to the kids getting on or off the train, but there's this one guy I know, who knows what he's doing. Got a skiff going up and down Lake Huron. I get enough to make sure no one gets sick."

Bob Butterfield said, "Then why're ya going to see the yardmaster?"

"Maybe you can tell me. It's kinda early in the morning for him wanting a visit from me."

"What if I told ya Pullman and New York Central slipped me a fin to work ya over, then report back to 'em?"

"Report what?"

"Detective Fred Heinz is on his way to the yard now. They want to stop the ruckus on board the trains 'cause a what happened to some college boy got stiff from wood alcohol they claim was sold by one 'a your porters. They're frightened they'll lose all their business to the Broadway Limited, as if no one's drinking on the Pennsylvania Railroad."

"Said it's *my* fault?"

"In so many words. Yardmaster said he don't give a damn but has got to show the boys upstairs that he's trying real hard so they can feel good about themselves making all that money. Something else, Liston. Before we departed LaSalle, a man comes up to my cab and asks me where he could get something to drink as if I run a broad-gauge saloon."

"That was an undercover train inspector, Bob, and they're

about as subtle as a lynching party. I guess the company's worried the engineers are now getting plowed under, too."

Bob Butterfield put out his cigarette. "Subtle or not, some smartass lawyer will be down at the yardmaster's day coach, today, nosing around."

"For what?"

"For whatever dirt he can find. So be careful. Detective Heinz might call you in, as well."

"Don't worry, Bob. I know how to handle him. He and I go back a long way." He stepped off the Elmsford. "Are you on our New Year's Eve run tomorrow?"

"On the last leg of your trip as always, Liston."

"Good."

"You expecting something to happen?"

"With Fred Heinz snooping around, you can be sure of that. Let's get out of here before we get swept up."

They left the Elmsford just as the cleaning crew boarded with dusters, brooms, and vacuum cleaners.

Chelsea, Manhattan

29

"**There are gossip** machines in this town that you know nothing of, and each industry has its own circle of tattlers who, every day, need something for their columns and lunch tables to feed on, so it's a good thing your photograph wasn't taken with Miss Swain on the way to that paddy wagon, or your face would've been seen by millions this morning."

"I didn't think a raid was going to happen," Shelby said as she stared out the cab. The streets of Manhattan rolled by in an endless stream of buildings and elevated trains.

"Shelby, you didn't know it could happen," Benchley said. "Now, your name is in the police blotters."

"No, I made one up."

"Were you fingerprinted?"

"No, I told them I was fifteen years old and was out with my parents when I got lost."

"Did they believe you?"

"My accent was enough to convince them I was from out of town and a total hayseed."

"Maybe," Benchley said, "but cops, the good ones at least, remember faces. And yours they won't forget. That's why I want you to get established with the right crowd. Get people to know and like you, because they'll protect you once they do. Then you may surface on your own, but if you hang around Miss Swain, this whole town will know you in no time, and you *do not* want to be known, unless you're a club owner."

"You forget Virginia's my friend. I stand by my friends, because that's the right thing to do. Or is the wrong thing more important in this town?"

"This is not a moral issue, Shelby, but a tactical problem."

"Yes, but Virginia is very important to me."

"How?"

"Never mind at the moment. I want to know why we're going to Barney Gallant's house and not his club."

"To pay him a visit."

"Why not at his club?"

"Shelby, it's the last place you want to be seen if it's not open for business."

The cab turned east on West 20th Street, between 8th and 9th Avenues, which was lined with nineteenth-century sea captain townhouses. A small Episcopal church made of Yorkshire flagstone with fairy-tale spires stood in the middle of the block next to a two-story brick rector's house. Benchley and Shelby walked up the stoop of # 339 and knocked on a front door that was recessed under a pointed Greek pediment. Barney Gallant greeted his two guests and took them to the first-floor salon that faced the garden. A pot of coffee and morning cake were on the breakfast table. Shelby thought the house was oddly quiet. The noise of home was absent. Its white walls were sparse, except for several contemporary works of art that had more to do about one's state of mind than of the natural world in its more "perfect" state. Gone were the Victorian florid reams of wallpaper, heavy-curtained rooms, bulk furniture, complicated rugs, ottomans with swinging tassels, side chairs with overstuffed cushions, and salon-inspired paintings of verdant landscapes with waterfalls and rolling valleys aided by muscular skies or canvases with shimmering oases mezzotinted in sand, with arabesque caravans followed by framed photos of vaudeville acts such as *Egypt's Cleo Patrick, The Tumbling Sisters from Canarsie,* or *The Widow Mrs. Rosenbaum.* The simplicity that replaced this smorgasbord of sentimentality was a stern rebuke, yet the pivot caused its own problem, because a rebuke invariably becomes a cliché when the posers get into the act; so Mrs. Rosenbaum, getting wind of it, married a gentleman who spoke English like the king—but like the king, he had no job.

Barney seated his guests and poured coffee. He noticed that the fumes, clatter, and chafing distilled into every New Yorker were wholly absent from Shelby's being.

Benchley said to Barney, "Hear about the raid at the Blue Swan last night?"

"Everyone has," he said as he turned away from Shelby.

"It's all over the morning papers," Benchley said.

"That's because Virginia Swain was there."

"Well, they broke down the bar," Benchley said. "Thousands of dollars in damage. I got a call this morning saying I might want to take a look at the loot. Dottie's down at the yard, taking inventory for next week's *The Talk of the Town* page, that is if the *New Yorker* is still in business."

Barney said, "That's what happens when an owner doesn't take care of business."

Shelby said, "What business would that be, sir?"

"People business," offering her a slice of Louisiana Crunch cake. "How long have you been in town, miss?"

"Almost a day," she said as she set her pint of rye on the table, impatient and not interested in cake, and not yet convinced of Benchley's advice.

"Bob tells me this is the best rye whiskey he's ever tasted."

"I leave that up for you to decide, sir."

Barney rose from his chair. His slender frame was flat in his navy suit, and his dark hair wet as if he had just left the barber. He poured an ounce of rye into a short glass and sipped it as if he were tasting tomorrow. "Is this pre-Prohibition product?"

"Nossir. It's from a two-year-old barrel. Not filtered. Made the correct way, because there is only one way."

"You have exclusivity of distribution?"

"Yessir."

"There's no one else?"

"No one, but I, sir."

Barney held up the bottle—the Magnolia Belle label removed. "Tell me about the man who makes this."

"Sir, I can only say that this is the best rye made. It is not wood alcohol nor is it made from corn as in Canada."

"And with whom do I negotiate?"

"With me, sir."

"And what if you go to college? Get bored? Or do something that leads to nowhere?"

"I already am nowhere."

"You mean...*bootlegging*?"

"Yessir." Her face clown sad, her mind of two thoughts.

"I appreciate your honesty...Why are you in it, then?"

"That's how you get out of it." Shelby said, thinking of the bet she had made with her father.

Barney poured her more coffee. "Well, we all have reasons for doing things we don't like. But next time you're up here, bring me a case."

"I could bring you more, sir."

"One case is fine."

"Why just one?"

Barney said, "Because the few who get this product will like it, and then everyone else will want it, and to keep the price up, we'll need to bring it to market slowly."

"I could bring you several cases. No one will know how many you have."

"One will be enough, Shelby. By the way, how much is a pint?"

"Eight dollars, sir. You can sell it for fifteen easily. I was in the Blue Swan last night and was offered lesser quality for the same price."

Barney said, "Eight dollars is high."

"Anything less than eight, I can't make a profit."

"I'll do business with you at six a pint. And have every pint sealed red for the first shipment. All other shipments will be of a different color."

"Why is that, sir?"

"Because if you don't have the right color, then you've got the wrong product. Once a product catches on, every bootlegger copies it. And call me Barney. No need to be formal."

"Yessir, but why do the bootleggers bother to copy good product if theirs is inferior and everyone knows it is?"

"The bottom-feeders don't care. They're only interested in money and nothing else. They will lie, cheat, and kill you to satisfy their self-interest." He moved one of several morning papers on the table toward her. "There's a million-dollar suit-in-law with the railroad about some very rich boy on the verge of death because of wood alcohol. His father happens to be a patron at my club. He also works on Wall Street, and when he stays in town, he drops by—and not alone. I could make his life very difficult, if you know what I mean."

"Six dollars is way too low, sir."

"When would I get my first shipment?"

"Three weeks."

"How about we start at six and see what happens?"

"With all due respect, sir, I need something more concrete than see what happens."

Barney said, "Send me four cases at six dollars a pint, each case sealed with a different color. Everything after that will be at seven."

"Two cases at six."

"Four at six."

"Three at six, and you keep this pint, sir."

Barney poured her more coffee. "You're a hard negotiator, young lady."

"At eight I'm better. So the compliment goes to you, sir."

"Four at six, or there's no deal."

Shelby gave in. "Only because you're a gentleman."

"You're very gracious, young lady."

"At eight dollars a case we both are."

Barney reached into his billfold. "One day it might happen. Here's a card to my club with a very low number. Anyone who works there will know that you are more than an acquaintance. Say nothing of who you are and what you do. You're a very pretty girl, but pretty girls don't stay pretty if they're dead."

Shelby took the card and rose from the table. "Thank you, sir."

"Leaving so soon?"

"Am I being rude, sir?"

"Certainly not."

"Did I say something wrong?"

"Not at all," Shelby said.

Benchley said, "We're just running a little late, Barney. See, I'm taking Shelby to see the Woolworth Building. Then we have to rush uptown to lunch with Dottie at the Algonquin."

Shelby said, "If you'd like to join us, it would be my pleasure. But if you have more pressing matters at hand, I completely understand."

Barney led the way out. "Maybe some other time when we can talk about life and not money. You're an interesting young lady—the kind interesting men like to be around."

"Rather than *having* around?"

"Exactly."

Shelby stopped by a canvass hanging on the living-room wall. The title of the work, *Die Journalisten*, was painted so that it seemed to be pinned to the canvas. The journalists were a rogue's gallery collage of cloaked, robed, one-eyed, and bug-eyed men with *listen* hyphenated as if their hearing was as well, and though the artist's tongue-sticking-out humor seemed childish, in application the dysfunctional professional class in question was morbidly adult. The artist's signature was at the bottom right corner well distanced from her caricatures. Shelby wondered, "Who's Hannah Höch?"

"Ein Berliner Künstler," Barney said.

"You speak German?"

"Something like it."

"Why is this art good?"

Barney said, "Because it visually links you to the truth instead of diverting you from it."

"You mean...what Norman Rockwell is guilty of doing?"

"I see you've studied art, young lady."

"I study everything, sir. Among illustrators, I prefer John Held Jr."

"Why is that?"

Shelby said, "Unlike Rockwell who paints a world that is forever, Held knows that it's not going to last."

"I never thought of it that way."

"I do—always, sir. Good day."

Barney closed the door behind them. A woman, just out of bed, appeared at the top of the stairway. She was gripping a morning tabloid tightly in her hand. "Say, what's this about the Blue Swan closing for good?"

"Virginia, your old boyfriend's no more."

The Woolworth Building, lower Manhattan

30

The isle of Manhattan was spread out like a board game fifty-eight stories below. Trolley cars, elevated trains, buses, automobiles, and water-crawling ferries inched their way across the vertical landscape. For every ship horn that blew, a tugboat answered. For every building going up with riveters and hoisted beams, demolition teams tore away at the fabric of nineteenth-century New York. Robert Benchley reached out his hand as if to change all that. "The building boom has been going on for the last twenty years, but when in 1913 the Woolworth building, the Biltmore Hotel, and Grand Central Terminal were built, they became the Holy Trinity of New York, and should anyone think of demolishing them, a curse will manifest itself in ways unimaginable and horrid and affect the families of those developers for generations to come, but then there are other projects where the curse is the building itself."

Shelby was more interested in the piers lined up like shoe boxes numbered with giant sizes painted on the gates and waterside ends that crammed the Hudson River with triple-stacked ocean liners. They went from Pier A Battery Park all the way up to Hell's Kitchen like one big breath of make-believe. The constant clash of horns, sirens, and ship bells; the jam-packed concrete; steel; cobblestone; tar; and grime, intersected by elevated train tracks housing fairy-tale gingerbread stations of steep stairways and long wooden platforms that shook underfoot whenever a train roared into a stop, made Shelby feel as if she were a babe in toy land. New York wasn't a city in as much as it was ledger of buildings, streets, and backroom proposals. It serviced five million plus through agencies, factories, showrooms, shops, schools, speakeasies, houses of ill repute, hospitals, prisons, bakeries, butchers, railways, taxis, churches, synagogues, all against the constant breakdowns, shutdowns, disruptions, parades, accidents, ambulances, and the perpetual curse of slow-moving traffic. Shelby turned away from the palpable murmur below and raised the pitch of her voice to cut through the whipping winter wind that even the pigeons avoided in the corners of terracotta gargoyles mounted on chimera front façades. "I see you really love this city, Mr. Benchley."

"It's not so much love," he said, "as it is the excitement. You hate the noise. I love it. You find the air hard to breathe. I find the mixture perfect. You find it too crowded. I find it just about right. You say it's too expensive. I agree but don't care. But there is something you like about this town, and you won't tell me."

"You're either stiff in the heels or stiff in the grave," Shelby said as she watched several tugboats guide a three-stack ocean liner into its berth. "Was Barney trying to scare me when he talked about dead pretty girls?"

"Not at all; he happens to like you."

"I certainly didn't feel any great warmth."

"You don't know Barney."

"He certainly wasn't melting any ice."

Benchley said, "You may not know this, but five years ago Barney's speak was the first Prohibition raid in New York City, and when they rounded up his staff and shipped them off to jail, Barney told the judge to jail him instead, since he was the owner. The judge abided and released his staff, and when word got out, he became the town hero. His staff is now loyal to him to the grave, and anyone who's anyone goes to his club. The criminals don't even bother him. So getting a card to his speak with his signature is like getting awarded a medal, and you just got one. If that isn't warmth, I don't know what is." Benchley moved off the railing. "We should be getting along. The wire Zola sent from Roosevelt airfield on Long Island said she'll be arriving at the hotel by noon. This time she's going to take that job I've got lined up for her, or I'll put her over my knees."

"How well did you *really* know my cousin, Mr. Benchley?"

"We're friends, *no* more, but our real attachment is her rambling mind and my ability to indulge it."

They headed into the crush of bodies and conversations that jammed the elevator. Shelby tried to push away a man who was pressing up against her, but he was in his own world, the first thing a New Yorker reaches for in his or her survival kit.

"Are there stables in New York, Mr. Benchley?"

"Of course, there are."

"Do I have time to ride?"

"You never have time in New York. Haven't you learned that yet?"

No, and she wasn't about to.

Mott Haven Yard

31

The December wind unloaded onto Mott Haven Yard and sent Al Nachman's hat flying past the auxiliary commissary where stewards were taking inventory of all the porcelain, glass, cutlery, and linen for the next trips north or west. First cooks were lining up with requisition lists for ten different varieties of beef, slabs of bacon, broilers, roasters, duck, veal, quail, clams, crabs, lobsters, not to mention chives, galax, leeks, squash, tomatoes, turnips, and asparagus. A professional butcher in Rochester had cleaved the racks of lamb. Every side of beef had been cut to company regulation. A fifteen-pound Virginia ham was split into ten double slices. All this fitted, baked, grilled, and plated in a dining-car kitchen no larger than 17.5 x 17 feet with a coal oven. Any room left was for sweat.

Outside the commissary, the roofs of the freezer cars were getting iced for the trips north and west. Al asked one of the workers atop the cars, who was pouring crushed ice into hatches, where he could find the yardmaster's office.

"The buzzard's roost is right down the track." He pointed to the 1890s' day coach, where a tall wiry man stood by the entrance of the coach with his bony knuckles resting on the handrail as he searched the yard for someone. Tom Cordley, the new director of the New York Central Railroad, and a renowned trial lawyer by the name of Max Steuer, were inside the day coach, impatiently waiting for that someone. Beau came around a decoupled Elmsford car and spotted Al crossing the tracks. "I see you made it up here."

Al turned toward the familiar voice. "It's like another planet. Good to see you."

"Good to see you," Beau said. "I got your message at Bristol. What brings you to the yard?"

Al said, "Have to see one of the executives."

"So do I."

"Look for a cigarette, Beau, and a match to give me so we can have a moment to talk. I don't want them to think we know each other." Al turned his back to the day coach. "What can you tell me so far?"

Beau handed Al a cigarette he saved for passengers who didn't want to buy a packet. "Cobb knows the Prevette girl is staying at the Biltmore. I saw him this mornin' in the lobby. When he tried to get her off the train at Bristol, he told Miss Prevette she was goin' to pay for all the trouble her family put him through all these years, and I think he means it."

"And just how is she going to pay?"

Beau said, "I don't know, but you know how bullies are. They say whatever comes to mind, and the only thing that sticks is the anger behind it."

"Cobb's staying at the Biltmore?"

"No, but he might as well be. I got the girl takin' the service elevator, and she ain't too happy for it. But at least we know where Cobb is, so it'll be easier to get him."

"Maybe not," Al said. "He's got a handgun, and somebody in

that busy lobby could get hurt if he uses it."

"You been there?"

"Checked in an hour ago."

Beau struck a match and cupped his hands. "I went to the Commodore Hotel down the street. Then the Ritz-Carlton on Forty-Sixth. Then the Windsor. The Murray Hill Hotel. Even the Drake, but Cobb could be goin' by a different name, or he could be livin' on the street or somewhere else. Who knows?"

"What exactly happened on the train?"

"I sent you a wire. Didn't you get it?"

"I got it. You just didn't say why Cobb was thrown off."

"Well, to make a long story short, he picked a fight with the wrong man. I'll say one thing."

"What?"

"Cobb's face is like a fire that reaches out into the night."

Al said, "You mean there's no way to reason with him?"

"He's way beyond that point."

Al heard the door of the day coach open. "They're getting restless in there. We better get going."

***

The yardmaster cleared the cigarette from his mouth and handed the teletype back to his assistant. "I don't care what they think. You tell the boys over at Grand Central if they got a problem with the two forty-five p.m. leaving late, I got Tom Cordley here, the new director of the company they can bitch to." Then he pointed to Al but spoke to Cordley. "This who you're looking for, sir?"

Cordley and the renowned lawyer, Max Steuer, turned to Al, who stood in the open doorway of the old day coach. Cordley looked over Al's shoulder. "Boy, are you porter LaHood?"

"Yessir."

"Come over here."

Beau stepped around Al and slowly approached the irritated train executive who was unaware of the track dirt smudged on the side of his coat and sleeve. New to the train business, he had tripped on the rails in front of all the workers. When they told him that the buzzard's roost was the other way by the dope monkey, he went the other way, because he had no idea which way was the other way.

The new director said to Beau, "Mr. Steuer's clients, the parents of the boy in this photograph, claim that you sold their son wood alcohol on the train from Chicago back in October of this year. The boy is now blind and paralyzed. How many pints of liquor did you sell him?"

Beau studied the photograph. "I don't remember ever seein' this boy."

"He claims to remember you."

"Anybody can claim anythin', sir."

Steuer interrupted, "Pardon me, Mr. Cordley, I think I can help resolve this."

Cordley, not too sure about protocol, said, "My lawyers said to wait for them."

Steuer said, "Then why did you ask the porter whether or not he knows the boy in the photo and how many pints of liquor he was sold?"

Cordley said defensively, "I was just making conversation."

"And that's exactly what we're going to do until your lawyers get here. We'll use this time to our advantage."

Cordley said, "As long as it's to our advantage and not yours."

"Oh, it will be." The lawyer approached Beau. "You *are* Beau LaHood? Pullman porter for the New York Central Twentieth Century Limited?"

"Yessir."

The lawyer pointed directly at the photograph of the boy in the hospital bed. "You told Mr. Cordley that you don't remember this swell young college boy, an all-around terrific kid, whom everyone loved and held dear to their hearts. And to think he had his whole life ahead of him when all of a sudden it got plucked away. Why did you just lie to Mr. Cordley, the head of New York Central Railroad?"

"Well, sir, I wasn't lyin'," Beau said. "There's a whole lot a swell college boys that's all-around terrific, so it would be real hard to remember which terrific kid you talkin' about."

"I'm talking about the boy in this photograph, Beau," he said, pounding his finger on it. "*How* does he know your name?"

"There could be lots of ways, sir."

"How many passengers do you serve a day, Beau?"

"Depends on the ride. Depends on the car. Could be twenty. Could be less."

"Twenty or less is not as if I'm asking you to remember ten thousand. This swell young terrific college boy only traveled with you this last October twenty-first."

"Well, sir, there been lots of trips since then. You talkin' hundreds, maybe thousands of passengers."

The lawyer said, "How many have you sold contraband?"

"I don't sell contraband."

"I find that hard to believe, since so many of your passengers drink."

"Well, sir, unless you been on the train countin' who drunk what and who brung what, I don't know as to how you know how many passengers drink, let alone brush their teeth."

The lawyer sat down by the edge of the yardmaster's desk and clasped his hands together as if he had just caught something. "What comes to mind when you see someone drunk, Beau?"

"Nothin', sir. I minds my own business."

"But you would know if someone was drunk from the consumption of alcohol?"

"I wouldn't know nothin', sir. I'm just a porter. I knows to turn down a berth under three minutes. I can show you next car over."

"Some other day. Are you prepared to say under oath that you couldn't recognize a drunk person from someone completely sober and that you've never sold contraband to anyone on the train?"

"Yessir."

The lawyer said, "Are you drunk, Beau?"

"Do I appear to be, sir?"

"I didn't ask whether you appear to be. I *asked*, 'Are you drunk?'"

"I wouldn't think so, sir."

"You *wouldn't* think so?"

"Nossir."

"No *what?*"

"That I'm drunk."

"So, then, you *do* know when someone is drunk?"

Beau looked up at the clever man. "Nossir. I don't put it to my lips, so I knows I can't be drunk. And I don't remember seein' that boy. I see so many it's like they all look the same to me."

"Are you telling me, Beau, that I look the same as everyone else?"

"Nossir."

"That you couldn't distinguish me out of a group of people?"

"Nossir."

"Then you're lying when you say all people look alike."

"Nossir, I ain't lyin', and I didn't say all people look alike, just that they seem to look alike since I serve so many on the railroad."

The lawyer ignored Beau's sharp grin and showed him a Pullman ticket stub with the car number and compartment on it. "This proves that you were the porter for my client's dying son. It also proves that you've been lying to me the moment you opened your mouth."

Beau said, "Far as I'm concerned, all it proves is that it's a piece of paper, sir. Nothin' else, sir. But I do know this. There's bootleggers up and down LaSalle Station sellin' to kids all day long, who can't wait to get their hands on hooch. Every fool knows that. So there's lots of maybes you got to consider before you go callin' me a liar, includin' that boy, who was probably too drunk to know what he's talkin' about."

"Porter, I've contacted all the other passengers who rode with you that day and enough swear that they had bought contraband from you, and when I put them on the witness stand, they'll swear to it under oath. So—" he jabbed his finger on the photo and, almost shouting, said—"can you truthfully tell me that you don't remember this boy?"

"I don't remember him."

Steuer walked over to Cordley as if he were now in the witness box and said, "Your porter is a liar, and I'll tear any credibility he has to shreds in a courtroom, and I don't care how dumb he can act; the jury will see through it. So I suggest you settle for the sum my client is asking, or I'll see to it that your company pays for the destruction of a young man who has been the joy of every crowd and the apple of his parents' sweet, loving eyes. No one will ever ride your railroad again." Steuer gathered his things.

Cordley said, "Aren't you going to wait for my lawyers?"

"There's no need to now," Steuer said as he left the coach and headed east to his waiting motorcar.

Cordley turned to Beau, "You're fired."

The yardmaster stepped in-between Beau and Cordley. "Mr. Cordley…I wouldn't fire the porter just yet."

"You're telling me what to do?"

"No, sir, but if you fire him, it's an admission of guilt."

Cordley, having been told what to do, stubbornly put out his cigarette. Al Nachman pulled a badge from his coat pocket.

Cordley said, "Are you a Prohibition Agent working with that lawyer?"

"Nossir," he said as he leaned over to take a light from Beau. Al blew out a long stream of smoke that gripped the cold air. "I have an interstate warrant to obtain a murder suspect who might be traveling on your train. I'll need accommodations and preferably a compartment in the Waldameer Observation Car on the New Year's Eve Train to Chicago."

Cordley wondered, "How dangerous is this man?"

Al said, "He's like wood alcohol. He'll blind you."

"Why the Waldameer?"

"The last car can be separated en route without further delaying the consist, should it need to be stopped."

Cordley turned back to Beau. "Just how many kids are drinking on our train? And don't lie to me."

Beau said, "Everybody's drinkin', sir. On every line across the country and more so than before Prohibition."

"You think that lawyer has a case against us?"

Beau was startled that his opinion had been asked. He replied as an equal to make his point. "I know this. You settle with that lawyer, you gonna get every shyster after our train iffen a passenger so much as gets a sniffle. So I'd fight him tooth and nail with the best lawyers you got. Let 'em all know they can't mess with the railroad. You do that, you'll have every worker in this yard 'n across the country on your side. This is an opportunity for you to show everyone what you're made of 'n' make a name for yourself. Because the issue here ain't the kid. Every single one of 'em drinks. The issue is the stupidity of Prohibition and that lawyer tryin' to use it to line his pockets, and I can assure you, you ever get the chance to search his house, you'll find contraband in some bottom drawer somewhere."

"The porter's right," the yardmaster said to Cordley as he pointed to the executive's coat sleeve. "You put up a fight, the boys in the yard will beg to clean your coat the next time you trip."

Cordley brushed off his coat sleeve. "All right, we'll fight 'em." He said to Al, "You've got that compartment on the Waldameer." Then turning to Beau, "If you can find a way of getting into that lawyer's house, let me know."

Biltmore Hotel, Suite A

32

Robert Benchley wasn't sure what to make of the vamp in the dark-red silk coat embroidered with fronds of black, green, and gold with sleeves that draped a foot wide. The coat was shapeless as a window curtain, but its long fox collar, bushy and wide, snowy and soft, turned something formless into exotic fanfare. "Fancy meeting you here, Bob."

Benchley, half asleep, reached for the glass of soda water and rye. He gulped down what was left of it and waited for it to induce the mood needed to take in the vision before him. "Zola?"

"Yes. Your wife finally kicked you out of the house?"

"*Loin de vérité*, madame," he said as he put his hand over a stubborn yawn.

"That's what *you* say."

Benchley got on all fours to search for his other shoe. "You have a dirty mind, ma'am."

"But without the guilt." Zola eyed her cousin sprawled out on the suite's best piece of furniture. "What's going on here, Bob?"

Benchley said, "I came in early this morning to give your cousin a tour of the city. We thought we'd take a quick nap before heading over to the Algonquin." He found his shoe and struggled with it. "Welcome back."

"This time it's for good. Now tell me how you two found each other?"

"Didn't you get the wire I sent you at Roosevelt Field?"

"Yeah, I got it. Are you always on the prowl?"

"I resent that, Zola. I was in the bar downstairs and heard your cousin's voice, and it reminded me of the sweetest little girl I had ever met with the same sweetest little accent."

Zola said, "You should've been a bond salesman." She turned back to her snoozing cousin on the long, blue velvet divan with gold-carved scrolls. A copy of the struggling *The New Yorker* with all its quips and gossip of Manhattan was clutched in her hand.

Zola said to Benchley, "Did you speak to the editor of this magazine?"

"Yes, and Harold's very keen on having a woman take over the column. He just wants Dottie to talk to you first."

"Dottie?"

"Dorothy Parker. You met her last week at Tony Soma's speak. Short dame with a bob almost as good as yours."

"Why do I have to meet her again if I have already met her?"

"Zola, take it as an honor, not an insult."

She turned to her cousin. Gone was the little girl with black stockings, laced ankle boots, sailor suit, and a doughy Edwardian flesh of time that stood still. In its place was a sublime creature that detonated with each blink of the eye. "Long time no see, cousin."

Shelby slowly opened her eyes; everything was a blur. "Who're you?"

Zola said, "Do you always leave the door open?" Benchley quickly got up. She stopped him. "I already locked it, Bob."

204

Shelby, still sleepy, said, "You didn't answer my question."

"I'm the old lady used to give you piggyback rides way back when and taught you how to sail on Moon Lake. So what's this column all about, Bob?"

"It's a real tough job, Zola. You have to go out six nights a week and write about all the speakeasies, good and bad, highfalutin and hoi polloi."

"Sounds more like fun than a job."

"It is," Benchley said, "and if you don't take it, I will—even if I have to wear a dress."

Shelby reached for the White Rock Ginger Ale that had long lost its fizz. "*You* sure have changed."

"So have you," Zola said.

Shelby, never the quick hugger, handed Zola one of the Western Union Telegrams that were on the floor by her new box of bootleg labels that she had picked up on the way back to the Biltmore. "Your sister just gave birth."

"Euphia?"

"Who else?" Shelby stretched out like a scarecrow and yawned.

"I suppose I should give you a hug or something," Zola said. She waited and then said, "Come over here, you little brat," and took hold of Shelby. "It's been a long time." She kissed her delicate but stirring face, wishing it were a mirror instead of someone else. "My...have you grown."

"I was eleven when you left for the war."

"Thanks for writing me all these years. Your vivid descriptions of home made me glad I was stuck in the mud."

"You said you wanted to know everything, so I told you."

"Except what had happened to you."

"I don't want to talk about it," Shelby said as she irately looked out at the tall office building across the street. A man was sitting at his desk. The light over him was ripe with monotony.

Zola said, "I only wish I had been here to help you."

Shelby went to the bathroom. She cued Zola to follow and whispered, "*Shut* the door." Shelby let loose. "That son of a bitch, Marston, should've been lynched. No matter how many baths I take, I feel *dirty*. I have goddamn dreams of what he did to me."

"My mother told me that you wanted to break up Euphia's marriage."

"Your parents are idiots," Shelby said. "Neither has ever read a book of substance nor has had any thought of their own, and, like all clowns, they've got opinions on everything. Instead of asking me how I was after getting brutalized by Marston, they whined like babies about how well off our family is. As if their misery is our fault and our obligation to fix. So my father threw them out of our house and said if they ever set foot in it again, it would be their last day on earth."

"My mother's jealous, Shelby. Everyone knows it."

"Well, had it been the other way around, neither of your parents would be grieving over their good fortune and our lack of it."

"People are like that."

"People are full of *shit*. I *hate* them." She tossed her cigarette into the toilet and left the bathroom. Zola was right behind. Benchley was getting off the phone.

He said, "Everything all right, girls?"

"Everything's fine," Shelby said with more than a touch of anger.

"Good," Benchley said, "because I just spoke to Texas Guinan, and she's very much interested in your business proposition."

"What did she say?"

"You've been invited to her club tonight to sit at her table." Benchley turned to the door suspiciously. "Did you all hear something?"

Zola said, "I've learned to tune everything out in life, so it's hard for me to hear anything."

Benchley said, "Must've been the maid then."

"Not this time of day," Shelby said as she nervously watched the door handle jiggle.

Zola said, "I saw Marston in the lobby when I checked in."

"Why didn't you immediately tell me?"

"I had my luggage and everything to deal with," Zola said, "and when I got here, you were knocked out."

"Are you sure it was Marston?"

"Positive."

"How can you be positive when you haven't seen him in years?"

"My mother showed me Euphia's nuptial album, soon as I walked in the door, to remind me how happy they were. If that

207

wasn't Marston downstairs, then it ain't you upstairs."

Shelby took the telegram off the table that her father had sent to Meridian and showed it to Zola. "It seems my mother told your mother that I was going to New York and so she told Euphia who, out of spite, told Marston. When I get back home, Euphia's going to wish she were never born," she said, now holding the Lemon Squeezer in her hand.

"Where did you get the gun?" Zola asked.

"From a friendly little place called Hessler's." Shelby headed to the door. "Next time you're in Bristol, Virginia, stop by. They *aim* to please—listen to him wail."

Zola said to Benchley, "Call the operator and get room four one two."

"Why?"

"*Do* it."

Benchley picked up the phone and waited for the operator. "Room four one two, please."

Zola took the phone. "Al? I'm in Suite A. Marston's at the door. Shelby's got a gun." Zola said to Shelby, "Al says *not* to use it."

"Tell him to go to hell."

"Marston's banging on the door, Al...Well, get here as fast as possible." Zola hung up the house phone.

Shelby said, "I heard you and that Nachman are real tight. Is that true?"

"What if it is?"

"You know he's a Jew."

"So was Jesus. If it was good enough for him, it's good enough for me."

"Yeah, well, people still aren't going to like it back home."

Zola said, "I'll worry about that when and *if* I ever get back home."

Cobb was now shouting. Banging. Shelby said to Benchley, "Call the goddamn house dick."

Zola said, "Nachman knows what he's doing."

"I don't care," Shelby said.

"Marston's got a gun, too."

"Good for him."

"Shelby, that's not possum out there."

"It will be when I get done with him," she said, aiming the gun at the door.

Benchley said, "Vengeance is a dish best served cold, young lady."

Shelby put the muzzle on the door. "Yeah? Well, no dog enjoyed a hunt unless he could do some barking."

A rumbling followed in the hallway. The stairwell door slammed. An echo followed. Then an ensuing silence for what seemed to be an eternity. Benchley got up. He put on his hat and coat and headed to the door.

Zola said, "Where're you going?"

"If you want that job writing for *The New Yorker*, we better hurry. I don't know how long Dottie can wait, and I don't know how much longer we'll be in business." He cautiously peered out the door as Shelby followed.

Zola said to her, "Leave the gun here."

"That would be like leaving the door open." Shelby put the Lemon Squeezer in her handbag and locked the door behind her.

The Algonquin Hotel, West 44th Street, Manhattan

33

A man-about-town entered the Rose Room with a gambler's stride two drinks in, and quickly noticed that two women had taken over *The New Yorker*'s reserved lunch table. One of them was beautiful. The other blindingly so. For some reason she was quickly writing and revising on the edge of a newspaper like a bookie before the first bugle call. The man-about-town was determined to find out why.

Benchley said to Shelby, "Don't you worry. I'm sure that Nachman fella will get Cobb. He didn't have much of a head start down that stairwell."

"That's what *you* say."

"She's right, Bob," Zola said. "Nachman's a country boy. Cobb's from Chicago and has spent some time here. All he had to do was to get out of the hotel, and he's gone. Especially if he went underground in the tunnels leading in and out of Grand Central Terminal."

Shelby said to Benchley, "Who's that man staring at me?"

"Oh, he should be staring at Dottie."

Zola said, "Who is he?"

"A man-about-town by the name of Walter Burns."

Shelby said, "What's a man-about-town?"

Dottie leaned over and said, "A man-about-town is five feet eight. Well dressed. Has a trust fund. Is never more than thirty—though this one's getting close—and is always hard to find." Then to

Zola she said, "And now that you'll be working for *The New Yorker*, you'll be finding the likes of him in all the best speakeasies."

Shelby said, "Why would he be hard to find?"

Dottie said, "Well, when Walter's not attending prize fights, the revue, or eyeing the temporary tenants at the racetrack, he's usually at a dinner party eyeing those tenants."

"Does he live in town?"

"Walter floats."

"I don't understand."

"Neither does the headwaiter who's taking his order."

Shelby said, "Is a man-about-town a native New Yorker?"

"Indeed *he* is," Dottie said. "The other night Walter and I visited one of those speaks that are always popping up all over the place. This one was in Beekman Place by the East River, and he had the most terrible shock. On his way out of the bathroom, he noticed the Humpty Dumpty wallpaper and realized that he was in his childhood bedroom. I made the mistake of saying, 'Let's go home.'"

Benchley said, "They're what's known as the *Lost Generation*."

Shelby said, "The *what*?"

Dotty said, "See, once there was this little itty-bitty war that made a mess of everything, and when it was over, a woman, in Paris, went to pick up her automobile and was told by the owner of the garage that his two mechanics—soldiers of the war—had left for the day. She wanted to know why. The owner replied, 'Madame, they're the lost generation'—and it stuck. But we're not lost at all. It would only be true if we were on our way somewhere. We're not. Nowhere is just fine with us."

Shelby said, "You were in the war?"

"No. The draft board found out I was a woman and declared that I was overqualified. Hey, Walter, I'm over *here*!"

Benchley said, "Remember you're having fish for lunch, not him."

"I'm having fish because he's too well done."

Benchley said, "Not too well done to have his eyes on Shelby."

"Then Walter and I are done, because he never had his eyes on me—just his hands."

Shelby looked up from a new issue of *Billboard*. "Miss Parker, the price of sweat in this magazine doesn't match the quotes in yours."

Dottie affected a drawl. "Miss Shelby, that's because we charge less for our rag, which may fold any day if business don't pick up any soon—by the way, if you order food and nothing comes, that's because I'm paying." Then turning to Walter, she said, "Please have a seat, young man."

Walter thought he heard a voice.

Dottie said, "Walter, I'm over *here*."

He searched for a light. "I'll let the waiter know," he said, his gaze still on Shelby.

Shelby warned him, saying, "Whatever you're looking for isn't here."

"You're in my seat, young lady."

"No one has complained so far."

"*I'm* complaining."

"I hate men who complain."

Dottie laughed. "You're not the only one."

Walter said to Dottie, "*Butt* out." Then turning back to Shelby. "Now, miss—whatever your name is—there's a theater director out in the lobby, yapping about a character's spine and the sound of trees falling in a cherry orchard. I told him he had no spine. You're not in that Russian play he's about to ruin, are you?"

"No. I'm a mathematician, not an actress."

"Really? You remind me of someone."

"Yeah, the last girl who dumped you."

Dottie sidled over for support. "Bob, I'm beginning to really like this girl."

Walter said, "*Butt* out, Dottie." To Shelby he said, "You're from where, miss?"

"Brooklyn."

"I thought so."

"Why?"

"You look like one of those Coney Island fortune-tellers whose misfortune is to always get it wrong."

Dottie said, "You're wasting your time with her, Walter."

Walter turned to Zola. "And who are *you*?"

"I'm a guest of Miss Parker."

Dottie intervened. "Miss Nicholas is going to write a column for *The New Yorker* about all the speaks in this town, so everyone knows where not to go and which people to stay away from," pointing her knife directly at Walter.

Walter said, "Tell Harold to save his nickel. I can tell him everything he needs to know, free of charge."

"Yes, but unfortunately, that's *all* you know. Zola, here, served in France during the war as a surgical nurse and knows something about life."

"Hey, I was over there, too."

"Obviously the Germans didn't think you were worth shooting."

Walter ignored the insult. "So *you're* a writer?"

"I am, now," Zola said.

"I know every speakeasy. Where's your first assignment?"

Dottie said, "Zola's taking the Twentieth Century Limited to Chicago to report on what goes in that nine-car saloon. We hear some college boy and his fancy-pants Greenwich parents are suing the railroad millions for having sold him coffin varnish that paralyzed him. Probably *your* stuff, Walter."

Walter ignored Dottie and said to Zola, "Traveling by yourself?"

Dottie said, "So will you, if you don't cut it out."

Walter sniffed at Dottie and said to Shelby, "You're going, too?"

"What's it to you?"

Walter said, "Everything, young lady. See, I have a long-lost cousin from Chicago, who's dying to meet me."

Dottie said, "You've *never* been to Chicago, and all your cousins hate you."

"Only the first part of that is true." Then to Shelby he said, "Now, my limousine is right outside. Why don't we go to the Columbia Club for lunch? This place is getting stuffy."

Shelby said, "No, thanks."

"Then dinner tonight. What time do you dine?"

"Way past your bedtime."

Dottie said to Benchley, "Let's hire her too." Then she said to Walter, "You're fired."

"From what?"

"From this table. Now *get out*, you two timer!"

Spotting his bootlegger, Walter said, "I'll be back in a minute."

Shelby said to Dottie, *Variety* magazine in hand, "It says right here that quality whiskey is going for as much as one thousand dollars a case in this town *if* you know the right people. Are any of them here?"

Dottie caught sight of a rich old daddy entering the Rose Room with a young showgirl on his arm. "Yeah, and I know some girls who go for a lot less."

Someone else entered. He had a worn look on his face. As he approached the table, Shelby stood up, her anger bare and visible to everyone. "You *didn't* get him?"

Al, out of breath, replied, "No."

Zola quipped, "Should've brought your coon dogs."

Dottie asked, "Who's he?"

"One of those good-looking boys who thinks work is a virtue."

Upper-East-Side Manhattan

34

The dim, narrow hallways echoed Hungarian, Yiddish, and German accents that came and went like a fitful sleep. The walls were soured with years of filth, and since people bathed infrequently, if at all, there was the added assault of foul sweat and end-of-hall toilet odor. A woman poked her head out a door. She stared at Cobb with his sores and bruises. He was someone else's husband. Someone else's problem.

Three more floors to go.

Apartment 6-S faced Third Avenue. Cobb knocked hard on the door as an IRT Third Avenue Elevated *Local-Express* train rumbled by and shook everything off its rivets. A neighbor, having heard the unfamiliar steps, opened her door and looked out into the dim hall. Her apron was her world.

"Hey, meester...!" Her voice strained from the language she would never master. Seven children crowded up closely around her. Cobb recognized the youngest who stood alone. He was barely three years old, barefooted, and dirty, his clothes unchanged with holes that increased with each wearing. She said, "You must be husband. She show me picture."

"Where is Grace?"

"She no here."

"Where did she go?"

"I don't know, but she talk of you always...how you work on

train." The immigrant woman looked down at the little boy. She patted him on the shoulder. "He your boy, meester." She gave the child a gentle push. "You take him, meester. I got my own. I like him. But I got my own."

Cobb looked up from the child. "Didn't she at least leave a note?"

"I told you, meester. She gone. You take him, or I get orphanage take him. He nice boy. Good boy. But he want his mama."

Cobb peeled several bills from his roll and gave it to her. The woman counted the money and slipped it in her apron pocket. Cobb said, "I'll be back."

Mott Haven Yard

35

The railroad had first gotten into Liston Truesdale's blood in December of 1897 when he hitched a ride from Beulah, Mississippi to Cleveland Depot, where boomers headed out to Chicago, Abilene, and as far west as Oregon for seasonal work. The more Liston heard about train life, the more it interested him, but soon the war with Cuba got underway, and he wanted to be part of it. He spent the next several years in the army. When he was discharged, he applied to the Pullman Company and, with his service record, was hired at once. Pullman not only offered a decent wage, but like the army, it was a world unto itself: a brotherhood that rode from town to town, where bakeheads, dingers, Big E's, boomers, bug slingers, grave diggers, mud hops, and porters knew each other by trade and reputation hard earned, and it was through these towns that he had met Beau in 1920. Liston Truesdale quickly saw there wasn't any edge, anger, or soreness to the porter. No uneasy ambition, sense of entitlement, fragility of ego, or unearned pride that could be easily bruised. Beau never showed impatience or peevishness as some other porters had when they believed, rightfully or not, that they deserved something better. He might have felt underappreciated at times, but it never turned him into someone with a chip on his shoulder, even though he was more than ready to move on to a better train, and Liston Truesdale was more than ready to help. Within weeks, he got Beau signed up with the New York Central Railroad's Twentieth Century Limited line that went from New York to Chicago and back. Within two years Beau made first porter and became indispensable, but there was another indispensable person on the railroad, and he was New York Central's Detective Fred Heinz, who had his worn brogues up against the Mott Haven yardmaster's desk. He struck a match against it and lit a cigarette. Outside, the sound of the yard shifted into a late afternoon key as Train 25, otherwise known as the Twentieth Century Limited, rolled in from Chicago and graced the yard.

Detective Heinz pointed to a chair opposite his. "Sit down, Liston," he said, his deadpan smile a result of having faced hundreds of yard thieves, prison escapees, train robbers, and lunatics over the years. He looked up at the big Southerner, their eyes meeting like oncoming cars in the night. "This won't take long."

Detective Heinz never made close friends with anyone, no matter how long he knew them. According to him, no one could be trusted, and sooner or later everyone could be bribed. Ethics meant little when people faced deadlines, loss of position, shame, indebtedness, rejection, or had a false sense of pride. As far as he was concerned, self-interest, honor, greed, and fear were more than occupational hazards; it was the human condition, and in the right condition, it made folks downright ornery, even deadly, no matter the rich banker, roving card shark, runaway kid, criminal, itinerant drummer, dowdy matron, ballplayer, nobleman, clergyman, blue blood, distinguished professor, or surgeon with unsteady but eager hands. Fred Heinz had met them all and would meet them again, no matter how many times they had been jailed or hung, because life was a vicious cycle with no future—just a dead-end spin of time. He reset the brim of his gray felt fedora and smiled the way a crab crawls: low and stingy. He pointed a finger straight up to the ceiling as if jamming it through. "They're all confused upstairs, Liston. They think this is a train yard, not a gin mill."

The conductor, still on his feet, said, "Maybe they're drinking the wrong stuff, Fred."

"Maybe they're drinking *your* stuff. You hear about that kid who got paralyzed from wood alcohol?"

"Yeah, Fred, and every time I hear the story, the beard on it gets longer. Get to the point."

"The point is New York is no different than Junction City nor any of the old territories we once rode. I told the boys upstairs your niggers live on tips and that motivates a man like nothing else, and that's fine by me. I got nothing against anyone trying to earn a living, and I don't give a damn what color he is." He stared at the Pullman conductor as if he was meditating on a pair of deuces. "So in case your brain is addled by all the coffin varnish you've been selling, we run a train operation here. But some fools got it in their heads it's a gin mill. The boys upstairs are pulling their hair out. Far as they can see, there's nothing but train cars in the yard," pointing outside, not even turning his head. "Now you tell me, Liston. Are those things out there Pullman cars or gin mills? Because if it's the latter, I gotta go upstairs and tell the money boys they've been parking their asses in the wrong part of town all these years."

Liston Truesdale flicked an ash. "Get to the point, Fred. We been through all this before."

Fred Heinz, now on his feet, said, "The point *is*, you or your niggers get caught selling contraband, you're all fired." His finger was now on Liston Truesdale's chest. "Do I make myself clear? And I don't care how long I've known you, and I've known you longer than my wife." He stared into the Southerner's face. "This warning is from Tom Cordley himself, the new fancy-pants director of the New York Central, in case ya don't already know."

Liston Truesdale moved the doorjamb off his chest. "Go ahead, Fred," he said, used to the routine. "Pack the trains with your undercover dogs. But don't forget. It's New Year's Eve tomorrow, and as far as the passengers are concerned, if it ain't a gin mill, they'll all be getting off at Harmon to get the first train back to town."

Detective Heinz said, "They wanna bring their own stuff on board and get plowed under, fine with me. It ain't against the law to drink the stuff; just sell it, buy it, and make it. And in case you've forgotten, there's a suit-in-law could bust this company in two. So if you and your niggers are caught selling contraband, your asses will be off this yard forever."

"Even if some dopey kid drinks his own poison and paralyzes himself?"

Fred Heinz saw the approaching yardmaster through the old fancy windows. "Especially if it's some dopey rich kid about to die whose folks, for some reason, think they're gonna miss him." The detective buttoned up his bulky overcoat as if he had just relieved himself and left the day coach.

The yardmaster climbed aboard and made his way to his desk, unaware that it had been used as a footstool. Outside, Detective Heinz stepped over the east tracks as easily as a winter cloud drifting on a gray failing day. Beau watched him turn the corner. Their eyes met long enough to stir the misgiving that had already filled the yard.

36

Beau headed the other way, west, into a Morris Avenue lunch wagon hidden behind fogged and frosted windows. The short order cook, an Italian kid from Mulberry Street with big dark eyes, ruddy skin, and an immigrant's eagerness to please, walked over to the big steel urn, pulled out a thick ceramic mug, and pushed back the enamel lever. Beau heard the cup gobble up the coffee as he walked in, but its aroma was thin against the noon roast thick with old-world aromas of long-cooked onions, garlic, stewed tomatoes, braised beef cheeks and shoulder simmered in beef stock, tomato paste, thyme, and real olive oil, not the grocery brand cut with canola for the American market. Beau took the stool at the end of the counter and waited. Moments later, Liston Truesdale opened the door and walked in. Another slice of ham was thrown on the grill along with a pair of eggs. He sat next to Beau, put up two fingers for coffee, and pulled out a folded sheet of paper. "Judy Gerber, the Pullman clerk up at the Distribution Board at Grand Central, says they've been flooded with calls all day long for the New Year's Eve run. Seems everybody in town wants to ride out the old year with us."

Beau studied the report. "I thought you and Fred Heinz was gonna be in that coach car all day arguin'."

"Some rich kid got wood alcohol in his gut, and some shyster smells money."

"You thinkin' what I'm thinkin'?"

"We'll get to it in a minute, Beau," he said as he pointed to the sheet. "Compartment C in your car finally got ticketed to a lady named Jessica Jill Turner. Judy Gerber said none of her clerks was allowed to book the Waldameer compartment until Miss Turner showed up. So she's our undercover this ride."

Beau, his eye on the sheet, said, "Happy Scoggins had her on the Boston and Albany route."

"When?"

"This past Monday. She's one of 'em contracted girls who gets work now and then. Happy said she was real eager. Like she had somethin' to prove. He found her business card in an empty ticket envelope. Wanted to know what a lawyer was doin' nose-sniffin' with all that education. Used her real name, too."

"Contract girls often do so the office can keep track of who's permanently on and not."

"I know," Beau said, "but most of 'em undercovers ain't that educated. Most of 'em is actresses tired of dreamin' of makin' it big on Broadway. Others, they got an eye on seein' the country at the railroad's expense. But a lawyer? I don't know. When's the last time you ever heard of a woman lawyer?"

Conductor Truesdale said, "Remember that girl rode with us every weekend last spring to visit her folks in Chicago? Always had a compartment to herself?"

"You know it's dangerous for me to remember anythin'."

"Well, dangerous or not, I got to talking with her one day. One of them flappers believes she can do anything a man can. Told me she had just gotten out of law school and not a single firm in New York would hire her except as a stenographer. I got a feeling Miss

Turner's got the same kinda story." He took the distribution report sheet from Beau. "I've got something else to tell you."

"I got a feelin' I know what it is."

"We ride dry this trip, Beau. Both ways. I'm checking every porter and every stash hole before and after tomorrow's boarding."

"I already told the crew, and they ain't too happy. New Year's Eve our biggest day."

"Too bad. This was going to happen sooner or later, Beau, so we'll deal with it now. I'll be in the Waldameer before push-off to set 'em straight. Meantime, you pass the word to anyone who didn't get it first time around—*no* contraband."

"Understood."

The Italian kid came over with another two cups of coffee. Liston Truesdale said, "We already got coffee." The kid shook his head. The conductor took a cup and sipped. "Tell your old man he makes good wine."

Clarksdale, Mississippi
December 30

37

Granny Ella got up from her rocker and made her way over to the cast-iron gates of the Pioneer Step Stove. "Get any colder in here, us all gonna be icicles hangin' off the roof come mornin'." She opened the Pioneer and stoked the bitter fire with a long iron poker. The flames rose and jumped across the floor as if they had been unduly disturbed. Beau's mother, Charlotte, held the youngest of her grandchildren near the fire and gently tapped the boy's back to help alleviate his congestion. The rest of the children were asleep on the floor, bundled up in woolen blankets that the Pullman company no longer deemed fit for passenger service. Granny Ella, back in her rocker, tossed another blanket over her lap. A wide shawl draped her powerful old shoulders. She brushed her broad hand over her short bristly gray hair and let out a sigh with a stillness of eye that had a long and deep memory and a notion that everything had a purpose, if not for good. The wind blew, and the tree branches rustled. She turned to Clementine, who was sitting in a straight back chair, facing the only door of the cabin. Her Remington Model 1889 shotgun was laid over her lap as if it were a Bible open for study. Granny Ella snapped, "Us had better cabins 'fore Surrender than this here slap shack. That's for sure."

Clementine moved the box of shotgun shells closer to her chair, while her mother-in-law, Charlotte, gently rocked the baby so he could breathe better. Clementine said, "Granny, all you been doin' is complainin' since us walked through the door. Iffen you don't want us here, I be more'an glad to get up and leave."

Granny Ella paid no mind to the young woman across from her. She continued her complaint. "Us had vittles and warms, yet us didn't have no money. Us needs a doctor he come down in no time. Marse John didn't want none of his slaves to die 'less he be out a heap a money."

Clementine said, "We ain't livin' back then, Granny. So why bother?"

"Because us was well took cared of then, not like now where they let us die 'cause us ain't worth nothin'. Us got freed all right, but us lost all our worth. Abe Lincoln never thought of that. Not one bit he did. Freed us without a penny to our pocket. Nowhere to go except that camp the soldiers shut us in where us starved, stole, and scrounged for vittles. That war ended all right, but our misery didn't. So us all went back home."

Clementine said, "Why don't you get some sleep, Granny? You're keepin' yourself up for no good reason." Clementine counted her children again.

"They's all here, Clemmie. Stop your countin'. Iffen them white boys out to kill us was all a comin', you'd a knowed it by the Screechin' Owl. When ya hears the Screechin' Owl, ya knows somebody gonna be dead come mornin'," Granny Ella said, nodding her head the way a churchgoer does in response to a rousing sermon. "But then I wouldn't be surprised them yackety white buckra fools is catched by old Raw Head and Bloody Bones and us be finished with 'em like *that*." She slapped her hands and howled with laughter as if it had already happened.

Clementine said, "You best go to sleep, Granny. It be a long time till mornin' come."

Granny Ella put her eye on the sick baby, and then she shook her head in misery. "Been a longer time since I been born."

Clementine said, "You don't even know when you was born, Granny."

"I sho'nuf do knows when. 1833 to be exact. On Marse John Stephen's plantation the same year his twins Isabella and Thaddeus was born and us growed up together and plays till I'se old enough to carry water to the fields. And I was jes your age day of Surrender. Day my world come to an end. Somethin' like that you don't *never* forget. And when them Blue Coats come a swoopin' down on Marse John's plantation and tells us niggers is free, I say to the Yankee cap'n, 'Where's I'se supposed to go with my seven chil'un? Ain't got a penny to my name. Ain't never touched money once my whole life.' Cap'n, he jes say it again, 'Y'all is free.' Then takes all the hams out the smoke house. Kills all the chickens. Drinks all the spirits. Come mornin', them horse soldiers gone jes like that." Granny Ella snapped at the fire. It snapped right back at her. "Marse John, he come the next day to tell us is free. Us could go where us wants. I say, 'Fine, Marse John, fine. Us is free but like a fish free of water. Us can't read nor write. Us is freed of knowledge as with the workin's of money. Marse John jes throwed up his arms and walk away. They sho'nuf freed us them Yankees. Freed us from one misery to the next." She waved her hand across her face. "Marse John was good, though…better than the rest. He never done whip us no how. So us didn't have it as bad as them did on them other plantations."

Clementine said, "I thought you said y'all got whipped all the time."

"They whipped Beau's granddad is what I said. Oh yes, they did. And he was sick of it. He lived over on the Prevette plantation, and you needs a pass to go from one plantation to the other in them days, or them paddy-rollers stop you on horse and whips you till your hide is raw. Jes like them Klu Kluxes do today. Ain't no difference 'tween the two. Back then, they paddy-rolled up and down every road of every plantation. Even the big cities had 'em in case a nigger was walkin' at night with no pass. But Beau's granddad, his namesake, he sho' wished he was on our plantation 'cause Marse John was good. Beau's master never let his niggers off Sundays nor holidays. But us always had time to frolic on Sundays, and on Christmas, Marse John give every nigger a jug a whiskey and meats and sweets and taters and the whole damn week off. Beau's granddad knew all about that and begged Marse John to buy him when he come over, but his Marse wouldn't sell him. No way would he sell a big buck nigger. Then one Tuesday when I was a waitin' on Beau, he don't show up. See, Tuesday's the day all slaves is allowed to travel iffen they got 'em a pass. I waits the whole Tuesday for my husband, Beau, and then finds they got the coon dogs out for him 'cause of him comin' the next day, a Wednesday, with no pass. Say they gonna whip him till the skin come right off his back. I heard it myself from the overseer. I seen it myself. And that night the damn overseer he come a walkin' in every cabin, searchin' for Beau's granddad with his whip shakin' in his hand. And lemme tell you, you can jes hear a slave scream for miles round when the lash is on him. But they didn't find Beau no way, and they had 'em a heap a dogs, but us never heard a scream, so us knowed he wasn't catched." Granny Ella fixed her shawl and went back to rocking. "I ain't never see'd my husband, Beau, since that day. I'se still a waitin' on him. Still a waitin'." Granny Ella heard the little baby cough again. She got up from her rocker and headed to the front door.

Clementine said, "You best sit down, Granny. Ain't nothin' but trouble fixin' to come out there."

Granny Ella put her hand to the door. "I had me enough of what I'se suppose to do. I ain't gonna let that baby die. Not long as I can stand on two feet."

"I didn't hear no Screechin' Owl, Granny."

"No, but I hears the cough, and it jes as bad."

Clementine blocked the doorway.

Granny Ella said, "What that baby needs is herbs, Clemmie, and I got to get to the thickets to get 'em and make the tonic for him to drink."

"Granny Ella, it's mighty cold out there, and the wind is strong. Good enough to get sick and die iffen 'em crackers out there don't snuff you out first."

"I don't see a damn soul out there, Clemmie. It's too cold for 'em to come get us tonight."

"I don't care, Granny. I can't let you out. Can't have Beau hearin' I let you die."

Granny Ella grabbed the door handle with both hands. There was a fire in her eyes deeper and hotter than the one in the step stove. "But you can let him hear his chil' is dead?" She opened the front door and was gone.

***

The eerie howl of the wind was at Granny Ella's back all the way to the woods. She reached down and felt for the shrubs and roots that snagged at her feet. She read each plant, leaf, and root with the tips of her fingers as she picked, pulled, tore, and tossed away anything not of quality. She made her way through the thicket with a marked speed and thoroughness and a determination that made her more fearsome than any creature nearby or on the way. Darkness and old age seemed less of an obstruction than a companion, and it was never more felt when a flash of light beamed harshly into the trees. It bore through everything and made the bare winter branches look like Old Bones afoot as it settled on the old slave like a suspicious eye. Granny Ella hollered, "Take that away 'fore ya blind me."

Thaddeus Stephens lowered the light. "That you, Ella?"

"Yes, it is." The hogweed and sampson snake root, gnarly as the wind that battled the bare trees, were bundled tightly in her arms.

"It's mighty late for you to be out here, Marse Thad."

"It's mighty late for *you* to be out here, Ella."

"Our age it's always mighty late. What'ch ya doin' out here, Marse Thad?"

"You collecting herbs, Ella?"

"I got me a sick chil' in the cabin. Don't get him some root, he gonna die quick soon."

"Let me see what's in your hands, Ella," he said, putting the light on the herbs and then lowering it back onto the hard winter ground as old memories revived. "We know this thicket pretty well, don't we, Ella?"

"Sho' enough do. Us played here when us was young and sprightful way 'fore the Rebellion, 'fore everythin' good us had got took away."

"Yes, but we're not here to play, Ella. And we're no longer young and sprightful, though I do remember all the good times we had before Surrender."

"I'm sorry about Miss Isabella. I was over to pay my respects last week, but you wasn't there. Say you was in Tupelo. Some kinda business, but you was rushin' home quick soon. I sure did love your sister. Remember how us used to play together as chil'un? Isabella in her pretty white dress, always 'fraid somethin' gonna mess it up. I had to pick her up and carry her to keep her clean. Then us all jump naked in the river. Thems was the days, Marse Thad. Thems sure was the days. Life was good. And then like a trick that got your eye on one thing forgettin' the other, it swoop down and brung misery and plight."

"Yes, indeed it did, Ella."

"Remember how us used to chase them ghosts at night? You come crawlin' out the window. I be waitin' for you and Isabella. I had with me my magic bag to keep the rat snakes away, while us all be swimmin' like the fool over the moon, and you be a worryin' a right smart them paddy-rollers come find us and whip us blood red."

"The patrollers didn't whip us children, Ella. They never did that."

"They never whip white chil'un, you mean. But us loved that river. Remember when your pappy done hid his box of silverware and gold in yonder swamp when them Yankees come a look for it on their way to Vicksburg—or was it Atlanta? I don't remember which, but I do remember the day when my brother Julius and your daddy went down to the swamp. He trust no one else but Julius. Took 'em all of five trips to get all the valuables hidden from them blue coats. Then Julius come down with the fever and dies two weeks later with the map in his head."

"The silver and gold are still hidden there. My father never could find it. It would be worth a fortune today. That war certainly ruined us, Ella. We should've made that deal with Lincoln to keep slavery just in our states, but we got stupid. And now our old plantation is part of Addison Prevette's. You and Charlotte are all what I got left of it. We did our best, though."

"At teachin' us to be slaves, y'all did your best."

"I meant with what he had."

"With what *y'all* had. Us had nothin'. But even with nothin', us still had fun. You can't take that out of a person, no how. No matter what you do to folks, you can't keep 'em from tryin' to have fun. Us had everythin' but freedom, and when you balance the two, us had more fun than freedom and more work than worry. But your pappy was a good master. Not like them others who loved to whip. Your pappy never once did raise a cane. Never once put a black man to rest unless it was the Lord's doin'."

Thaddeus Stephens said, "I know, Ella. And had we done right to y'all from the beginning, we wouldn't be standing here freezing in the cold. But men are blind until they lose everything. Then regret comes upon a fool." Thaddeus Stephens shone the light on her. "You shouldn't be out here, Ella, this kind of weather."

"I told you, Marse Thad. I got me a sick chil' to take care of."

"It's still not good for you to be out here, Ella."

"I got me my magic bag to protect me. One my husband, Beau, done give me time 'fore he run off. You ain't forgot Beau now, have ya, Marse Thad?"

"That was before Surrender, Ella."

"*Way* before Surrender. Remember when he come over to our plantation without a pass one day and them paddy-rollers come after him?"

"It was the patrollers' job, Ella."

"Was his job to get away. And I'se still a waitin' on him after all these years. I know he be out there somewhere. There was no Screechin' Owl that night. It was silent except for them horses and coon dogs. Us all a listenin' in the cabins. Followin' it like us on horseback, too."

"They killed him, Ella."

"*Who* killed him?"

"They did."

"They *never* catched my Beau. Ain't *no* man can catch Beau LaHood, Marse Thad. He like them ghosts. You see 'em, then they's gone."

"They caught Beau in the swamp that night, Ella."

She walked closer to the lantern, anger deep in her eyes. "*Who* catched him?"

The lantern went off.

Thaddeus Stephens said, "Clay Nicholas, the Prevette overseer. He caught Beau in the swamp, but Clay knew there'd be hell to pay for killing a buck niggra, so nothing was said."

"I *don't* believe it. Beau knew that swamp better than a rat snake. Better than all them Nicholas and Prevette folk."

"I'm sorry, Ella."

"Nobody knowed that swamp better than you, me, Beau, and Julius. *Nobody*. You *hear* me, Marse Thad? *Nobody!*"

The old man's cane struck the hard winter ground as he walked away.

He spoke with his back to Granny Ella as he headed toward the clearing. "It was a long time ago, Ella…when the world was no bigger than where we lived. But that has all changed."

In the distance, flames lashed high above the trees. Granny Ella watched them rip apart the sky overhead. "It was *you* who told them paddy-rollers where to find Beau in the swamp, *wasn't* it?"

Thaddeus Stephens opened the rear door of the Model T Ford waiting by the edge of the thicket. "Watch your step, Ella. You don't want to fall at your age."

"*You* killed my Beau."

"You don't want to fall now."

"Beau loved you like you was one of his own!"

"Watch your step, Ella."

"How could you kill our Beau?"

He turned toward her. "They scared me, Ella."

"How could they scare the son of Marse John Stephens?"

"By scaring the father of Thaddeus Stephens."

Clementine, Charlotte, and all the children were huddled in the backseat. A man she didn't know was in the driver's seat. He was Vince Brocato.

Granny Ella said, "You should be ashamed of yourself, Marse Thad. *Ashamed* to the bone!"

"I am, Ella, I am. Now get into the car before they find us."

Broadway, New York

38

A blur of nighttime marquees rushed by the taxi heading north on Broadway where, in the squeeze of lights and fierce competition, everything had to be said more than once. In clashing support were newsstands shingled with rows of magazines, storefronts with recessed entries, and glass showcases that boasted second-rate suits, cheap fur coats, discounted theater tickets, ice cream sodas with shots of something else, shoes, frankfurters, and cheap diamonds with off-centered tops and asymmetric sides flaked with gletzes—all without any notion of commercial continuity or permanence except claiming the best deals in town and some room to bargain. The more grander stuff was reserved for second-floor offices with block lettered windows of steamship lines that sailed to rum-running Cuba, English Bermuda, or white beach Bahamas, where native coin divers swam up to docking ships while passengers, pale and suited, tossed pennies from the promenade deck and watched human porpoises dive into the green depths to come up with coin in hand.

Shelby said, "How many Broadways are there?"

Benchley reached for the fare. "Just the one."

"Where are we now?"

"Right in the middle."

"Where did we have supper?"

"Downtown."

"Where's that?"

"Behind us."

The taxi pulled up to the curb.

"What time was that?"

"I don't remember." Benchley opened the door. Shelby accepted his hand.

She said, "Nobody remembers anything in this town."

"That's the whole idea," Zola, right behind, said as a string of taxis and limousines nosed for the curbside that was packed with swells dressed in top hats, black or white tie, ladies pitched out in beaded and sequin dresses, drop-waist lamé imports, opera cloaks of blazing orange silk and purple velvet. Evening coats embroidered in gold, pink, and black metallic yarn with cut steel beads. Some trimmed in fox. Others with raccoon at the collars, wristlets, and hems, or a simple closed neckline with a jazzy scarf. The more exotic nightlife arrived in opera capes of folding collars and explosive patterns as if they'd been spilled straight from mind to cloth as jazz from mouth to horn.

Shelby said to Benchley, "Are all these folks going to Texas Guinan's?"

"My dear, at this time of night, they wouldn't be caught anywhere else except for Barney Gallant's."

Shelby said, "Who are these people?"

"They're asking the same of you, my dear," Benchley said as he showed the doorman his low-numbered membership card that was personally signed by Texas Guinan.

Now inside, they found the speakeasy packed with tables so

close together there was hardly any room for the waiters to work. Orders were taken from several tables at once and dashed off to the kitchen. Texas caught sight of Benchley and the girl whom he had said made Evelyn Nesbitt look less than homely. He had warned Texas that Shelby wasn't a gentleman's mistress: the submissive beauty of nickel and dime wit with a pinch hitter's eye for rich stage door Johnnies. Texas climbed on her table, as was custom, and screamed *Hello Sucker!* to the incoming guests. Then the orchestra stopped. The dance floor cleared. The lights dimmed to a floor-level glow as a professional dance team swept across, hoofing it as cock-eyed as a Tin Lizzy on a country lane with a pig in the trunk.

Benchley whispered to Shelby as they took seats at Texas's table, "They just stopped in from Nebraska."

The skinny male hoofer wore black tie; the svelte female, lame´. He combed with Brilliantine. She bobbed to the neck. Their footwork went beyond thin dancing slippers, spread satin, and head feathers. They used chairs, drinks, hats, hankies, walking canes, struck matches to tease, prod, or playfully annoy. They treated dancing like it was a walk in the park, made pouring a glass of milk hotter than a first kiss, and took each other's arms like lovers on an unmade bed. The hoofer tipped his hat like he was taking off her dress. The hooferette fluffed her bob as if she were only in her teddy. They took the simple acts of everyday life and turned them into art. Those patrons who later danced out the club like swans were excused for their exuberance.

Benchley said to Shelby, "The skinny cornhusker goes by the

name of Fred. The limber worm at his side is his sister, Adele, and they take in as much as six thousand dollars a night canoodling with their toes."

"Doing *what*?"

Benchley pointed to the dance floor. "*Canoodling* with their toes."

Zola, already tipsy, said, "Our darkies do it for nothing."

"Ours don't," Benchley said as Fred and Adele cleared off the dance floor. The band struck up *Indian Love Call*, and everyone jumped out of their chairs. Shelby noticed a tiny man across the floor hoofing it with a tall woman who seemed to be auditioning for something other than lover.

Shelby said, "Isn't that the Tramp?"

Benchley replied, "If you mean Charlie Chaplin, yes, but without the mustache."

"What about those people over there in the back? They don't seem to belong here." Shelby meant the hard-boiled-looking characters tightly gathered around a table with even tighter molls by the dark edges of the room. Their manners seemed out of proportion to their clothes and their clothes out of proportion to everyone else's. They wore sneers all the way down their sleeves and wouldn't stop playing with their supper knives. The big boy, at the center of the table, with a smile as deep as a wound, sat next to an eye-batting dame who acted like she'd been elected dog catcher. She went after waiters and anyone else who piqued her fancy, including one of the men sitting next to her with the Halloween glow, whose napkin was tucked in his shirt collar Mulberry Street style.

Benchley said, "Those boys are the obligatory anti-socials, but everyone in this speak has been handpicked by Texas and not the Social Register. There's no prejudice here. She chooses from Vaudeville, Yiddish Theater, Tin Pan Alley, the Bowery, the Lower East Side, and a place called Sing-Sing on the Hudson, where the landlord's name is Uncle Sam and never bothers with your rent, just your time. The rest of the folks drip in from Berlin, Paris, and Flatbush—welcome to New York, Shelby. This ain't Mississippi."

A surge went through the club as if someone had pulled a switch. A negro band hustled in and played the Charleston with the ferocity of a tommy gun on full automatic. The tables, the pairing of couples, and the scrambling waiters all dissolved into a big spill, and the splash got everyone wet. Outside, people were begging to get in, but there wasn't any room as 1925 drew to a roaring close.

Texas leaned over and said to Shelby, "I spoke to Bob, young lady, and if your shine's panther piss, I'm sending you home to bed, right now. So let's sample your product before we go any further."

Shelby slipped Texas a pint with a new label: *Trusted Rye Whiskey*. Then she abruptly left the table and headed over to the Tramp who was doing the Charleston and shaking his rear end like it was spring cleaning. He felt a sharp tap on his shoulder and got steered away by someone as tall and as quick on the feet.

Miss Guinan said, "Where'd you find that little girl?"

Benchley said, "I like to think she found me."

Taking a sip of the rye and liking it, she said, "Who's supplying her this busthead? And gimme the real dope. This kind of product don't pour out of a faucet."

"I have no idea, Texas."

"Why's it called *Trusted Rye Whiskey*?"

"Read the small print—*Quality You Can Trust*."

"I still don't understand."

"All I know is that Miss Prevette has got a fierce hatred for wood alcohol. A friend of hers back home died from it."

"Okay," Texas said, "but I've met a lot of crazy bootleggers in my time, never a kid right out of short pants."

"She's just the distributor. Someone else makes the product. Now, if you don't like it, let me know."

Texas poured herself another shot. "Sure, I like it and so will all the swells here. We haven't had real rye whiskey since January sixteenth of 1920, but I know a few goons who won't like it, and they're sitting right over there, and they're the ones supplying me with busthead as well as giving me protection, and if you don't believe me, just ask the garbage man who was sniffing empty bottles in the trash can the other day, telling me if I don't pay him off, he's gonna to turn me in. As of this morning, he can no longer walk. I wouldn't want that little girl to get hurt. Especially if she, or whoever it is, can make product this good."

Benchley said, "I completely understand."

"Yeah, but does *she*?"

"No. But for now that's beside the point. I explained the deal to you. What say you?"

Texas said, "She's gotta be willing to learn, and she better have patience and a steady head with a nose for business and men, because they're all crooked."

"You're not talking about *me*, madam?"

"No, Sir Lancelot, you're the exception, but when it comes to a partnership men always think it goes one way, no matter what they say to you in bed."

"What about out of bed?"

"Don't get cute, Bob. If I like her, I'll look out for her and teach her the ropes *if* she can get me more of this stuff and *if* she'll listen to me," Texas said, looking over at the thugs up against the wall with manners as soaked as their brains.

Benchley said, "Are you in or not?"

"What's my percentage?"

Benchley said, "Eight dollars a bottle which you can turn over for fifteen. Pretty easy money for just making a call to all your society pals considering the product never passes your hands nor enters your club: just the money in an envelope. Good-bye Prohibition agents and the goons over there will never know a thing."

"I don't know about never. And I don't know about good-bye. She better do something about the price. Eight dollars is a lot."

"Fifteen dollars a pint; eight is about right down the middle."

"What do you get out of this?"

Benchley smiled. "I? Why, nothing but eternal delight. And Shelby's as crazy as Owney. She'd shoot her foot off if it talked back to her. I ask you again, are you in?"

Texas climbed on her table, threw her arms straight up to the ceiling, and cried: *Hello Sucker!* The slick mayor-elect Jimmy Walker, who hated Prohibition, got a rousing cheer as he made his grand entrance into the speakeasy. The waiters grabbed a table that was flat up against the wall, pulled out its legs, threw on linen, and seated the mayor-elect and his female companion on the chairs just brought in from the kitchen.

Benchley helped Texas down. "I see Jimmy left his wife at home."

Texas said, "The girl's someone he picked up during the election."

"She's a real landslide."

"If you mean dumb? Yes. And don't you say a word about Miss Prevette and me in your new magazine or to anyone else. I may be sick of Owney and those mugs lording over me, but fair play ain't high on their list, and we don't wanna get on it. Understand?"

"Yes, ma'am." Shelby was on her way over with the Tramp. "Let's break the news to her."

Texas said, "I'll handle this," and made the rounds of her club.

When she returned, she slipped a stack of business cards into Shelby's hand. Each one had an order on it and a delivery address. Shelby quickly did the math: five thousand dollars in change. Texas said, "You've got one month to fill these orders. Any later, don't bother coming up. Folks up here don't wait, and they don't remember."

Stunned, she nodded her head and said, "I understand, Miss

Guinan."

"Good." Texas handed Shelby a club card with a very low number and her personal signature. "There are some things you need to learn. Stop by my home for breakfast tomorrow morning." She handed Shelby another card with her home address. "We need to talk. Not here."

The chief goon was approaching the table. Texas put on a smile that didn't fit. "Let me introduce you to Owney Madden. He's the king of beer in this town. He's from England. That's why he talks funny."

Charlie Chaplin, a fellow Brit, got up to shake the delinquent's paw.

Owney said to Texas, "Mind if I dance with your kid sister?"

Texas slapped Shelby on her bottom. "As long as you bring her back in ten minutes and not a second longer. It's already way past her bedtime." Shelby was swept across the dance floor into the crush of 1925.

39

A Central Park rider cantered down the eleven block 5th Avenue section of the bridle path. It was bordered by a large reservoir and a long row of tall shady trees. He called out to a young lady on the chestnut mare, "Are you Miss Prevette?"

"Why, yes, I am."

"There's a Miss Guinan waiting for you at the stable in a taxi."

"Who are you?"

"A stranger happy to be of hand." The young man tipped his hat and, unknowingly, rode off with more than that.

***

Texas Guinan said, "You've got to learn that everything in this town is conditional—including appointments." She got out of the taxi. Shelby was right behind. They entered a Greek Revival captain's house off 10th Avenue and 21st Street in Chelsea. Shelby was stunned by what she saw in the parlor. A lost-and-found of canes, spats, fedoras, and cloches, some belonging to people no longer alive. Cigarette cases, lighters, and gloves were piled on the coffee table. All from the club's late-night sweeper, including medicine bottles, compacts, lip paint, jewelry, house keys, watch fobs, and English, French, Italian, and German passports. Two from Tsarist Russia. Framed photographs of racehorses with garlands. Babe Ruth's baseball bat, stamped left-handed. Horseshoes tacked on the door frame and a 1919 two-reel movie poster that read ***Boss of the Rancho*** Star-

ing Texans Guinan, A Western Story of Feminine Comradeship and Courage hung on the opposite wall. Shelby had seen the flicker and had liked Texas's gutsy, nervy attitude. So different than Lillian Gish and Mary Pickford who, Shelby felt, were delicate little squabbles. Still, the house was a mess lost in thought.

They headed downstairs. Texas found the cook asleep on the prep table, her arms spread over an opened newspaper. "Move your ass, Lillie. We got company." Texas's tumbleweed accent was sharper than thorns. She said to Shelby, "Lillie will have us something to eat, in a second," and headed back upstairs. Texas said, "I never go riding in the city, but I know what it is to sit in a saddle all day under the sun and use a rope at a gallop." They reached the third floor. Texas's bedroom faced the back where the garden trees were reaching over the next yard in an attempt to escape. Texas flopped on her big chair. She let out a grunt and lifted her bottom. A long, sharp hat pin was painfully extracted. "Once day I'm gonna fix this place up right," Texas said. "Get one 'a them high-class decorators to come over and move things around." She kicked off her shoes and crammed her feet into a pair of tired old red pom-pom slippers that were parked at the side of her chair. She slept for five seconds and woke up. "You know that louse you danced with? The beer king?" Texas pulled at her curly blond hair. She was feeling all of forty-one years from too many late-night bouts and early morning bedtimes.

"What about him?"

"He's a murderer," Texas said.

"A real murderer?"

"Is there any other kind?" she asked, staring at the nineteen-year-old kid, whose face belonged in Botticelli's *Mary with the Child and Singing Angels*.

Shelby said, "Why isn't he in jail or at the end of a rope?"

"It's different up here than back home."

"How?"

Texas said, "They got more lawyers, so everyone lives longer." She reached for a hand mirror and took a gander at her pretty but tired face. Shelby noticed the unmade bed. The silk Chinese robe that had been over the back of a chair for a month now. The new vanity mirror table with sleek lines and a big round look-in. Only two walls had been papered. The fireplace was used for storage. It had been a year now, and Texas still hadn't unpacked.

She said, "I've drunk every shade of panther piss that's been made since Prohibition went into effect. Yours is the best. That's the good news."

"What's the bad news?"

"You're beautiful."

"Why is that bad?"

"Every man's gonna wanna sleep with you, and we can't have any of that. So for now, you're Barney Gallant's niece."

"His *what*?"

"Listen, hon, Barney's a saint in this town, and being related to him is your protection, and you'll need it."

"How is he my protection?"

"Because going after a man's kin is off-limits with the goons."

She shut her eyes for five seconds and then opened them. "So this is the deal. When you come to town, you're gonna stay at Barney's. He's never home, so don't worry. And he's a gent. He wouldn't touch you if you jumped into bed with him. He's like that with everything he does. I just love the man and so does everyone else. You just leave some clothes there. Your job is to get to know people. The right people. We're gonna get you into the circles of the very rich and powerful and establish relationships so they'll protect you, because you can't go to the law if something happens in our racket. You gotta know people—especially to make money in this town." She shut her eyes again, snoozing for five. Lillie entered with a tray of ham-and-cheese sandwiches and a bottle of whole milk with cream on top.

Shelby touched the stale bread. "I don't mean to be rude, Miss Guinan, but I have a train to catch. Plus Charlie's waiting for me at the hotel."

Texas woke up. "Where ya going? Ya just got here."

"You said to come over for breakfast. It's past noon."

"I told you—appointments are conditional in this town."

"Well, the train isn't, and it doesn't wait for anyone, and I have to catch one."

"When're you coming back?"

"End of January, and I'm staying with Virginia Swain, not Barney."

Texas was now wide awake.

Shelby said, "Yeah, I know; you and Virginia don't get along.

But she and I are best of friends, and I won't have it otherwise."

"You're staying with Barney, young lady. Virginia's worse than a horse thief, and she can't act for beans."

Shelby said, "I don't care about her acting, and I'm *not* being anyone's niece. If you want to spread the rumor that my sister is married to one of Barney's siblings or whatever, go ahead. I can deal with that. Just don't tell anyone that it's Martha, because she's five years old and in kindergarten."

"So you're not gonna listen to me," Texas said. "You're gonna be a big shot around here."

"No, Miss Guinan. I'm going to get to know all the people as you said. Lay low until the time is ready. But I will *not* live in a man's house. I once got stuck in a cabin with one, and it's not going to happen again."

"You're making a big mistake, young lady."

"No, I'm not."

"Why are you such a prude?"

"I am *not* a prude," Shelby said. "I'm an independent soul. And if you don't know the difference, that's because you're way older than I am."

"Are you saying I'm stupid or something?"

"I'm saying men are stupid because they have no choice. Women are stupid for the wrong reasons."

"Where are you from, again?"

"Mississippi."

"Yeah but where?"

"Coahoma County."

"Lemme ask ya something. Why on earth ya wanna be a bootlegger with all its dangers? I don't get it. Anyone can tell you got proper education and good breeding soaked into you. Maybe tons of dough too. You don't need this. So why go looking for trouble?"

Shelby heard the throaty horns of tugboats drifting up and down the Hudson, each sounding a warning of its own. "I made a bet with someone, and one that I shall not lose."

"What kinda bet?"

"I can't say. But go ahead and tell Barney that I'm his in-law. When I return we'll go to church. Meet the pastor. Let everyone think we're some kind of family. But I am not living with Barney, and I will not be his niece."

"That boy's a Heeb. He won't go near a church."

"I'm talking Sundays, not Saturdays. But I'll visit him. Pretend I'm family. Spend evenings in the parlor. Go to church picnics. But I'm *not* sleeping there. Now, excuse me for rushing, Miss Guinan; I have to catch a train. I've got a month to fill some orders, and when I make a promise, I aim to keep it." Shelby rose from her chair. Texas was dead asleep in hers. Lillie was at the bedroom door.

"I got a taxi waiting for you, miss."

"Is she always like this?" Shelby pointed to the rancho boss knocked out in her big chair.

"Oh yes."

Mott Haven Yard
1:15 p.m., December 31

40

Seven porters in dark-blue jackets were waiting in the Waldameer, a 1910 observation car that had a Twentieth Century Limited drumhead attached to the deck gate. The Waldameer was furnished with big leather couches, deep slumbering chairs, and soft carpeting that soundproofed it from the outside world. The polished mahogany, brass fittings, and cut glass gave even the most insecure passenger a sense of dignity. Pullman conductor Liston Truesdale and first porter Beau LaHood entered through the observation deck. The porters stopped their chatting. Conductor Liston Truesdale posted himself by the corner buffet bar and went through the pre-trip quiz.

"McGallion, passenger asks for a ginger ale or any bottled brand of beverage. How do you serve it?"

Porter Apollo McGallion of the Delta Baggage Lounge Car stood up. "Use the ten-ounce glass, sir. Two or three ice cubes, no more. Wipe the bottle down in front of the passenger and only open it in the presence of the passenger while pointin' the neck away from him."

"Rees, what's the first thing you do when preparing a section-berth?"

Porter James Rees stood up. "Close the windows, sir, or put up the screens as the passenger requests, sir."

"You forgot something."

"Yessir, ask whether the passenger wants to sleep with his head or foot toward the locomotive engine."

Liston Truesdale pointed to the new man. "Paisley, what about towels in the men's room?"

Porter Samson Paisley said, "You never wait for a passenger to ask for a towel. When he's done washing, you immediately hand him one. And you never use a towel for cleanin' purposes such as wipin' down the wash stand."

"Nor shining shoes."

Samson turned to Beau and then back to Liston Truesdale. "Yessir."

"First porter LaHood. Passenger asks for a shot of whiskey. What do you tell him?"

"I tell him it's cheaper by the pint."

The porters laughed. Conductor Liston Truesdale put up his hand. "The New York Central Railroad and Pullman Company have put an undercover inspector on our train tonight, and it's a lady. Her name is Jessica Jill Turner. She's ticketed for the Waldameer. I want y'all to be on alert. There's a suit-in-law pending against the company, and the big boys upstairs are looking to catch any porter selling contraband. Anyone caught will be summarily fired and discharged from the train. It'll be a long walk home in the snow. Is that understood?" The porters gave a collective nod. "I'll be checking every porter in every car. We ride dry until otherwise notified. Turning to Porter Heywood Hodges, he asked, "What are the rules about smoking?"

"The privilege of smokin' in cars is permitted as a favor to passengers, not as a right…"

The crews, outside, gave way to the electric T Engine heading south on the center track of Mott Haven Yard for its hook-up with the Twentieth Century Limited that rode electric until Harmon, New York, where it was coupled with a coal steam locomotive for its journey west. The yardmaster notified the downtown beehive that Train 25 was on its way for the New Year's Eve run to Chicago. When the hook-up with the electric locomotive was complete, the consist rolled south until it reached the Park Avenue tunnel at 97th Street, where it descended and rode underground for fifty-five blocks to Gate 27 located on the main floor of Grand Central Terminal at 42nd Street.

41

The Biltmore Hotel, at the Vanderbilt Avenue entrance, was defended by bellhops in dragoon waistcoats, tight billet trousers, and quick shoes. The offense came out of the huddle in taxis, private limousines, and sedans on Vanderbilt Avenue where Grand Central Terminal—a limestone fortress of vaulted ceilings that strung shafts of light into the main level—stood in anticipation of the migratory impulses of southern Manhattan. Fixed atop the terminal's front façade was the statue of Mercury, the God of Financial Gain and Thieves. Below, the head Biltmore bellhop, keeper of luggage and kit, led his formation across Vanderbilt Avenue toward the west entrance of Grand Central Terminal, where Red Caps took the luggage and brought it to the north side where it was ticketed and forwarded to the baggage elevators for immediate loading.

Marston Cobb was waiting under the automobile loop that connected Park Avenues north and south by the Vanderbilt entrance. He looked withered, homeless, swollen. His suit unchanged with oily slicks at the elbows and knees, pocket flaps dog-eared, and his shirt pasted against his chest from moments of intense sweat. His eyes were sullen and heavy after having been chased the day before, down two dozen flights of stairs into the reckless Manhattan streets of jaywalkers, crosstown traffic, and short-tempered natives, yet New York was forgiving of such misdemeanors. It had bigger things in its current to channel than a scofflaw. Somewhere in-between a green Fifth Avenue Coach Company double-decker five-cent bus and a wave of hurried pedestrians, he melted away into the city's deep human purse—his hat, among thousands, bobbing up and down the avenue.

The Biltmore bellhop tried to avoid Cobb who was waiting for him under the Vanderbilt canopy. But Cobb, in his heavy-handed manner, pounced on him.

"Where's Miss Prevette?"

The bellhop pushed him away. "She just walked in."

"Is she in her room?"

"She left her trunk to be picked up and went off with Charlie Chaplin."

"Charlie *Chaplin*?"

"You never heard of him?"

"Fuck off. Where'd they go?"

"They kept it a secret."

"Maybe you just want more money?"

"Maybe you don't have any."

"Why are you picking up her trunk?"

"Since she's got a new boyfriend, who knows?"

Cobb grabbed the bellhop. "The hell do you mean *new* boyfriend?"

"Hands *off*, mister," the bellhop, no sissy, slammed Cobb hard against the terminal's exterior wall. "You wanna know anymore, it'll cost ya eight bits."

Cobb tossed him a dollar coin. "She's on her way to the Twentieth Century Limited."

"Did Charlie sleep with her?"

"Put it this way. Housekeeping checked her bedsheets and then called the newspapers tell-all-boys for the five-dollar tip-off."

"So he did sleep with her?"

"Unless he wasn't asleep."

Cobb hurried through the side-entrance door of the vast configuration of Grand Central Terminal, only to be stopped by a mass of people spilling out of the maze of stairways and gangways steeply angled for the ease of moving small, big, round, heavy, and too much luggage. The deluge of heels and bodies echoed off the astral heights of the terminal. Cobb remembered that the Red Caps were taking the luggage north where the big elevators hauled everything down below to the trains, but, first, he stopped off at the telephone exchange and called J. Benito at Lansing Garage in Chicago. Cobb told him, "Meet me at Buffalo New York Central Exchange Street Station December thirty-first at eleven forty-five p.m. eastern time, and bring the heavy rope, the animal tranquilizer, and a road map to Canada. If Prevette wants his little girl back, he's going to have to pay huge."

Benito asked, "How huge?"

"Five hundred thousand huge."

"This better be real. If you're bullshitting me—"

"Look up Prevette in the Who's Who if you think I'm kidding. He's my uncle, and he's worth millions."

"So then ask for a million."

"Don't get greedy." Cobb hung up and walked out of the big grand wooden doors of Grand Central Terminal like a man leaving a saloon one drink too many.

Grand Central Terminal
1:45 p.m.

42

The arrival and departure gates were wrought with arrow-tipped lances that were all the rage in new apartment construction, where polearms of corseques and glaives were installed at street-level windows to give the tenants a notion that they were living in a Tudorian castle—it was what argyle was to golfers. Inside Gate 27, Pullman porters in dress blues and white gloves were making final arrangements with the carriers swarming in from the loading gates with the last of the luggage. Conductor Liston Truesdale made his way through the swinging personnel doors that led from the tunnels below to the main terminal. He said to Al Nachman, "Do you have authorization to apprehend Cobb?"

The cold air, filtering in through the tunnel, stuck on Al like tape. "Yes."

"And New York Central knows this?"

Al handed the Pullman conductor a typewritten business letter. "You know Tom Cordley?"

The conductor's face turned nasty. "Yeah, what about him?"

"Cordley made arrangements for me on the Waldameer. The observation car."

"I know. He gave you a compartment right next to the Prevette girl and the undercover."

The anticipation of the crowd heightened as the Pullman conductor, with one big heave, lifted up Track 27's gate. A pleasing sigh came from the battery of punchy, light-footed, toe-leaning passengers, who had been fearful the train would leave them behind with the old year.

Al said, "What about this undercover?"

Conductor Truesdale weaved through the crowd and said, "She's right over there."

A young woman was loitering near the Waldameer, the last car of the consist but the first one on the platform. She wore a wispy brown bob, black round glasses, and a nondescript overcoat the shade of moth. Her eyes were serious but determined to be pleasant.

"How do you know she's the undercover?"

"Same way I know the girl over there ain't."

"I hear your porters are selling contraband," Al said. "The stuff that blinds folks."

"Where did you hear that?"

Al said, "When I met Cordley, there was a high-powered lawyer claiming his client was sold bad liquor on your train that caused a rich college kid to get stiff."

"That's what *he* says."

"What say you?"

"I say baloney. The notion is as dumb as walking across No-Man's-Land expecting a warm welcome on the other side. Everybody drinks, and you can smell it like French cheese. So why blame it on the working man?" The conductor posted himself on the far side of the platform to keep an eye on the train.

Al said, "You were in France?"

"Yeah."

"On the front?"

"Yeah, and I still can't figure out why the screwy politicians declared a war we had no business being in. We had no army, no experienced officers, no NCOs. Just a whole lot of fools singing Yankee Doodle Dandy."

"You'd been in the service?"

"Yeah, and when I told the draft board I was too old to go to war again, they said thirty-eight is just starting out in life."

"You were in Mexico?"

"Cuba."

"Saw action?"

"Joe Wheeler's Cavalry, 2nd Brigade. The army pushed me through, but leadership and selflessness are the hardest things to teach a kid overnight and even harder when your lieutenant's just out of college and scared up the ass if he's to be or not to be."

Al flicked an ash. "Good thing I didn't take poetry in college."

"You were a lieutenant?"

"Yes."

"France?"

"Belleau Wood."

"Oh."

"Whaddya mean oh?"

"Captured a Hun from the Kronprinz Gruppe. Said you Marines were *erschrekend*."

262

Al laughed. "So I'm scary."

"You speak German?"

"Something like it."

"Well, you won't be needing it on this train."

Al reached into his coat pocket. "You need to take another look at Cobb's photo?"

"No. I looked at him long enough and so did my men. If they see him, they'll let me know."

"I hope they were paying attention when you showed them the photo."

"Mr. Nachman, a lot of people say bad things about colored people, but when you gotta get the job done, they're as good as a white man, and they do it for a lot less. We'll get this Cobb if he's on board." The first call for the train went out across the platform.

Al said, "I'll stay here a minute, if you don't mind."

"Suit yourself."

***

Shelby walked through the gate wearing a camel polo coat, hunter green wool riding britches that flared at the thighs, and a beige felt cloche with a taupe ribbon. Her custom-made russet leather field boots, discolored at the ankles from months of horse sweat, fit like a second skin over her lean long legs, but it was the rural pursuit of windswept pleasure that had put the blood back in her veins and the buzz in the air. Her retinue—a personal valet, assistant, and bellhop provided by the hotel—stopped at the boarding steps of the Waldameer Observation Car. Beau was busy helping passengers board. He said to Shelby softly, "The undercover's right behind you, miss."

Virginia rushed along, "How was your ride in the park?"

"New York stables should be ashamed of themselves. They rent you a horse and give you a jackass." Then to Beau, as if they had never met, "Make sure everything of mine is on board, boy."

"Everything is, miss."

Zola came along. "I'll see you on the train."

Shelby said, "Where are you staying?"

"All *The New Yorker* could afford was an upper berth."

"Then you'll stay with us."

"Thanks, I love you."

Shelby noticed Al on the far side of the platform. His biblical eyes shone bright like the prophets when they go blind and see the future. Her mother called him the *Jew* as if she were spitting out the dense monosyllabic Anglicized Hebrew word. Her hatred of his people was deep, and when Shelby asked why, Mims said, "How do you explain hate? You feel it. That's all there is to know." Shelby walked over to Al, telegram in hand. She showed it to him. "How did you know Tom Nicholas was hiding in the old slave cabins?"

"The dogs found him."

"Yes, but who gave you my cousin's shirt?"

"Does it matter?"

"It does to me. My aunt certainly wouldn't have given it to you. Did Euphia?"

"You'd have to ask her."

"I don't have to," Shelby said. "Julius gave it to you."

"He didn't give me a thing." Al had fallen into her trap.

"So then you do know him." Shelby boarded the train, thinking not of Julius's betrayal but at how easily he could be compromised.

The final bell rang. Conductor Liston Truesdale leaned out of the Waldameer's vestibule and sang *All Aboard*. The porters pulled the chains of the heavy steel steps. Al hopped aboard the observation deck and closed its gate as Train 25 headed into the tunnel. Those mingling on the platform watched the drumhead of the Twentieth Century Limited recede into the long dark tunnel under Park Avenue that led north to 97th Street.

***

Compartment C

Structural steel-workers, also known as "bridge-men," balanced themselves hundreds of feet in the air, without safety nets or lines, on steel beams no wider than six inches and sometimes in gale wind conditions. There they piloted steel girders into place while snatching red-hot rivets tossed from rivet boys to link them all together— Zola looked up from her magazine. "Thought I'd drop by."

Al shut the compartment door. "I doubt I'll be getting much sleep tonight. So if you want, I'll get the porter to bring up your things. The section-car's no good for shut-eye. I'll tell him we're married."

"You might as well tell him we're divorced. That's not why I'm here."

Al slipped off his coat.

Zola said, "The head bellhop told me that Marston entered Grand Central Terminal, and it wasn't to take the subway. Said he was crazy like a man lost inside himself. I looked for you in the hotel, but you had already left. Maybe you can tell me."

"What?"

"The hell is wrong with him?"

"Who?"

"Cobb. Why are people like that?"

Al took the opposite couch. He reached for her magazine. "You read *Modern Science*?"

"Everybody does. What's wrong with Marston?"

Al turned the magazine over and thumbed the pages. He glanced through the article about the dangers of walking on a steel beam way up in the sky without any harness or safety net. Then he looked up at Zola. "I suppose Cobb lacks the ability to distance himself from himself and stare into the ugly truth of what we all are."

"And what is that?"

"The porter let you in?"

"Beau let me in."

"Nice fella Beau."

"…You were saying about Marston?"

"He's a mass of contradictions," Al said.

"I already know that."

Al put down the magazine. "Those contradictions and flawed beliefs are what compromise our best intentions and subvert whatever rational capabilities we may have, and from there it's easy to step into the void of twisted logic where violence, because of the finality of its action, self-empowers as it simultaneously self-destructs."

"In other words…he's nuts."

"Yeah. You're staying?"

"For now."

"What about that new job of yours?"

"Working on it now." Zola put down the first sentence of her new column on her new writing pad: *The approaching New Year had lit a fuse to the day, and it was burning short.* The train emerged out of the tunnel. She looked up from her pad, her eyes no longer wasted on things lost. "I think I found myself, Al."

He put down the magazine. "It's about time. You're not any good at extortion."

43

The Twentieth Century Limited pulled out of Harmon, New York, at 3:38 p.m. after it had coupled with a Pacific Class K-14f coal steam locomotive. Its last stop north was at Albany at 5:49 p.m. Then it turned west to Chicago.

Passengers in compartment cars were still getting themselves settled in as they rang their porters for hangers or bars of soap already in their closets or bathrooms. Others rang for the sheer pleasure of having a butler for the first time, only to find out they had to share him. Beau entered Shelby's drawing room with a tray of ginger ale and soda water. The drifting scent of her delicate perfume made him suddenly yearn for the compatibility lovers sustain over time. He quickly took hold of himself. "You wanted to see me, miss?"

"What took you so long?"

"There's other passengers, Miss Prevette."

"Miss Swain and I happen to be two of those other passengers."

"I don't see her here."

"That's because she's somewhere signing autographs." Shelby walked over to the closet. "Where are the hangers?"

Beau reached into the walnut closet trimmed in gold leaf, "You got to reach over to get it." He handed her one.

Shelby said, "Guess who came whipping by, in the lounge, saying she was dying for a drink?"

"The undercover?"

"Yeah, and I told her to get her own sweat. Turns out her compartment is next to mine. I suppose that's to keep an eye on you, Mr.

La Haut."

"Well, I suppose it is, miss."

"I want you to open her door right now."

"Excuse me?"

"I need to get in there."

"Oh, I can't do that, miss."

"Yes, you can," Shelby said, her hand straight out. "Give me the passkey."

"It's not for passenger use. I could get into a lot of trouble, and I'm in some already," Beau said.

"It won't cause you any trouble, if you stop wasting time," Shelby said. "I need to make sure this girl is really the undercover you say she is, because I've got a trunk full of contraband, and I don't want her near it tonight when our party gets going."

"That might be hard to do."

"Not with Virginia at the door. We're putting a half-hour limit on all guests before letting them in again. That girl isn't getting in at all."

"I understand, miss, but it would be very unwise of you to go in her compartment."

"Baloney. She's in the first car with all the other celebrity gawkers. So don't waste any more time. Give me the key."

"Look, miss, I been on the train long enough to know she's the undercover. So you don't need no goin' in there."

She sternly approached Beau. "I *want* that key."

"Miss Turner, for sure, is the undercover."

"We're wasting time, Beau."

"With all due respect, miss, some might even say you got a lot of nerve."

Shelby said, "Look who's talking. I heard all about the performance you gave at Mott Haven Yard yesterday. Nachman said that you missed your calling."

"What calling?"

"Said you should've been a lawyer."

"Well, maybe there's still time for that."

"Not if you don't give me that key." Shelby took it out of his hand and left the drawing room.

Beau said, "You got a lot of nerve, miss."

"I got more than that."

Beau went on up to the men's lounge, by the vestibule, to keep an eye on the car, ahead, in case Miss Turner was on her way back. Two very long minutes elapsed before Shelby tapped him on the shoulder and brought him into her drawing room. She showed him a business card: *Jessica Jill Turner, Juris Doctor, Private Eye – Pullman Affiliate, No Case Too Big, No Case Too Small, Plaza 2333 New York.* Shelby said, "Here's the copy of Miss Turner's contract with the Pullman Company and the New York Central Railroad, which gives her free pass on this train and this train only for the next two weeks. Here's a photo of you, Mr. La Haut, Pullman hat and all."

"You better hurry and put that all back, miss."

"No. She will only think she misplaced it," Shelby replied and led him to the door. "Now, excuse me," and showed him out. "I must

270

dress for supper. We shall talk business, later."

"Porter, what time is first seating?"

Beau looked over his shoulder. "Six o'clock, miss."

"Good. I'm hungry." Miss Turner closed the door to her compartment.

44

The Pullman dining car was filled to capacity with gentlemen in black ties and ladies in slim drop-waist evening dresses that touched the knee: a cause for arrest just a few years earlier. Glamour competed from table to table with joy and flashes of the eye. The dining-car waiters, in their starched white jackets, swiftly maneuvered silver trays that carried painted porcelain specifically designed for the New York Central's Twentieth Century Limited. The menu indexed an array of mouthwatering fare from Lobster Newburg, Lake Trout Maitre d'Hotel, Planked Spring Lamb Steak, Broiled Shrewsbury Squab, New Wax Beans Fermiere, Shrimp Cocktail Lorenz, and these represented only a portion of the menu. The heady aromas in the dining car caused gastronomic stress even among the least-discerning diners. Shelby, exasperated, looked up from the menu. "I'll have it all."

The waiter, compressed into a starched white cotton jacket, gave Shelby the ruling with the caution of a gamekeeper feeding his lions. "We're only allowed one sitting at a time, miss, but we'd be more'n happy to serve you again later."

The headwaiter approached the table, with the undercover trailing behind. "Pardon me, Miss Prevette, but unfortunately, we cannot serve single passengers on a four top, so would you allow this kind young lady to be seated at your table?"

Shelby said, "Miss Nicholas is on her way, and Miss Swain is unfortunately detained at the moment, but I'm expecting her shortly."

The headwaiter, fully aware who Miss Swain was, wondered,

"Is she not feeling well?"

"She's not feeling anything." Shelby scanned Miss Turner's stringy bob and then her dress that was baggy at the waist and loose at the shoulders. It had a broad white Dutch collar popular a few years back, but it was her smudged rouge that made her a puddle to avoid despite her having eyes that were intelligent, alert, and weighted down by long hours of reading and interrupted sleep. There was something odd about Miss Turner, and Shelby wasn't sure if it was intentional.

Miss Turner sighed. "I'm so terribly sorry to disturb you. If I am intruding, please tell me. I would be more than glad to return to my compartment and have dinner alone."

Shelby enjoyed the self-inflicted torture. She said to the mouse, "I so love your dress. It's so different than anything I've ever seen."

"Well, I wasn't sure what to wear. This is my first time on a train."

Shelby smiled at the little liar. "Then you should have knocked on my door."

Miss Turner said, "I wouldn't have wanted to disturb you."

"A neighbor in need is never trouble."

A buffet porter entered the dining-room car with a handwritten note and gave it to Shelby. "A passenger, in a forward car, requested that I bring this to you, Miss Prevette."

Shelby opened the note and read it. The expression on her face went from high fun to burning fury.

Miss Turner said, "If you'd like me to leave—"

Virginia arrived. She took the gum out of her mouth and looked for a place to stick it. She almost put it on Miss Turner. Shelby pushed back her chair and left the dining car.

***

The snow-covered hills of upstate New York glowed under the starry evening sky as the new frost covered everything with a velvet chill. Zola bookmarked the moment for later. She was more concerned with Al, who was getting dressed for supper and who was undisturbed by whatever she was feeling. His sense of duty was greater than any of her needs, which were always intimate and complicated.

Zola said to him, "When did you find this out?"

"Beau came in with the wire while you were in Shelby's drawing room."

"Is Tom completely blind?"

"Yes."

"What about his confession? Did you shoot that out of him, too?"

"We didn't have to."

"What exactly did my brother say?"

"That Cobb befriended him while he was visiting Chicago. Seems years earlier your Uncle Addie's sister ran away from home."

"She didn't run away," Zola said. "She got pregnant at fourteen and went to Chicago to have the baby and stayed."

"At *fourteen*?"

"Yes."

"Was your uncle's sister raped?"

Zola said, "The Prevettes don't tell us everything."

"Well, I've got other news for you." Al turned to the mirror to fix his dinner tie. "Unless, of course, Euphia already knows."

"You're bringing my sister into this now?"

"Cobb did. Not I."

"What're you talking about, Al?"

"Did you know that Cobb was already married?"

"What do you mean *already* married?"

"He was married when he married your sister."

"When did you find this out?"

"Right before I left Clarksdale. His first wife went to court for child support. She put out a warrant for his desertion and then had it desisted. Cobb left New York and returned to Chicago where your brother, Tom, wasn't having any luck holding a job. So they left for Clarksdale to stay with your folks. You were in Europe, so your parents gave your room to him. Soon he was after Euphia. It seems Cobb used your brother and sister the way he uses everyone else."

Zola dropped her robe on the couch. "And my family knows nothing of this other marriage?"

Al turned away. "As far as I know."

"How did Marston use my brother?"

"He told him, in explicit detail, that he had seen Lindsay Coleman kill Grover in the cotton fields. When word got out that there would be an acquittal, because of new evidence, Tom was primed to kill Lindsay Coleman."

"Primed?"

"Psychologically."

Zola took her evening dress off the hanger.

Al continued. "My point is, your brother had been manipulated to do something he would not have done—or should I say, *might* not have done."

"You're not saying Marston is the one responsible for Lindsay's murder?"

"An argument can be made that he was instrumental in it happening."

"Then my brother might not be hanged?"

"Let's just say this could affect the sentence."

"How?"

"If the defense can prove that Tom had been primed to murder Lindsay Coleman, then that changes everything, *if* the jury buys it."

Zola slipped on her dress. "That's a big if."

"Depends on the court." Al handed her the shoe she was looking for. "But it definitely changes or at least shifts reason for motive, which is central to the case." He stepped to the side to let her fix her bob in the long mirror on the inside of the closet door. "I'd go as far to say there's a possibility Tom might not do any time—I'm not guaranteeing it."

Zola reached for her double-rope pearls and slipped them over her neck. "How do you figure that?"

276

"He might only have to do institutional time, at most," Al said, "but then I'm talking about possibilities, not certainties. He still might be hanged."

"Thanks. With your kind of thinking, maybe no one's guilty, and everyone will be hanged."

"I don't think so."

Zola said, "What if Marston's lawyer makes the case that he too was primed to kill Grover, because of his upbringing? That he came from a wealthy family and that his exclusion resulted in criminal behavior? I mean, this could turn into a nasty little game where words mean more than actions—or is it the other way around?"

Al said, "No one primed Cobb."

Zola hitched up her dress and snapped a loose stocking to her garter. "You know what I really think?"

"What?" There was a knock on the door. Al said, "Who is it?"

"Beau."

"Come on in."

Beau opened the compartment door and said to Al, "Porter McGallion, up in the Delta car, saw Cobb walk out of baggage and take a seat in the forward lounge."

"When?"

"Just now."

"How did he get in the baggage car?"

"Must've come through the north side of Grand Central Terminal where they got the big elevators. That's why you missed him on the platform. He was already on the train with the first loadin' of the big trunks."

"Didn't you look for him there?"

Beau said, "There was no way I could've pulled apart a car full of trunks and valises, let alone freight before we left."

"Is the forward car crowded?"

"The whole train's crowded."

There was another knock on the door. Shelby entered and handed Al the note that had been delivered to her in the dining car. He read it and then looked up from the scribble. "Who's Dr. Jennings?"

"I don't think I'd want to say that out loud."

"When did you get this?"

"In the dining car, now—you're going to *sit* there?"

Compartment B

45

Beau's last call Miss Turner complained that she had left her flask at home and was at a loss for a drink. He reminded her that the whole country was at a loss for a drink and went on his way. This time he had a feeling she might try to entrap him, so he turned his head away before gently rapping his knuckles on her compartment door.

"Have you been to my room, Porter?" Miss Turner said as she held the door wide open.

"Why, yes, miss," more than surprised at what he saw in the periphery of his eye. "I was here to see about all your other requests."

"I mean after that. When I was in the dining car. I'm missing something."

"Ironin' maid still on duty 'cause tonight's New Year's Eve. I'll have whatever it is brought over real soon."

"I'm not looking for a dress."

"Your shoes, miss?"

"No. An envelope with my pass from the railroad."

Beau smiled best he could. "Oh, I wouldn't know nothin' about that, miss."

"You damn well should. There was a photo of you in it."

"I wouldn't know nothin' about that, neither."

"I left it right in the corner by the couch in my briefcase."

"Wasn't it there when you returned and dressed for supper?"

"I didn't need it then."

"Maybe you ought to check again, miss. Things can just disappear on a train. Happens all the time."

"Boy, if I don't get it back in ten minutes, *you'll* disappear," as she had done with herself and her round black Harold Lloyd glasses, stringy bob, and frumpy smock. The new Miss Turner wore a sleek navy blue lamé chiffon drop-waist dress with a flowered hip sash that made the curves of her body supple, sharp, and eager to get attention. She was done playing the pipsqueak.

"Well, miss, I can't promise you nothin', but I'll go look for it."

"You're goddamn right you'll go look for it, boy. Where's Mr. Nachman's compartment?"

"It's just up ahead, miss, but he ain't in it."

"Where is he?"

"I wouldn't know other than I saw him go up the train with New York Central Conductor Pete Huley."

Miss Turner took a wire off the table and left her compartment. She found Al in the telegraph room with Pete Huley. "Excuse me, sir. Are you Mr. Nachman?"

"I am, miss."

"I'm Jessica Jill Turner. I work for the railroad. I'm with Undercover Inspection Unit 6." She showed him her papers. "I just received a wire from Tom Cordley, president of the company. When we reach Buffalo, the New York Central Railroad Police will be boarding the train to apprehend a suspected murderer by the name of Marston Cobb."

"I know all about that, miss."

"Good, because New York Central doesn't want you to interfere with the investigation."

"I have an authorized letter from Tom Cordley to pursue the suspect without constraints."

"I don't care what he gave you, Mr. Nachman. You're not to get in Detective Heinz's way. He has railroad jurisdiction, not you."

"And just how would I get in his way?"

She showed Al the wire from Cordley's office. "Because you do not have legal jurisdiction on the railroad. You may use the train for transporting criminals but not in any activity related to railroad law enforcement, such as apprehending or restraining suspected or known criminals unless in accordance with penal code eight ninety-five. And you, Mr. Nachman, do not have any such authority."

"Why didn't Cordley tell me this when I visited him?"

"Because he was unaware of railroad procedures when issuing you the letter. He may be the new president of the company, but he's not a train man. He came over from Wall Street."

"And you, miss?"

"What about me?"

Conductor Pete Huley interrupted. "The kid's on the level, Mr. Nachman."

Miss Turner added, "Despite your unfamiliarity with railroad law, Mr. Nachman, I will afford you the courtesy of introducing you to Detective Heinz when he boards the train. You may work out your situation with him concerning Cobb, and if there are any legal questions concerning procedure, I will be available for further consultation if Detective Heinz, you, or the railroad should require it, or if I deem it necessary within the legal context required."

Al put away her business card. "So you're a lawyer as well."

"I'm a lot of things, Mr. Nachman."

"How old are you?"

"Twenty-four."

"Why railroad inspection?"

"Law firms don't hire women in executive positions, but the railroad has a use for us."

Al said, "When will Detective Heinz be boarding?"

"Buffalo, eleven forty-five tonight, eastern time." She put the telegram back in her purse. "I hope you enjoy your stay as a passenger, Mr. Nachman, and remain in the best of comfort. Other than that, you are to do nothing."

"And if I should run into Cobb?"

"You are to do *nothing*, Mr. Nachman."

Al scrutinized the girl: five-feet-three tops without heels. "Cobb's a lot bigger than you, miss. He's carrying a weapon. If threatened, he will use whatever it takes to escape the law."

"What are you saying, Mr. Nachman?"

"I'm saying that unless you have the experience and training, regardless of your size, you'll be putting yourself at great risk. You're young and bright with a solid future ahead of you. It would be foolish of you to jeopardize that and remiss of me to allow that."

Miss Turner said, "That's why Detective Heinz is on his way."

She went back to her compartment. The letter of transit and the photograph of Beau were in an envelope by her briefcase. A handwritten note was attached: *You dropped this in the aisle. Your neighbors, Drawing Room A.* Miss Turner quickly left her compartment with her passkey. Two could play the game.

46

Pullman conductor Liston Truesdale and New York Central Conductor Pete Huley were wedged in the vestibule that led to the Delta Lounge Baggage Car. The consist's steady *rat-tat-tat* tapped itself out—what the Big E's called train music.

Liston Truesdale said, "It's dumb if ya ask me."

Pete Huley didn't care. "The lawyers don't want Nachman involved, so that's it."

"And what if all of a sudden this Cobb should go nuts on us before Fred Heinz boards? Leave it up to that kid? Nachman and I were both in France. We know how to handle a weapon under stress. She's never been in a situation. That nut puts a move on her, we're going to have a dead little girl on our hands and the world up our asses."

"Speak to the lawyers, if ya got a problem."

"I spoke to *her*," Liston Truesdale said, "and according to her pickled brain, unless she's gets killed, she's in charge."

"That's the law."

"Sure, it is, but we have a dead little girl on our train, the press will go nuts."

"What do you want me to do, Liston?"

"Look, I know you a long time, Pete. You'll do the right thing when the time comes."

"Sure, I will. Meantime, you just go in there and ask that nut if everything's all right with him. And if you can get him in the men's lounge, all the better, because he's stinking up the whole car. Tell him there's a shower on board and the water's hot, and it's better than what he's got at home. And if he don't have a razor, I'll get one of the porters to sell him one, but go easy on him, Liston. He's carrying a piece."

"Maybe I should speak to a lawyer, first."

"Maybe you should, Liston." Pete Huley opened the vestibule door for the Pullman conductor to get going. The train's *rat-tat-tat* urged him on.

Conductor Liston Truesdale made his way up the Delta Lounge Baggage Car as if he were out for a Sunday stroll. Cobb was in the big leather chair, his hand stuck in a peanut bowl. His face was raw. His oily unwashed hair was matted over his forehead with the glean of wet paste. He was unevenly shaved so that half of his head looked a day older.

"I see you like those peanuts, sir."

Cobb looked up at the conductor with a sleepy scowl. "Tell your nigger I like 'em unsalted."

"Well, that's the only way they come, sir—the peanuts, that is—but I'll speak to the white fella over at the commissary, see if he can prepare 'em unsalted for ya on the next run." Then with a big phony smile, he said, "We want our passengers to be happy."

"I asked the nigger to get me something to drink."

"Apollo's filling up a whole pitcher of cold water just for you. Gonna bring it right over. Had your supper yet, sir?"

Cobb said, "Where're you from?"

"Mississippi."

"No shit?"

"You've been there before, sir?"

"What a dump."

"Is there anything else I can do for you, sir?"

"Go to hell."

"I'd be more'n glad to, sir, but first I want you to know we're in New York now, not Mississippi, and one of the good things about being on this train is that we got a real overhead shower with hot water. If you don't believe me, I'll show you myself. And I'll bet a dollar to nothing you'll like it. Just don't tell nobody else, or they'll be lining up to rob me."

Cobb said, "Get me a steak and mashed potatoes."

"How would you like it?"

"Cooked."

"Excellent. You go freshen up, sir. I'll have it brought to you soon as you come out the shower."

Cobb didn't move. He stayed where he was with his hand in the peanut bowl. Liston Truesdale went up to the bar and told Apollo to hurry up with the water. Then he opened the door of the vestibule and told Pete Huley, "The gun is in his right coat pocket. Puts his hand over it every time he gets jumpy, which is most of the time."

"Stay here and keep an eye on him. I'm going to the wire room."

"If I do that, Pete, he'll know we're onto him, and since there's no way we can prevent him from taking a walk without risking violence, I think it's better we leave him alone. The person he's after is in the Waldameer. If he ventures over there, Beau and I will be on hand."

"All right. Go down to Beau's car."

"By the way, Pete, you hear from Fred Heinz?"

"Just wired in. He's on his way."

***

Telegraph Room

Al Nachman said, "Excuse me, Mr. Huley. Would you have a second?" A pile of wires that were to be sent out were stacked next to the operator. One of them was in Pete Huley's hand.

"What's on your mind, Mr. Nachman?"

"What can you tell me about Detective Fred Heinz?"

"Didn't that girl say you should stay out of this?"

"Yes."

"You're not on your way to the Delta car, are you?"

"Just taking a walk."

"Well, don't go too far, Mr. Nachman."

"Do you know anything about this Heinz fella?"

"You best stay in your compartment, Mr. Nachman. Let us railroad folks handle this."

"I just never met the man," Al said.

"Look, Mr. Nachman, I know ya want that fella up there. But there's nothing ya can do about it."

"You're not ordering me to stay in my compartment, Mr.

Huley?"

"No, sir, I'm trying to be nice."

"Okay," Al said, "but Cobb causes any trouble, you know where I am."

"Sure, I know where you are. And I know where he is, and I'd like it to stay that way—if ya don't mind."

Al headed down the train. He got brushed by several young women on their way up to the Delta Baggage Car. They were telling each other that the porters had been passing word to all the kids that there was going to be a big New Year's Eve bash in a famous actress's drawing room. When they got to the Delta car, one of them said, "I don't believe it's Virginia Swain."

Another said, "Well, I saw her in the dining car myself, so I know she's on the train."

The last girl said, "Let's go to her party. She kicks us out, we can always come back here."

Cobb was thinking the same thing. He leaned over and asked one of the girls, "Where is Virginia Swain's party?" They quickly went back down the train.

Porter Apollo McGallion approached Cobb with a pitcher of water. "Here you go, sir. Ice cold, just as you requested. You need anything else like a cigar, cigarettes, or maybe the evening post, you let me know. We aim to please aboard the Twentieth Century Limited."

"Cigars stink. I hear there's a party on board. Which car is it?"

"Well, sir, there's lots of parties on board, bein' it's New

Year's Eve."

"I'm talking about the one in Virginia Swain's car."

"I wouldn't know, sir. She ain't in this car."

"Those girls are going to her party."

"Well, I didn't hear nothin' of it, but don't you worry, sir. When I get word, you be the first to know."

"Don't waste your time," Cobb said as he checked his watch. Buffalo was the next stop. It was time to get moving.

47

Virginia's time limit of thirty minutes for all guests was running out and so was the patience of the kids waiting outside for their turn to meet the famous actress. Beau, standing in the aisle, said to Conductor Truesdale, who was next to him, "What time will Detective Heinz get here?"

"Before eleven forty-five and somewhere short of Buffalo."

"I thought I heard Miss Turner say he'll be boardin' at the station."

Conductor Truesdale let another kid squeeze by as Virginia let a boy inside the drawing room as another one left. "She can say what she wants," the conductor said as he turned to Al who was on his way down the aisle. "Mind if I step into your compartment and have a word with you, Mr. Nachman?"

"Don't mind at all, conductor." Al opened his compartment door.

Conductor Truesdale closed it behind him. Zola was on the couch. "I didn't know you had a wife?"

"I take her along sometimes," Al said as he sat across from her.

"Is that why she's ticketed for a section-seat?"

"That's exactly why."

"Look, Mr. Nachman. You leave this Cobb fella to Detective Fred Heinz of the New York Central Railroad."

"That's what I plan on doing."

"Good. I have no doubt either one of us can handle the situation, but we got one suit-in-law on us already, and we don't need another. You'll get your man, long as he don't get off the train."

"Do you know Detective Heinz well?"

"We go back a long way."

"How long?"

"Used to ride together when they was still robbing the railroad on horseback, and every mail train he rode always had a coffin in it."

"He's that good?"

"Real good." Zola was taking down the conversation on a writing pad hidden under her throw. "And anybody wants to mess with the railroad knows him, and if they don't know him, they'll know him soon enough. And I hope you don't mind me giving you a word of advice," he said, staring at Zola, wondering why she had such a busy hand.

"Sure. What's on your mind?"

"The train is its own world, and we got our own way of doing things. You just leave this Cobb to us."

"That's what I'm doing, conductor."

"Good. I didn't think I'd have a problem with you." His eyes were still on Zola as he left the compartment.

Albany, New York

48

The December wind blew hard and fast across the airfield as New York Central Detective Fred Heinz made his way toward the flying machine some fifty or so yards away from the way station that was nothing but a shack hastily nailed to a light bulb. The wind tore, nipped, and tugged at the detective, sending anything unattached high into air. He pressed on toward the US Government Airmail JN-4H open cockpit two-seater biplane. The notion of going up into the dark evening sky was not all that inviting, especially since he had never flown before. The foul weather made the JN-4H look as stable as a kite in a hurricane. The airfield superintendent, a big man who grabbed the lapels of his coat like a Tammany Hall politician, said to the cinder dick, "Billy Hopson is your pilot. He can fly through any weather and land in a field full of cows. He's the best damn pilot on earth. So forget about a parachute."

Fred Heinz looked out into the pitch-black airfield and wondered if Billy was also the best damn pilot in the air. "What's with the cows?"

The superintendent said, "Pilots are supposed to make a pass over any field to let a farmer know he's going to land."

"Billy doesn't?"

"Farmer ain't always around, and Billy ain't afraid of cows."

"What do you mean he ain't afraid of cows?"

"I mean he ain't afraid of cows."

"Sounds like he's crazy."

The airfield superintendent said, "No one's forcing ya to go."

"I'd still like a parachute."

"Parachutes add weight. Weight cuts into fuel. With two men flying, you can forget about it."

"What if we get into trouble?" The airfield superintendent headed back to the way station, his hand on his hat. "Hey, you didn't answer my question," Fred Heinz said.

"When I have one, I'll let ya know."

***

Billy C. Hopson was a big athletic fellow with good looks, but he smoked his cigarette as if it was his last one. There was a glint in his eye that went from friendly to carelessness, and it gave Detective Heinz no little consternation as he watched Billy, who seemed to be in a world of his own, suit up next to the JN-4H. The detective put his hand to the biplane's flimsy material that covered the wings and fuselage. It felt no thicker than his undershirt. He said to Billy, "A horse's hide is thicker than this."

"Yeah, but a horse can't fly." Billy pointed to the fur-lined leather flying suit lying flat on the grassy field. It had the distinct shape of a man's body: one that had just been vacated. "This one's for you. Better hurry up. I run a tight ship." He kicked over a pair of arctic boots with big buckles. "Put them on, or you'll get frostbite."

"How cold does it get up there, Billy?"

"Cold enough for your toes to fall off when you pull off your socks tonight."

The detective reached down and lifted the heavy leather flying suit. It was like picking up the carcass of a bear. A couple of milk cows mooed in yonder barn as if they were having the last laugh. Billy tapped the detective on his shoulder and said that east was right and west was left. Then he pointed toward Buffalo (their destination) with his thickly gloved hand.

Detective Heinz said, "That might be so with your feet on the ground, but what about up there?" He stared into the nighttime heavens where there were no road signs, just the Big Dipper in the chaos of stars drilled into a sky, soon to be smothered by approaching clouds.

Billy pulled back his leather glove and showed the detective the ink on the back of his hand.

Detective Heinz said, "The hell is that?"

"Our compass settings."

"You're *joking*," he said, feeling like a short dog in high grass.

Billy pulled down his fur-lined leather head cover until it touched his eyebrows. Then he lowered his goggles. "You better put your head cover on, or your noggin will turn into a block of ice—and don't forget those goggles. You don't want your eyeballs to fall out, either."

"It's gets that cold up there?"

"Oh yeah."

The detective suited up like a groom with more than a second thought about the bride coming down the aisle. "You mind my asking?"

"What?"

"You ever crash-landed?"

"Tons of times," Billy said.

"No, what I mean is crashed. Ya know," pointing his hand straight to the ground like one of those World War I fighter planes tailspinning into flames.

Billy said, "Well, the lead carrier on the way to Cincinnati crashed yesterday."

"Was he flying at night?"

"Oh yeah."

"Was he killed?"

"Haven't heard from him."

The detective almost smiled. "Which is more dangerous? Flying at night or during day?"

"Whaddya think?" Billy took his passenger by the arm. "You'll be riding up front."

"*You* sit up front."

Billy said, "Ya want the plane to crash?"

"No," peering down the front cockpit as if it were a snake hole, thinking he would fall out if Billy veered too hard right or left, or if Billy just wanted to have a little fun flying upside down, because Billy looked like the kind of person who would do those kinds of things. Detective Heinz warily placed his foot on the flimsily lower wing of the biplane. "How long ya been flying, Billy?"

"Five years going on six."

"Is that a long time or a short time?"

"It's a helluva time," Billy said as he put his hand on the detective's back and guided him into the peashooter. "See, what people don't like about flying is not the flying."

"No?"

"I take people up all the time. They love it," his smile ten drinks deep.

"What don't they like?" The detective lifted his stubborn foot and steadied it on the fuselage grip.

Billy said, "Crashing. People wanna die quietly like they're going to sleep for the night. Far as I'm concerned, they're crazy."

"I'd rather die quietly," the detective said. "Crashing gives a man too much to think at once." He slowly took the next step into the front cockpit—with more than a little help from Billy.

"I got news for you." The careless glint was back in the mail pilot's eye. "There ain't no time to think."

Billy made sure the cinder dick was strapped in tightly before dropping himself into the rear cockpit. He checked his instruments and gave his ailerons and elevator a few wiggles and then made contact. The biplane suddenly shook as if it had been hit by a jolt of lightening. Prop wash beat against the fuselage. Two small windshields, fore of each cockpit, were useless against the spray of engine oil that streaked their goggles. Billy steered the big bumblebee out of the wind and bounced it over the uneven field. Then something happened. At roughly sixty miles an hour, it got pulled off the ground. Fred Heinz looked straight down as if it were for the last time. Earth was a galaxy of lights like the one above. Little headlamp bugs, some of them Packards and Willys, were scuttling below. Then something hard bounced off the fuselage. Fred Heinz looked back and shouted into the wall of wind, "A farmer's shooting at us."

Billy laughed. "Not this time of night."

***

Well into nine o'clock, Billy C. Hopson pumped his hand over the fuselage. Detective Heinz took it as a distress signal, sure that they were going to spill out as the JN-4H banked hard right and plummeted rapidly to earth. Buffalo's city lights came at them like an oncoming planet multiplying in size by the second. The flimsy biplane slapped and bounced high into the air against a gust of wind that dropped the JN-4H several hundred feet before rolling over and hitting what felt like the rubble soldiers stumble over after towns have been shelled for days on end. Billy brought in the fuel. For a moment the aircraft floated in space before touching ground. The propeller ratcheted into a soft blur. The pistons decelerated into a choking cough. The engine spurted. The biplane came to a halting stop. Detective Heinz, who had the sound of the universe humming in his ears, pulled himself out of the cockpit and felt born again into the world. Billy asked the novice with half a smile, "How was the ride?"

Detective Heinz crawled out of his flying suit. "You're one

helluva pilot, Billy," he said, and departed for the 1923 black Ford Tudor sedan parked under the exterior light bulb of the way station. He shut the passenger door as if he were escaping a mad dog. Sergeant Bobby Klee, a New York Central cinder dick just in from Utica, said, "You look awful, boss."

"So do you."

Bobby Klee turned the engine over. "Train 25 comes in at eleven forty-five eastern time, and Pete Huley knows we're boarding."

"Who's the conductor on Train 25?"

"I just said Pete Huley."

"Bobby," Heinz said, leaning into the younger man, "I happen to be a little hard of hearing at the moment."

"What happened?"

Not bothering with the obvious, he said, "We're gonna clean this up in ten minutes. The boys upstairs want the train to leave Buffalo at midnight, latest, and I know Pete does, too."

"Eastern time?"

"Yeah."

Bobby Klee said, "This guy armed?"

"Handgun."

"Is he dangerous or just another goofball?"

"Both," he replied, lighting a cigarette. "What's your drink of choice, Bobby?"

"Why?"

"Just answer me."

"Anything that won't blind or paralyze me."

"Good." Detective Heinz leaned back and, for the first time, felt like he was really on earth. "Right before I leave Albany, I get a wire from the undercover on board, saying one of the passengers is a bootlegger."

"So what? There's bootleggers on board that train all the time. It's the Lake Huron express."

"This bootlegger's a girl."

"She's not the first."

"What I'm saying, Bobby, is that the undercover goes into the bootleg's drawing room and finds a trunk. One of the bottles smashed and the room reeks."

"Happens all the time."

"Let me finish, Bobby." He shifted his weight and pulled out a 1920 Colt Army Special .41 L.C. revolver. He checked to see if it was loaded. His backup, a Colt Police Positive Special, was in his hip holster. He loaded it from a box of 50 Peters .38 cartridges 158 grain. "You know that problem we got with the pending suit-in-law? Says one of our niggers sold contraband got some rich white kid stiff?"

"What about it?" Bobby asked as he took out his revolver to make sure his was loaded, too.

"Well, this girl, the bootlegger, her drawing room is in the nigger's car, and the undercover says they seem to know each other real well. So I got a feeling there's something going on between them, and if there ain't...? Well, I ask you again. What's your drink of choice, Bobby?" slipping his Colt back into his hip holster, taking a flask from his overcoat pocket, and wishing he could've gotten to it while he was in the air.

"As long as it don't blind or paralyze me, I don't care."

"Good, because if it ain't wood alcohol, we're gonna be into a lot of hooch tonight."

Bobby Klee smiled. His boss always knew how to make the most of a situation.

49

The New Year's Eve party in drawing room A was in high gear as the slinky kid, up against the window with the ukulele, strummed *choo-choo* while Virginia Swain sang, "*Told the porter I had no money, He said then what're you doin' on the best train on earth? Told I'm lookin' for a rich man for whatever it's worth.*" The fact that Virginia was staying in a drawing room, the most expensive ticket on the train, and not an upper berth, hadn't affected her ability to wail like an orphan. She reached for a bottle of champagne sitting in the ice bucket, by the window, but then felt something clammy underfoot. She looked down at the floor and immediately understood what the problem was. "Pardon me, Jezebel," she said as she wiggled past a girl from Bryn Mawr, who was studying theatrical literature and openly wondered if Charles Hale Hoyt was outdated. Virginia said, "Your question is," and then leaned into Shelby, "we got a little problem." She pointed to the closet door where the leak originated.

One of the boys hollered, "Hey, Miss Swain, were you in that play at the Sam Harris Theater when someone broke down and cried in the last act?"

"Yeah, it closed opening night." She showed Shelby the widening stain on the floor and whispered, "Looks like a few pints got widowed."

Shelby said, "You don't mind I break up the party?"

"I was just about to do that." Virginia gave a quick speech, promising the festivities would resume at full force in fifteen minutes, then she threw everyone out.

Shelby rang for Beau, who promptly arrived. At first he thought Cobb had gotten into the drawing room. Then he saw the big stain and the broken bottle in her trunk. "Them baggage boys at Grand Central Terminal can be pretty rough," he said. "But now we'll know what to do in the future."

Shelby said, "What about my trunk? It reeks of liquor. Is there any way you can get rid of the smell?"

"Well, we got some solutions we keeps in the men's lounge for all sorts of stains. Some 20 Mule Team Borax, if that don't work."

"I don't think any of it will."

Beau said, "We can try."

"No. There's only one thing to do."

"What?"

"I want you to throw my trunk overboard."

"I wouldn't do that, miss. The rest of the stuff in there is good."

"See that other valise in the closet?"

"Miss Swain's?"

"Yeah. I'm going to put all my product in there," Shelby said. "When we get to Chicago, I'll buy another trunk."

"Does Miss Swain know?"

Virginia walked out of the bathroom. "Do I know what?"

Beau said, "You mind we use your valise? Miss Prevette got a problem with hers."

"Hell, no," Virginia said. "Business comes first." She pulled her valise out of the closet. "I'm in charge of the Broadway crowd."

Beau smiled at Shelby. "Then let's get to it."

They emptied the trunk and moved all the rye whiskey into Virginia's valise. Beau checked the aisle and quickly made his way to the vestibule. He opened the heavy steel door of the Waldameer, heaved the trunk overboard, and watched it tumble down the embankment onto the hard uneven frozen ground. Then he felt something equally uneven press into his back.

"We meet again, nigger."

Beau turned around. Cobb's whacky crazed eyes, aggressive and impatient, were slick with a madman's confidence and a killer's belief in lucky streaks, and like all crazy people, he had no notion of shared time other than his own, which he shared with no one.

"Did Charlie really fuck her?"

"Charlie *who*?"

"Charlie Chaplin, you dumb nigger. I saw the three of you at the Biltmore."

"Oh, him. You ain't got nothin' to worry about. I was just in Miss Prevette's drawin' room."

"*Fucking* her?"

"Nossir. She ordered a ginger ale. Was sayin' somethin' about some doctor by the name of Jennin's told her after what he done to her, she couldn't have no relations for a year or two or she might break somethin' inside and never bear no chil'un. So she wasn't messin' with nobody at all."

"You're a smart nigger."

"Yessir."

"Try any shit, and I'll blow your nigger brains out."

"Yessir."

"Which room is Miss Prevette in?"

"Third one in, sir."

"You got the passkey?

"In my pocket."

"Good." He nudged Beau into the Waldameer.

Drawing Room A

50

Virginia and Shelby pushed their fannies down until the snaps of Virginia's valise locked. "Look," Virginia said as she sat up and let out some air, "I know everybody on Broadway, and they're all bitching about their bootleggers overcharging for busthead they wouldn't give to a dog."

"Yeah," said Shelby, "but how cold does it get in January?"

"Helluva a lot colder than it does now."

"How cold is that?"

"Cold enough for chickens to lay hard-boiled eggs. But we'll warm things up by having a big party in my nine-room apartment on Park Avenue when you return, and I got one helluva room for ya. Big as mine." They got up off the valise. "We're gonna have a riot—you and me. And if you're here by the nineteenth, that's my birthday, I'm gonna have a real swell party with all the right people. By the way, what's your Zodiac sign?"

"My what?"

"Your birthday, silly. Everybody's into astrology."

"September seventeenth."

"Perfect," Virginia said as she sprawled out on one of the couches, "you're a Virgo. I'm a Capricorn. Astrologically, we're perfectly aligned. Too bad you're a girl and not a boy. Then I'd be all set."

"Did you say the nineteenth?"

"Yeah."

"That's the undercover's birthday."

"Whose?"

"Jessica Jill Turner. Next door. I saw it on her railroad papers."

"Hey, I wasn't the only one born that day, ya know."

"Maybe," Shelby said, "but our darkies say that people who think coincidences have no meaning are like people who look into a mirror and think their reflection is an accident."

"Well, when you find out what the meaning is, let me know."

"I'm not too sure I want to know," Shelby said as she took a stick of gum from Virginia. "Too bad you don't get along with Texas Guinan. Her birthday's the twelfth, and I've got one helluva gift for her if she doesn't conk out on me again."

"Well, I'm glad you told her you're staying with me and not Barney Gallant. That'll teach her a lesson."

"The hell do you have against her, anyway?"

"Everything," Virginia said, "and I'll get more orders than ya got from that loud mouth."

"Yeah, but why don't you like her?"

Virginia sneered, "Because."

"Because isn't a reason."

Virginia fanned herself with a copy of Shelby's *Science and Investigation* magazine. "Hey, you really read this stuff?"

"Yeah, and what do you have against her, anyway?" Shelby asked, taking the other couch.

Virginia fanned herself up and down with the magazine. "That big idiot won't let me into her club anymore."

"I know, but *why*?"

"Because she's a frog."

"That's some answer."

"She's *some* frog." Virginia pushed away the glasses on the table and stuffed a pillow behind her head. She slapped her tootsies up against the big wide window and let out a big fat sigh.

Shelby said, "You *still* haven't answered my question."

Virginia laughed. "The frog thinks I stole some rich fella from her."

"Didgya?"

"How was I to know he was going out with her also? Sends me jewelry and a limousine to pick me up whenever I want to go somewhere. I wasn't thinking if he's got somebody else. I'm thinking there's more where this comes from."

Shelby said, "Are you still seeing him?"

"I'm not seeing either one of 'em." She blew out a long stream of smoke that careened off the window. "She was once my best pal. Now I hate her."

"Yeah, but you make a ton of money. You don't need a man to look after you."

"Hey, if some bimbo wants to spend his money on me, I'm not gonna stop him. By the way, you throw away boys like peanut shells."

Shelby planted her tootsies on the window like her friend. "All they want is to grope."

"Say, *don't* you?"

Shelby said, "Yeah, but on *my* terms. I'm not a football they can toss around." She stuck out two fingers. "You learned the lines to that play yet?"

"Nope." Virginia slipped a Murad into Shelby's first two digits and then grabbed a hand mirror.

"Hey, I need a light."

She tossed Shelby a box of matches and then reached for the script. "Instead of the Nobel Prize, they oughta have a No Bull Prize," Virginia said as she opened the play upside down. "You know what that dumbbell director tells me middle of the party?"

"What?"

"Says he hates parties. Can ya believe it? I told him there's a funeral in the third car. Get lost!"

"Something's wrong with him."

"No kidding." Virginia picked an annoying tobacco flake off her lip. "So I tell him the reason ya hate parties is because you're so insecure with women. So Mr. Smarty Pants goes and blabs on how he and the theater are going to change the world like that moron who was the head of the Anti-Saloon League…Hey! Didgya hear what happened to him?"

"Who?"

"That piker William Hamilton Anderson head of the League."

"No. What?"

"Mr. Morals Up the Ass got convicted for fraud and is now in jail—like *anyone* should be surprised."

"Did he go on about your war play?"

"Who?"

"The director."

"*Did* he? Christ, he wouldn't shut up about it," Virginia said. "Wasn't even in the war. Had the measles or something." She looked for her mascara.

"What did he say?"

"Oh, some hooey about the main character leaving his soul somewhere in the Battle of Whatever and needs to go back to France and retrace his steps downstage or he'll turn into a pumpkin upstage." Virginia threw her head back and laughed. "Ya know what I told the jerk?"

"What?"

"Better make sure the main character is good-looking this time, or I won't kiss him."

"They casted him yet?"

"Yeah, they casted him," Virginia said, "but pretty boy goes and lands a part in Hollywood, where he's the juvenile character in love with some dumb older woman who's married to some dumb older fella who's in love with some dumb younger girl who's in love with the dumb juvenile with *all* the dough. Like we never heard that one before. I can't wait to hear the organ grinder in the movie theater play all that soppy music so the girls from the Bronx can cry their hearts out."

Shelby said, "Couldn't they find another juvenile?"

"You'd *figure*. I mean, Hollywood's full of delinquents." She turned to the door; someone was knocking. "Kid can't tell time. Fifteen minutes hasn't even passed yet." Virginia yelled at the door, "*Ten more minutes, son!*" She primped her bob and checked her profile in the window to see how big her nose really was. "Say...ya really slept with Charlie, or did I hear something erroneous?"

Shelby painted her lips in the window reflection. "Wants me to visit him in California like I'm some letter you drop in a mailbox."

"Say, if *Charlie* wants ya to visit him, it means he wants ya to star in his new picture. He always does that with his girls."

"Yeah, well, I told him I hate moving pictures. They're as predictable as a boy on a first date."

"Who cares?" Virginia said. "There's tons of dough and easy living out there. So what they're all full 'a shit? Ya tell him about me?"

"Nope," Shelby said. "I offered the Tramp a job is what I did."

"*No*, ya didn't."

"Sure, I did. Gave him my new business card and told him if I get checks with orders from all his Hollywood pals, then I might visit him."

"What'd he say?"

"Said I'll have tons of orders in a fortnight." Shelby, hearing someone knocking on the door, hollered, "*The party's on break the next half hour.*"

Virginia said, "Ya'd think they're all deaf out there."

A voice from outside said, "I got someone here would like to visit you, Miss Prevette."

310

Cobb stubbornly fumbled with the key in the latch. Then he angrily gave it back to Beau.

Shelby, thinking it was Miss Turner, said, "Tell her in a half hour, Beau. We're taking a break."

"It's an old friend."

Beau fitted the key into the latch.

"Tell her—" Shelby, realizing who it was, took her Lemon Squeezer out of her handbag and got off the couch.

Virginia said. "Hey, where'd you get that!"

"Tell me if Marston's out there."

"Maybe you oughta put down the heat."

"Just do what I say, Virginia."

She got up and brushed herself off. "Look, hon, I'm beginning to like you. I don't want you to die or anything."

"I'm *not* dying. Now, go out and take a look." Shelby kept the Lemon Squeezer aimed dead on the door.

Virginia slipped on her T-straps. "I don't like this one bit," she said as she cautiously approached the door. "I was in a play once, and the gun didn't go off, and the actor died like it did. Walter Winchell went nuts in his column the next day, saying it was the dumbbell director's idea and not an accident. You better not have one here." She watched the drawing-room door open.

Beau said, "Your friend got impatient, so I had to use my passkey."

Cobb pushed Beau to the side. The sight of Shelby should have made him feel what the saints experience in moments of intense ecstasy, but since Cobb was no saint, it was torture. He said with a thin you-don't-scare-me sneer, "So you went out and got a gun."

"Yeah," Shelby said, "and if you want to see how it works, let me know." She took the couch furthest from the door and told Beau, "*Get* Nachman."

Cobb said, "Nigger stays here."

"The only way he stays here is if you kill him, and to do that, you'll have to move your gun away from me, and if you do, you're dead." Her gun was aimed point blank at Cobb's head. Her finger hugged the trigger. Beau moved past the open closet and left the drawing room with something in hand. Cobb took the couch opposite Shelby. She said to him, "Ever hear of a Mexican standoff?"

"What about it?"

"You're in one, now." He was in more than that and knew it.

***

Telegraph room

Beau interrupted conductor Pete Huley and said, "Sorry, sir, but we got a little problem in drawing room A."

"You don't mean the nut was up in the Delta Car?"

"Yessir, he's now in the girl's room. Both is armed."

"I'll wire Buffalo. Meantime, I want you and Liston to get everyone out of that car and then block its access. If those two do anything stupid, it'll stay there."

"I already seen to that, sir."

Miss Turner entered in a hurry and very angry. "I can't get into the Waldameer. What's going on?"

Conductor Huley was in no mood for getting lawyered. "Speak to first porter LaHood about getting in his car."

Miss Turner said, "I don't have to speak to any damn porter about getting into a train car."

Pete Huley said, "On my damn train, you do. And by the way. You ever use a weapon, Miss Turner? And I don't mean at some Coney Island shooting gallery."

"What does that have to do with me getting into my car?"

"Because we got a problem in drawing room A, miss, and if something goes awry before Fred Heinz gets here, I'm sending in Nachman to deal with that nut, not you. He was a Marine in France."

"That's against the railroad code," Miss Turner said.

"Look, *I* run this goddamn train, not *you*, and that's in the railroad code, and if you don't like it, you can walk home in the snow and see how you like that. Is that understood?"

"Mr. Huley—your jurisdiction changes when a crime is in progress. I'm the one who's now in charge. Read the law." She left the car.

Buffalo, New York

51

Sergeant Bobby Klee parked the bureau's 1924 Tudor Ford behind a 1922 Dorris Touring car that belonged to a Mr. J. Benito from Chicago. The passenger seat of the Dorris hid a coiled rope, a gag, a hypodermic syringe case, several vials of a potent animal tranquilizer, and a road map, with the route to Canada marked out in pencil. Bobby Klee said to his boss, "Maybe we should tell that guy, up ahead, the train's gonna be late."

"Then he'll want to know why."

New York Central Exchange Street Station was an adequate two-story nineteenth-century building, soon to be demolished for something grander like Utica Station that boasted tall marble columns and long rows of streamlined wooden benches, whose rounded edges gave the impression they were endlessly circulating. Bobby Klee and Fred Heinz pushed themselves through the tight doors of the Western Union office. Fred Heinz said to the manager, "You got anything for me?"

"Two wires."

"When did they come in?"

"Just now." He put them on the counter.

Detective Heinz read through each one.

The manager said, "You want something to eat while you wait, McLeod's Hotel got a New Year's Eve special for train personnel tonight."

Bobby said to his boss, "I could go for some lamb chops."

Detective Heinz put the telegrams in his coat pocket and said to the manager, "Take down this wire and have it sent to all trains in transit, east and west, immediately."

"Go ahead."

"*All trains in transit through Buffalo will immediately halt in receipt of this wire STOP I will wire all trains once the situation on Train 25 heading west is back to normal STOP NYCRR Lt Detective Fred Heinz.*"

"You made lieutenant?"

"I came in lieutenant." He gave the manager a typed list of trains riding that night. "Send it to all consists, and don't leave out a single one, or a lot of dead people will be your problem. I want you to send an additional wire to Train 25, telling Conductor Pete Huley to stop his consist at Clarence crossroads. I'll meet him there." Detective Heinz turned to Bobby Klee. "You have gas in that Tin Lizzy?"

He followed his boss out the door. "You know I always fill it."

"You know I always ask."

They got into the Ford Tudor. Fred Heinz reached under the seat for a box of .41 caliber cartridges. He stuffed it into his side pocket.

Bobby said, "I put another one under there, just in case."

"Fifty rounds is enough."

They drove out of town onto Route 5 east of Buffalo. Most of it was hard-packed snow or ice. The Ford, with its skinny tires, spun out with very little prodding. Several times it felt as if the world had dropped out from under them. "You know how to drive this thing, Bobby?"

"Sure I do…"

The Ford skidded over.

Forty-five minutes later, they turned right on Clarence crossroads and waited by the tracks for Train 25.

***

The Twentieth Century Limited

Conductor Pete Huley, not liking the idea of his train losing any time, studied the telegram that just came in from Buffalo's New York Central Exchange Street Station that had been sent by Detective Heinz.

Conductor Liston Truesdale said, "Look, Pete, the two of 'em are in that drawing room, about to kill each other. I wouldn't worry about the train arriving late to Chicago. I'd worry about—"

"I know, I know. I'm just thinking, Liston. A man's gotta think. That's all."

"Well, don't take all night, Pete."

"I'm *not* taking all night. I'd just like to know what Fred's up to this time."

"I'll tell ya what he's up to. He knows the sooner he can stop the train, the sooner he can control the situation, and he can't do that in the middle of Buffalo. That's why he wants us stopped at Clarence."

"I suppose ya talked it over with him, Liston."

"We did it all the time on the Texas Special."

"What do you mean *we*?"

"Fred and I worked that line twenty years ago."

"You was a cinder dick?"

"No, Pete, but we once had an escaped convict board a train in Oklahoma Territory. He got in the mood for a cigar and went up to the smoking car. We stopped the train, decoupled it in McAlester, and sent him back to prison. That's what Fred will do here."

"Well, he's got fifteen minutes to do it, or he can go back to Oklahoma Territory."

"We'll do it, Pete."

Conductor Pete Huley headed up the train.

"And, Pete, don't forget to tell Bob to flick his engine lights as he approaches Clarence crossroads."

"Whatever you say, Liston. I'm running this train."

***

Clarence Crossroads

Detective Heinz pushed Bobby Klee's hand away from the headlamp knob. "Keep the Ford running, Bobby. I want you to flick the lights on and off when Train 25 comes down the line so Bob Butterfield knows we're here." The cinder dick opened the passenger door.

"Where ya going, boss?"

"Some kids up the tracks are spooning in a Marmon." He trudged through the snow and tapped the window of the roadster with the stock of his Colt. The kids were on their way. Then he relieved himself and got back in the Ford.

Bobby said, "Funny."

"What?"

"Ten years ago you got caught spooning with a girl, she became the town whore."

"Yeah, well, ten years ago might as well have been a thousand years ago." He lowered the window and peered down the long tracks with snow on either side that extended to the woods. "You hear her, Bobby?"

"Who?"

"The train."

It materialized as if a curtain had been pulled away. The big nose light painted the tracks a blinding white, and it made the steam locomotive look fiercer than the plumes of thick smoke rising into the evening sky. The engine's big disk face with fist-size rivets and misty vapors sweated stacks of flaring clouds into the cold December air.

"Flick yer lights, Bobby."

Bob Butterfield, the Big E on the last leg of the trip to Chicago, blew the engine whistle in response. Steam hissed out from below the boiler by the water tank, and the consist came to a hard breathing stop. The Big E leaned out of his cab from way high up and looked down at the two cinder dicks coming his way. "How long's this gonna play, Fred?"

He yelled back, "I'll let ya know soon as it's over, Bob."

"Hey, Klee, ya leave any lamb chops for me at McLeod's?"

Bobby looked up at the engineer, whose goggles were pushed up to his forehead. "One day I'm gonna climb up that cab and punch yer brains out."

"Yeah, *one* day."

Detective Heinz went right by Miss Turner and said to Conductor Pete Huley, "Where's the nut?"

"Drawing room A, Fred."

Miss Turner hurried through the train's interior lights that were windowed onto the snow. "Detective Heinz, I'm Jessica Jill Turner with Undercover Unit 6."

The cinder dick ignored her and said to Beau, who was coming down the line, "Haven't I seen you before?"

Beau said, "Mott Haven Yard. The other day, sir."

"You the nigger causing all the trouble with wood alcohol?"

Beau looked down at the white man: six feet tall and on the gray side of fifty. His easy, almost lazy, use of the word nigger, had it been spoken at a higher decibel, would have meant a lynching party had arrived. Beau said, "One causin' all the trouble is in the Waldameer, sir."

"Drawing room A?"

"Yessir. Mexican standoff."

"How are they positioned?"

"Well, sir, when you open the door, the man should be in front of you, sittin' on the couch by the window, his right side to you."

"Where's the girl?"

"She's on the couch too, with her left side to you. The table, between them, was up. There ain't no obstructions on the floor. The man's sightline is to the girl directly in front of him."

"How do you know all this, porter?"

"I was in the drawin' room but was able to get out just when they set themselves down."

"She's the bootlegger?"

"I wouldn't know nothin' about that, sir."

"I'm talking to the girl."

Miss Turner said, "Yessir," and handed him her credentials. "Miss Prevette's trunk was reeking of strong liquor."

"In the drawing room?"

"Yessir, and she's in cahoots with this porter."

Liston Truesdale stepped down the train car steps and stopped at the embankment. It was covered with a steep drift of snow. He said, "Hurry up, Fred. The toast is about to burn."

Miss Turner said to Detective Heinz, "Sir, I want you to know that Miss Prevette broke into my compartment and stole my transit papers and that this porter is a thief and a liar."

The cinder dick headed to the Waldameer. "You're supposed to keep your papers on you at all times, Miss Turner, not leave them lying around. I should fire you for that."

"That's not the point, sir."

"As far as New York Central Railroad's concerned, it is. Did you see her take them?"

"Who else would take my papers?"

"Maybe you dropped them."

"I didn't drop anything, sir. She and that porter are working together."

"You have any proof I can take to court, or are you like every other idiot in this world who thinks being pissed off is enough to make you right?"

"Sir, I'm not an idiot, and you don't need proof to fire the porter. We have legal jurisdiction to do it this very moment."

"Miss Turner, you wanna rile up the best porters on the railroad just because you got a score to even?"

"Sir, Miss Prevette's actions only further prove that she's involved with the porters selling wood alcohol. The same poison that paralyzed the boy, whose family has brought the million-dollar suit-in-law against our company."

"Miss Turner, you seem to be more interested in killing the girl than saving her."

"I'm trying to do the right thing."

"Bullshit."

"Sir, she and that porter are selling contraband. They *all* do. It's about time we did something."

"They also sell aspirins, and I could use one." Detective Heinz boarded the Waldameer and removed his .41 caliber Long Colt from his shoulder holster. Then he put his hand on the Police Special at his hip to make sure it was there. "How crazy is he, Liston?"

"Remember that fella on the Dixie Flyer back ten or twelve years ago? Got on at Waycross?"

"You mean that nut preacher who said the world was going to end unless he killed every atheist before sunset?"

"Yeah, Fred, we got the same kinda nut up here, but with a pistol instead of a shotgun and a sneer instead of a Bible."

"Have you spoken to him?"

"Yeah, and like all nuts, it was a waste of time."

Detective Heinz boarded the Waldameer, Colt in hand.

Drawing Room A

52

It was getting hard for Shelby to sit still and hold in all the hooch that she had imbibed at her New Year's Eve party. Cobb's wretched stink didn't help any. The crazy look in his fast-blinking eyes. His lurid, volatile, degrading, discordant rants and shouts only gave her more resolve to do what she might have to do, but Cobb did have a vision: an aggressive, tedious, grinding rehash of demands that were as mind-numbing as those stir-crazy people who crouch in the corner and weave the invisible with their fingers for hours on end, and Shelby, exhausted, aching from the irrational and delusional harangue now had to endure even more. "That was *my* baby you murdered. *My baby!*" he cried, having overlooked the desertion of his first wife and child—and now his second, the reason being the mothers of those prior conceptions hadn't been worthy enough of his long-term commitment—the way it is when suddenly the person you think you love commits the smallest offense, whether it be of hygiene or an overlooked habit, that spoils intimacy forever. Cobb's New York wife, deeply hurt by his desertion, put out a warrant for his arrest, and when he got wind of it, he sent her bits of money with quick letters of how he had become a boomer on the railroad and had endured break-ins, thefts, loads of rotten luck, all the while moonlighting in Clarksdale, Mississippi, paying Illinois Central porters on their way west to mail letters postmarked from specific cities, towns, and boondocks to prove that he was hard at work so that she would desist the warrant for his desertion. He even sent his wife a map with all the towns to track his alleged migrations across the continent. That is until one of the Illinois Central porters, redirected to another line, had absentmindedly sent Cobb's letter from Montreal. It was supposed to have been postmarked Junction City, Kansas, and in it Cobb had written how cowboys still shot up saloons and sang "She'll Be Coming 'Round the Mountain," but the game was up. Abandoned, lied to, ignored, she snapped, and not a single synapse, but all of them at once. She fled, her mind on fire. Their little boy left hungry and alone with a little shirt wallet for milk money.

Cobb yelled at Shelby as if she was at the other end of the train and not inches in front of him. His argument was his own, which made it even more absurd. "Was it a girl or a boy?"

"You'll never know," Shelby said.

"What did you do with my baby?"

"What you've done with your life."

"Did you at least bury it?"

"I buried *more* than that."

His oratory was now off the pulpit. "Then you're going to pay for your crime! Because it is against God and man's law to have an abortion!"

"It's against God and man's law to rape!"

"You *murdered* my baby!"

"You *murdered* Grover!"

"You're a *cunt*."

Shelby felt the numbness of someone whose mind endlessly

orbits on itself. You could not break it with reason, and she could not, if she tried, wear it out or she would plunge within it never to get out, and she had not the time for that now anyway. Someone else was now in the drawing room. He said to Cobb, "Anybody ever tell you you're a fucking asshole?"

Cobb, as with any bully, had a sense of honor touchy to a fault. No slight was ever too small but any advantage he had had been ejected like a brass cartridge as he reflexively turned to the intruder who stepped so quietly Cobb thought he had no bones in his feet. An explosion ensued that ripped of sulfur and potassium nitrate and tunneled deep into everyone's ears as the discharge lit up the room and sent Cobb hurling to the floor. His head became soft with blood. His eyes were like film that had never been exposed. Shelby moved her .32 over to the man in the doorway, ready to do away with him next. "*Who* are you?"

"Railroad police, miss," Fred Heinz replied, as he slowly and cautiously opened his coat to reveal his detective shield. "It's over, Miss Prevette. You can put the gun down. You have nothing to fear."

Shelby cautiously set the .32 on the table, the impression of the stock deep into her left hand. She got up. The door to the bathroom slammed shut. Bobby Klee, chewing on a sandwich he had found in the observation lounge, poked his head into the drawing room. Conductor Pete Huley walked around him and glanced at Cobb and then at his watch. "How long will it take, Fred?"

"I'll have you up and going in five minutes." Then to Bobby, standing in the aisle, schmoozing it up with Zola, who was taking down every dumb word, he said. "Bobby, cut the gossip. Get the Ford."

Bobby tipped his brown hat to the magnificent lady as if they'd be seeing each other again.

Shelby exited the bathroom.

The cinder dick's hands were deep into her closet.

"*What* are you doing, sir?"

"Looking for Sodom and Gomorrah, miss." Detective Heinz's other hand pointed to the liquor stain on the carpet. "Your whole room reeks of booze."

"It's New Year's Eve. What did you expect? Chocolate milk?"

Not impressed with her humor, he asked, "Where's the trunk full of wood alcohol that you and the porter are selling to all the kids?"

Al walked in and showed Detective Heinz his badge.

"What do you want me to do with that?"

Al said to him, "I'm following procedure."

Detective Heinz turned to Shelby, "Where's that trunk, miss?"

"If you can find a trunk on this train with contraband, it's all yours."

"Trunk or no trunk, you're coming in with me. The judge would love to meet a lady bootlegger and gunslinger to boot."

"I'm going home and nowhere else." Shelby left the drawing room and slammed the door. Al blocked it.

Detective Heinz said, "You're in my way."

"You're in your own way," Al said.

"Look, I know all about you and that Mrs. Brewer, and I couldn't give a damn."

"What do you know, Heinz?"

"She called the head of the New York Central and told him she's a personal friend of the girl and that she better get special treatment. You were sent up here to take care of everything."

"Mrs. Brewer is the girl's godmother," Al said. "You'd do the same."

"Are you going to move?"

"You have proof the girl is selling contraband?"

"What if I told you it's an offence in this state to carry a weapon unless it's licensed?"

"How do you know the weapon belongs to the girl?"

"I don't."

"Her cause was self-defense, and that's the greater issue."

Detective Heinz said, "She just blew someone away, and until the courts deal with it, self-defense is just a defense and nothing else. Then there's her bootlegging problem. My undercover is positive, and now so am I, that she and that porter are selling wood alcohol to kids and killing them, only confirming what everyone else is already thinking, including some hot shot New York lawyer who hasn't lost a case since Grover Cleveland was president."

"Suspicions won't hold up in court," Al said.

"We'll go to court and find out."

"All right, if you want it that way, and should some big-shot lawyer who never lost a case, since Grover Cleveland was president, puts me under oath, I'll tell him that you told me that you and Miss Turner are positive that a certain porter is selling wood alcohol on this train. Then it'll be all over for you and the New York Central Railroad. Remember, I'm a federal agent. No jury will go against what I say. So before you go after anyone, don't forget I can make your life miserable, and if that isn't enough, so will New York Central."

Bobby Klee entered the drawing room with a canvas body bag.

Detective Heinz said to Al, "You know what the problem is with young guys like you who think they're smart?"

"I already know. They meet up with old guys who aren't." Al left the drawing room, but not before telling Bobby Klee, who was stuffing Cobb into a body bag, "Your boss is one helluva shot."

***

Zola hurried after Al down the Waldameer aisle. "If you'd listen to me instead of acting like Jesus Christ himself, maybe we could have a relationship one day."

Al tried to step around her. "I'll think about it."

Getting in front of him, "Look, Al, I got a job I really like for the first time in my life, and I'm not going to blow it."

"You can't write about something else?"

"*No*. There's only one story, and I've got if first hand."

Shelby and Virginia were sitting on the far couch near the observation deck.

"You're writing about family, Zola, not some stranger." Al took the seltzer bottle off the buffet rack and filled a glass.

"That doesn't change the fact of what happened here."

"Zola, you write anything about Shelby, and I'll make sure your brother hangs. That's the bigger story." Then to Shelby, "You're going home."

Zola pressed on. "I finally find something I really want to do in life, and you want to deprive me of it!"

"I didn't say you couldn't write about what happened but that whatever you write could be used in court."

"How do you know?"

Al said, "I think you can answer that for yourself."

"I promise to be careful of whatever I put down."

"Zola…people think a promise is a qualifying statement, when all it is wishful thinking so they can avoid the truth. There are a lot of other things to write. Why don't you publish a book about your experiences in the war, from a woman's perspective?"

"You think it's easy getting published?"

"Nothing's easy," Al replied, heading up the Waldameer to the telegraph car.

Beau appeared by the buffet stand and beckoned Shelby. "You okay, miss?"

She came to him. "I'm all right, Beau. Thank you."

"Just so you know, I put Miss Swain's valise where nobody can find it."

"Good." She took out a list of names and addresses from her

handbag. "When you get back to New York, I want you to deliver the rye in Virginia's valise to these people."

"Consider it done, miss."

"If I don't see you at LaSalle, I'll see you back home."

The train whistle blew long and hard. A shout of *Happy New Year* rolled down the consist as it lurched forward. Shelby hurried to the window and watched the Ford Tudor ride away as Detective Heinz reached down for a pint that he wasn't sure how it had gotten there. Virginia kneeled right up beside her. "You okay, hon?"

"I'm fine."

"I know this may not be the time, Shelby, but...I need a real special favor," she said, showing her a black manuscript. "Could you go over my lines with me?"

"Sure."

They headed up the aisle and opened the door of their drawing room. Zola was on the couch, writing away. Shelby said, "Hey, I thought you weren't supposed to be writing about me."

"Don't worry. Neither your name nor mine will be ever used in this column."

Virginia said, "How do you write a column without a name?"

"Oh, I've got one. It's just not Zola."

"What is it?"

"Lipstick."

"I suppose you're gonna call your cousin mascara?"

"Maybe."

Shelby shut the door. "Go ahead and write that column. I don't want you to lose your job, but you're not going to publish it until I first read it."

Zola closed her pad. "What're you up to now, dear cousin?"

"Since you're going to be covering all the speakeasies for *The New Yorker*, you're going to be my inside girl."

"And what if I don't want to be your inside girl?"

"You forget that I gave you a lot money so you could find a nice place to stay in New York and pay the rent till you get going."

"I thought you gave it to me out of your heart, not your pocket."

"I did, and now it's *your* turn."

"I don't want your money."

"Then give it back."

Zola shifted in her seat. "I…I can't."

"Why?"

"I've already spent it."

Shelby grabbed Zola's pad and read what she had written, then said, "We're going to have to make some changes here."

"Over my dead body."

"You mean your brother's."

Zola quickly picked up her things. "Sometimes I *hate* you," and left the drawing room.

Virginia said, "What's with her?"

"She'll get over it," Shelby said, as she plopped down on the big couch.

"Well, she better not put me in that magazine of hers. She's a *nobody*." Virginia moved over Shelby's riding boots that Beau had polished, then she hopped on the couch. "Say, you really know how to ride? Or are you one of those phony baloney types who dress up and make believe…?"

Clarksdale, Mississippi
January 5, 1926

53

The winter morning was high with fight as Shelby grabbed the withers of her favorite mount and galloped off. She jumped a four-foot meadow fence, sprinted through a field, leaped a five-foot stone wall, galloped another quarter mile, and jumped a fence that led to a dirt road that opened to a wide open view of her family's house so white it blended in with the drifting clouds. Her mother, father, younger siblings, John and Martha, and one of her suitors were in the breakfast room that faced the sprawling garden out beyond the tall French windows.

Mims offered the suitor more coffee. "Are you going to be home all of January, Howell?"

Howell McDermott said, "Most of it, ma'am."

"I don't want to steal you away from your mother," Mims warned, "but Ruby is the finest cook in the county, and if you don't supper with us Saturday night before the hop, she'll be very much insulted."

"Yes, ma'am," he replied, his weary eyes on the doors that led to the family rooms upstairs.

Mims motioned to Julius, who understood to go look for Shelby, again. "My daughter caught a frightful cold in that Yankee suburb of Manhattan. I told her more than once to bundle herself up like an Eskimo, and as usual, she's regretting not having listened to me.

She'll be down any second, Howell. She can't wait to see you."

Howell McDermott rose from the breakfast table.

"Is there something wrong, Howell?"

"No, ma'am," he said as he dusted off his lap and sat down again.

Mims left the breakfast room. "You sit right there, young man. Don't you budge till I return."

Addison took up where his wife left off. "I hear from your father that college is going well for you?"

"Yessir," he replied, his eye on Shelby's empty seat next to her father's.

"Shelby's delaying Radcliffe for a year. But she's very excited to hear you're doing so well. She can't wait to join the college crowd herself."

Brother John, chewing on his toast, had heard all the talk about Howell McDermott the night before, but it was his bright blue 1925 Buick Master 6 Sport Roadster, sitting outside, that made him important. "I want a ride in your new roadster, Howell."

"Well, I planned on taking Shelby for a ride."

"Oh, you can take her for a ride any old time."

Addison interrupted, "Taking any business courses, Howell?"

"Yessir."

"Good. Your father tells me he can't wait for you to join the bank."

"Yessir."

"Any young man would give his right arm to be in your place."

"Maybe I should get going, sir."

"No, no, you stay right there, Howell. Shelby will be down any second. You know how it is with girls."

Martha, with milk on her lips, asked, "How is it with girls, Daddy?"

Addison said, "I'm talking to Howell, Martha."

"He's not a girl, Daddy."

"I'm *talking* to Howell, not you."

"Shelby said you know nothing about girls, Daddy."

"Martha, it's uncivil to interrupt."

"What's 'uncivil', Daddy?"

Brother John explained, "Mind your own business."

An angry rider, dressed in a blue cavalry lieutenant's tunic, reared her mount just short of the breakfast room's tall windows. Martha gleefully yelled, "Shelby!" and ran out the door into her sister's arms and rode away.

Howell McDermott, on his feet and staring out the window, said, "I…I thought Shelby was sick."

Mims briskly entered the breakfast room, unaware of what had happened. "Oh dear, dear Lord, I just don't know what to tell y'all. I can't get Shelby out of bed. I'll have to call the doctor, but don't you worry yourself, Howell. I expect her to be fully recovered for the winter hop come Saturday night, and she just can't wait. You know how Shelby just loves to dance," Mims said, retaking her seat at the end of the table. "You're *not* going?"

Getting up from the table. "It's getting late, ma'am. I have to meet up with friends."

"But you haven't finished your breakfast, Howell. You'll catch your death without something warm in you."

"Oh, I never get sick."

"But Shelby will be down any second. She just told me so herself. She's dying to see you."

Howell, embarrassed, fastened his jacket and adjusted his tie. "Tell her to call me later, if she'd like. Thank you for breakfast, ma'am. Good to see you again, Mr. Prevette. I'll tell my father you say hello." The boy went down the hall and left the house.

Mims stood up. "Well, just don't sit there, Addie! *Stop* him."

"It's too late. Your plan backfired."

***

Shelby's mount left a trail of thunder as its hooves struck the hard winter ground. She galloped through a row of cotton trees and then crossed a long narrow rickety plank bridge over a fishing pond protected by tall grass that hid some very unfriendly snakes. The clearing dipped into a shallow man-made gorge that opened up to a meadow. She and Martha jumped another fence and turned off the path that led back to the carport where Addison was searching his pockets like a man chasing an itch. Looking up, he saw his two girls charging down the road, and he couldn't help but admire how well and confidently Shelby rode, but it was her anger, not her skill, at work this morning. She cantered and then trotted around her father as if taking him prisoner. "Looking for this?" as she tossed him a flat box of Murad Turkish cigarettes that was illustrated with an Egyptian noblewoman lying on a golden daybed protected by two stone jackal-headed gods on each side. "Don't be so sour, Daddy," as she handed Martha to the maidservant who had come running from the house.

Addison caught the Murads. "My dear, even a blind hog finds an acorn now and then."

"Then get a blind hog to go over your books this afternoon, if I was just lucky in New York."

"You're family. I can trust you, Shelby."

"I can add in my head. That's why you can trust me." Then almost yelling she said, "My brother *can't*. But that's not stopping you from leaving *him* the family business!"

"Why are you wearing my army blouse?"

"Because Mama said I couldn't," circling even closer. "You and I made a bet, and I've come for the payoff."

"What you're doing is illegal, child."

"Why didn't you stop me before?"

"Because, like you, I'm angry at the government for shutting down Magnolia."

"And I'm angry at you for squelching on your bet. You promised that if I come back from New York with any real orders, I'd inherit your business when the time comes, and the time has come."

"What about young Howell?"

"What about him?"

"He wants to take you to the winter hop this Saturday night."

"Who cares about that? You made a promise, Daddy. I get your business if I come back with any substantial orders. If you don't think earning over five thousand dollars is substantial enough, then I'm committing you to an insane asylum."

"I didn't think you'd walk away with that much, let alone in one night."

"Well, *I* did."

"Yes, child, but I made the bet on a more reasonable assumption."

"All bets are reasonable until you lose. Now man up." Her mount nibbled grass. He was convinced they were going to be there all day.

"Howell wants to marry you, child."

"Mama will not arrange my life, let alone the days, nor the hours in it. If you cannot inform her of that reality, then she'll have to learn the hard way. And the next time she invites a boy over for breakfast, she better tell me first."

"I'm not saying I don't understand the difficulty y'all are having at the moment."

"At the *moment*?"

"My dear, Howell McDermott is a very rich boy with good breeding. He's the captain of his college football squad. Candidate to be All-American. Very good-looking. Fun to be with, and he has revealed to me his ambitions. I wouldn't be surprised if he became president one day, and I wouldn't be all that troubled if he became part of our family, if you'd only let him."

"How nice of you to inform me."

"I'm being more than nice, young lady. That boy is in love with you, and he knows nothing of what Marston did to you. You're missing the opportunity of a lifetime by not marrying him.

"Mama is. Not *I*."

"You *both* are."

She rode tightly around her father. "Do you know what selling short is?"

"*Why* should it concern you?"

"One night, in New York, I overheard a conversation about a Wall Street banker pocketing thirty thousand dollars in one day. That's the opportunity I'm missing. And he belonged to the same club as you, at Harvard."

"What's his family name?"

"I'm not telling."

"Well, I promise you, when your brother gets out of college, I'm going to set him up with friends of mine in New York so he can really learn something about life before coming home for good."

"Wire one of your friends on Wall Street and set *me* up."

"No. Your job is to be a good wife to Howell."

"*Really?*"

"Yes. When a man gets home from a hard day's work, he wants his pipe and slippers and a hot meal, and if you marry Howell, I'll get him that job on Wall Street so that he can really expand his father's banking business."

"You've got it all wrong, Daddy."

"*What* have I got all wrong?"

"If I marry Howell, you'll get *me* that job on Wall Street, and *he'll* bring down my pipe and slippers after a hard day's work."

Addison laughed.

"What's so funny?"

"When I get home tonight, I'm going to undress you and put you in front of a mirror to remind you that you're a girl."

"I'll save you the time and do it right now." She started to unbutton her tunic.

"*Keep* that on, young lady."

"Then don't threaten me."

"I *wasn't* threatening you."

"I won't be anyone's slave."

"A wife isn't a slave, Shelby. Her job is ages old, and if you don't know that, I'll have to teach you."

"You've already taught me *every*thing I need to know, including riding, shooting, hunting, gambling, negotiating, reading a financial statement. I've read all your books from Aristotle, Protagoras, Sextus Empiricus, Marsilius de Padua, Machiavelli, including those two lunatics, Rousseau and Marx, with their crazy notions of a single moral universe, where history is a linear movement that matures into perfection over time. Their slayers—Vico, Herder, and Fichte—put an end to all that nonsense, only to come up with their own. The only thing you never bothered to teach me was how to cook, but I *won't* hold it against you."

"No, you probably wouldn't. There's something I have to tell you…"

"It better not be Howell McDermott."

"It concerns Marston."

"Bringing up the dead *now*?"

"He has a wife and child."

"I know that."

"In New York."

"*New York?*"

"Maybe other places as well."

"What on earth are you talking about?"

"Marston was already married when he married Euphia."

"Oh, I *can't* wait to tell her," Shelby said, lifting her mount's head from the grass, ready to ride off to her cousin's house.

Addison grabbed the reins. "*No*, you won't. Marston tried to visit his first wife when he was in New York, but she deserted their little child, who's now in an orphanage."

"I think Euphia and her new baby would love to hear that, as well."

"You'll tell her *nothing* of the sort, young lady. Now, the orphanage sent me a letter."

"About what?"

"They want to know if the mother's family won't have the boy. Would we?"

"What did you tell them?"

"I said I would consider it. I mentioned it to your mother, but she wants nothing of it. What say you?"

"What you're asking of me is cruel."

"I didn't say it would be easy," Addison said as he reached into his billfold for a small photograph. "A good-looking little boy, isn't he? He's my great nephew. Your kin, as well."

Shelby refused to look at it. "And what if we find out Marston has other wives? Other children? Should we take them *all* in?"

Addison said, "That means you want me to leave the poor little boy in the orphanage?"

"No. Find him a home with good people who can't have children and who'll give him love."

"What's wrong with our home?"

"Nothing, except that I killed his father."

"You can always say that railroad detective did."

"You make lying sound easy."

"It still doesn't change the terrible loneliness and pain that little boy is going through."

"Well, imagine the pain *I'll* be going through when you give him the family business, because he's a *boy*."

"Shelby, this is a serious matter."

"And so was the deal we made about inheriting your business. And if you give it to my brother, you'll regret it. He's brainless as Mama. Martha and I are the ones who think like you."

Addison gave up and got into his Pierce-Arrow 7. "We'll continue this later."

"You'll continue it by yourself."

"That means you're not stopping by the office for lunch?"

"Only if you don't squelch on your bet. Otherwise, I never want to see you again."

"Now, you're the one who's being cruel."

Shelby rode over and leaned into the open rear passenger window. "Daddy, if you gave a thousand people a test to see who was best qualified to run your business, whom would you choose?"

"I suppose the one who tested best. Why?"

"Suppose I tested best?"

Addison said, "That's not fair."

"*Why* isn't it fair?"

"I want my son to run my business. How else will he support a wife?"

"You're totally irrational, Daddy."

He tenderly smiled. "Ah yes, but that's what the world is built on, dear. Better to learn it now than later. See you this afternoon." He and Julius rode off.

Ruby came rushing out the kitchen door with two baskets, but the Pierce-Arrow was already down the road. "Julius done forgot your daddy's lunch, again."

"Call my father's secretary and let her know."

Ruby handed Shelby the other basket. "And don't you go jumpin' over no fences with this, or your breakfast gonna get ruined." She headed back to the kitchen.

"Ruby?"

"What?"

Riding up to her, Shelby said, "I've been meaning to have a word with you, and I think the time is now."

"What about, chil'?"

"I know all about Julius and what he did."

"What did he do?"

"He gave Al Nachman cousin Tom's shirt."

"Julius didn't do nothin' of the sort."

"Then how did Nachman get his shirt?"

"*I* gave it to him."

"*You* gave it to him?"

"Yes."

"You had no business doing that, Ruby."

"Cousin Tom had *no* business killin' Lindsay Coleman." She shut the kitchen door behind her.

Mims hollered over the second-floor balcony railing of Martha's bedroom. "*Shelby!* I want to have a word with you at once! You're in very big trouble."

"Mama! The only trouble is that which you make for yourself." Shelby galloped off and thought of Grover, Lindsay Coleman, Cobb, and now the little boy, and how nothing in life came and went without leaving a headstone and a lot of grief.

54

The sunken cracked floorboard of Beau's veranda wobbled underfoot. The problem was first apparent in the spring. More so in summer. By late fall Clementine had forbidden anyone from entering through the front door until repairs had been made. When the new flooring planks arrived, in November, they were stacked on the veranda, but Beau was on the road until December; now it was January.

Clementine said, "You fixin' on mendin' the veranda in 1926 or '27?"

Beau pulled aside the window curtain and looked out into the endless flat fields. "I'll have it done by the week's end."

Clementine said, "What about this?"

Beau took the pint of rye from her hand. "You remember that paddler, Magnolia Belle, rode up and down the Mississippi?"

"What about it?"

"Well, that girl takes a lot of pride in her family and tradition."

"Long as you don't take no pride in her."

"We're gonna be rich, Clementine. Very much so. Take pride in that."

"Rich or not, I don't like the Prevettes one damn bit. No one does."

"Clementine, when you're rich, no one likes you. When you're poor, no one wants you. Might as well be rich."

A cranky Ford Huckster wheezed down the dirt road. Granny Ella, in yonder planting yard, leaned on her hoe and put her chin on her stacked hands. "What's that boy want now, Beau?"

"What'ch ya talkin' about, Granny?" Beau asked as he hopped over the sunken veranda.

"You jes got home, 'n' here he is again."

"You always worryin', Granny. I ain't leavin' town."

"Then why's he here?"

"Got some chores to do, now that I'm home."

"He come to get you for the train, he is."

"Granny, you gonna plant them Cherokee purples or not?"

She poked the stubborn winter ground. "I got to hoe it first. Just can't throw it in, or us'll starve next year."

"I already hoed it for you, Granny. Have a look."

"I'se lookin' at Jess Earl, and he ain't takin' you back to no train, Beau." She raised her hoe at the Huckster and struck it into the air. "Ain't gonna let ya do that, Jess Earl. Ain't gonna let ya take my Beau! They already took one."

"Granny, I told you. I'm home for two weeks. Maybe three 'cause of the extra work I done for the holidays. They gonna send me a wire in the mornin' and let me know. Then y'all be sick of me soon enough."

Jess Earl pulled up by the planting yard with a big smile on his face. He hollered, "Hiya, Granny Ella!" She turned away like a girl does a pesty suitor.

Beau said to Jess, "The hell're you so happy about?"

"I'm happy 'cause it's my last day drivin' for the Alcázar. Tomorrow I'm headin' up to the Pullman trainee center. Gonna have me some real fun. And thanks for the good word. I knew you wouldn't let me down."

"I knew you wouldn't stop pesterin' me, Jess, so I told 'em everythin' they wanted to hear."

"Which was what?"

"That you're narrow between the eyes, and your tongue wags at both ends. They said you're just the man they lookin' for."

Granny Ella beaded a steady eye on Jess Earl.

Jess Earl whispered to Beau, "What's with her?"

Beau stepped into the Huckster. "Nothin' wasn't there before." Then turning to Granny Ella, he said, "Go inside. Clementine got hot biscuits, jam, and tea for you. You don't get it, the mouse will."

Granny Ella held up her hoe as if it was a spear. "Jess Earl, you take my boy to that train, I'se gonna come getchya."

Jess Earl ducked. "Easy, Granny. We just goin' for a ride to town and then back." He turned the Huckster around. "You ready, Beau?"

"Ready as I'll ever be."

Jess Earl stepped on the gas. "That old lady scares me, Beau."

"Scares herself most'a the time."

"How old is she, Beau?"

"Ninety some odd, with a lot yet to go."

Jess Earl headed down the long dirt road that separated the cotton fields. "Where in town we goin'?"

"You know the stream cuts through the Prevette plantation?"

"That ain't town."

"I know it ain't."

"So why we goin' there?"

"Blue suckers."

Jess Earl looked across the seat. "I don't see no rod. And blue suckers ain't in that stream, no how."

"A Pullman porter don't ask no questions. He just nods his head and smiles."

"At what?"

"At whatever."

They drove on for several miles and then turned at the crossroads where the First Zion Church stood with its frail white steeple. In the distance, they saw a splendid horse gallop in the meadow. Its rider held a basket in one hand. The sharp morning sun flashed off the nibs of her silver spurs as she jumped a four-foot fence that secured a large expansive field. She rode up the embankment and disappeared as the wind, saturated with cottonwood sap, blew through the trees and scented the country air.

Jess Earl said, "That's the Prevette girl."

"You know her?"

"Used to muck stalls for her at the county fair. See, her groom was too old to do the heavy work at the competitions. I'll say this for her. She's one hell of a rider. Rode her courses; never made a mistake. Never a stride too long nor too short. Rides like the devil, that girl. I was in charge of all her daddy's groomin' before I got this job."

"You never told me you worked for Addison Prevette."

"There was no reason to."

"When you said old groom, did you mean Roy?"

Jess Earl said, "Yeah, and he acted like he owned the damn barn."

"Roy's my great uncle."

"Uncle or not, he didn't like me. Thought I was goin' to take his place. So I stayed far away as I could from him. But Addison Prevette was sad to see me go. Not me. Drivin' a Huckster's easy. Now I'm gonna be a train man. See the damn whole country for nothin'."

"You and the girl still on friendly terms?"

"Yes and no."

"What do you mean yes and no?"

"Old Roy didn't like no one messin' with little Shelby, but hisself. Kinda thought she belonged to him, and in a way she did, since he taught her everythin' a person need to know about horses and the medicines needed when they get the sore hock or the ache. But as I said, her daddy, he was sad to see me go and never once treated me like I was anythin' but white, but the Alcázar paid better, and you gotta go where the money is, and drivin' is a lot easier than workin' a barn, and ridin' a train's a lot easier than livin' in this town."

Beau said, "Turn off the road and follow her."

"Beau, I wasn't tellin' you that so you go fall in love with her."

"Just do what I say."

"I don't think so, Beau."

"You see that barn in yonder clump of trees?"

"Yeah, 'n' I see a lot of other things too, and they's called trouble."

"Trouble or not, that's where we're goin'."

Jess Earl made a sharp turn off the road. The Huckster's chassis flopped hard into the field. Beau nearly fell out. "You tryin' to kill us?"

"I ain't tryin' any harder than you are, Beau."

They drove on past unconcerned quarter-thoroughbreds and warmbloods grazing in the fields.

"See it up ahead, Jess?"

"Yeah, I see it, and it sees me." Jess Earl stopped the Huckster short of the new barn and paddock. Parallel poles and cross rails for schooling horses at the collected, working, and extended trot were down one side of the ring. "What business you got with horses all of a sudden?"

Beau said, "Absolutely none."

"Then what're we doin' here?"

"When you get done trainin', wire me. I'll see to it that you get on my consist."

Jess Earl looked too confused to be happy. "You don't mean the Twentieth Century Limited? You can't mean that train, Beau."

"What other train would I mean?"

"I'm just startin' out, Beau. You gotta be the best to work on that line. It takes years to get on that train. You just can't get on that ride after a week a trainin'."

"Local boy like you should fit in just fine. Plus I can trust you."

"Beau, don't think I'm ungrateful or nothin', but tell me why you need somebody you can trust with absolutely no experience."

"You just answered your own question." Beau hopped out of the Huckster and headed to the barn. "Don't forget to wire me." Jess Earl waved and drove off, about all he could do.

Shelby rode up to the paddock, dismounted, and removed her saddle. She put a halter and a blanket on her gelding and then sent it out to graze with a slap on the hindquarter. Then she set her eye on the Huckster. "I know that boy."

"That's Jess Earl, miss."

"He was my groom when I went to competitions and a very good one at that. Why didn't he say hello?"

"Oh, he had to hurry off, miss. But he told me to say hello to you. He's off to the Pullman trainin' center and needs to get his things together."

"Will he be working on your train?"

"Well, now that you bring it up, that's what I'm plannin'."

"Can he be trusted?"

"Oh yes, miss."

"Good. Find more boys like him. Now, come with me, Beau."

He followed Shelby into the barn where she slid open the rear panel of a stall that led to a secondary room with tall cylindrical stills that had once made the renowned Magnolia Belle Rye before Prohibition. Beau could almost see the old Magnolia Belle paddleboat rolling down the Mississippi with its name just above the staterooms, so called because each room had been named after a state in the Union.

"Welcome to my distillery, Beau," she said, her eyes filled with the ageless allure of youth.

"It's a beautiful distillery, miss."

"Yes, it is," she said, weaving her agile body through the bottles, boxes, machinery, and walls stacked with barrels of two-year-old rye whiskey ready for market. The older, pre-Prohibition stock, with stamped dates, was kept for her father.

Beau handed Shelby an envelope. "You'll see everythin's accounted for, miss. Not a penny missin'."

"Thank you, Beau." She unbuttoned her blue cavalry tunic and sat on a bench. "We must get to work now."

He set down his lunch pail and took off his coat. "Jess and I saw you ridin' in the fields before, miss, and, well, see, I was wonderin' where you got that army blouse you're wearin'."

"It's my father's." She took a ledger from her saddle bag.

"From the Cuban campaign?"

"Yes."

"The Tenth Cavalry served there and fought hard," Beau said.

"I wouldn't know." She used a coded system to mark her orders for New York.

"My cousin Webb Stephens was in the Tenth. They charged San Juan Hill on foot. Took a lot of fire. Said it was witherin'. Lot of 'em fell down; never to open their eyes again. But they held the line for the white troopers who followed on up." Beau, his eyes still on Shelby's cavalry blouse, quietly said, "It must be hard, miss. Real hard to give up your life like that. But then, I guess, that's what real honor's all about. Leavin' this world knowin' you did the right thing even without no one else knowin' or carin'."

Shelby looked up from the ledger. "We can talk about it later. These bottles here, without labels, are for Barney Gallant. Every one has a red seal. You'll deliver them to his townhouse in Chelsea." Shelby took fifty dollars out of the envelope Beau had given her and put it into his hand. "Not bad for a day's work."

"No, not bad at all, miss." He put away the money: a month's wages on the train. "Please don't mind me sayin' this, miss…" Beau said, feeling safe to speak up, but he waited a moment.

Shelby was writing a letter to Virginia Swain about a boy whom she had met while riding in Central Park. She called the stable when she had returned to the Biltmore and asked for the young man's name so that she could leave what he had supposedly dropped in the bridle path with the hotel concierge for him to pick up. Shelby then went across the street to Abercrombie & Fitch, on 44th and Madison Avenue, and bought a pair of men's riding gloves and left a note in the box: *Thanks again for finding me in the park. If these gloves aren't yours, they would still look good on you. Miss Shelby Prevette, 399 Park Avenue, PH A*, c/o Virginia Swain. Shelby looked up. "Mind what, Beau?"

"While you and Detective Heinz was in your drawin' room, back on the train, I went and left somethin' in his motor car with a note attached."

"What?"

"A pint of your rye without the label."

"What did you write?"

"You're barking up the wrong tree. There's no wood in this shrub."

Shelby laughed. "I would've liked to have seen the look on his face."

"You mean before or after he took his first sip?"

"Both. Now, when are you heading back to New York?"

"Two, three weeks, miss. Whenever the railroad wires."

"I hope it's not more. See, I promised to have all this delivered before the end of the month."

"We'll get it there. Don't you worry, miss. You ridin' back with me?" Before she could answer, they heard a train whistle fill the valley.

She stepped toward the sound that filled the air with its piercing roar. He eyes softened of memory. "Seems so long ago that day we left Clarksdale, Beau."

He stood beside her and looked toward the valley. "Indeed, it does, miss," he said and thought of what his cousin Samson Paisley had told him on the Pelican Midnight Sleeper the week before: *You know how things was back then. I'd look that girl long in the face next time you see her. Seems us is all mixed up together.*

Beau wanted to tell his cousin that he was right, though it would have to wait. Not the Yellow Dog 10:13. It waited for no one as it blew its whistle through the Yazoo and Mississippi Valley.

www.raederlomax.com

99¢ Price Deals at **www.RaederLomax.com**. Get on the list **NOW!** And get notified of the exact day.

See how Midnight Sleeper, the prequel to Stand Your Ground, arose from this contemporary story.

"The legal premise of deadly force in the *Stand Your Ground* law is taken to it's limits."

KIRKUS REVIEWS: *Stand Your Ground*
"Lomax knows how to keep the plot moving...The clipped prose hums along, generating a blunt, edgy mood...A heist goes bad in entertaining fashion."

A PAGE TURNING THRILLER: Zany, chaotic, inappropriate—A comedy of bad manners about wicked people who abuse the Stand Your Ground gun law to double cross, steal, cheat, murder and cause plain old mayhem.

"There was a madness in Ronnie's eyes. The kind a vulture has when it circles the dead..." He had been betrayed. People were going to pay, and he knew just how to get away with it.

Roy LaHood was one of those getting in Ronnie's way.
"He had the energy of the hunter. The Stride of the cheetah hotfoot in the Savannah..."

Roberta said to Ronnie, "Tell Roy you saw a ghost. You won't have to kill him. He'll die laughing."

Get **STAND YOUR GROUND** now! and find out what happens.

Amazon   iBook   Kobo   Barnes & Noble

Made in the USA
Middletown, DE
14 December 2016